CHAPTER ONE

Climb every fountain

The walls of the narrow street seemed to melt like candle wax under the hot Roman sun. All around, tourists and locals meandered down the cobbled path among the chic boutiques and bustling pizzerias. Italians wearing dark shades sat outside cafés, sipping espressos and gesticulating as they spoke, as if performing in a play.

Along the route, against a backdrop of leafy vines, stood a fountain. Its single column was topped with the bust of Augustus, and just below, two stone dolphins dived outwards, water spouting from their mouths.

'Mum, Dad, watch me. I can go higher!' yelled a young boy who had clambered up the column and was swinging from a dolphin, his legs dangling a few feet off the ground.

As another deluge of water gushed down, the boy yelped and thrust his fingertips into a tiny crag hidden among the algae, just managing to hold on.

'Come on, my little one, let's go,' the boy's mother called as she sheltered from the oppressive heat under a nearby veranda.

As expected, the plea went completely unheard, and her son continued to dangle from the fountain like a giddy monkey.

'It's too hot. I've got to get out of here,' said the child's father, patting the bald spot on his head with a handkerchief. 'Desperate times ...' He turned, and with a glance, sought his wife's approval.

Reluctantly, she nodded.

'Arif, if you come here now, you can have as much ice cream as you want, OK?' he called out.

'Ice cream!' the child cried, his ears suddenly working again. He leapt down from the fountain and ran over, dripping glugs of water across the burning cobblestones as he went.

Together, the family wandered towards the Gelato Gelato ice-cream shop and disappeared among the crowds.

In the corner, alone once again, the fountain began to shift ever so slightly, as if the summer's haze were distorting its rigid lines. The moss to which the young boy had clung just moments before, started to drip, staining the stone column with a lime-green trail. The water, which had flowed from the dolphins, spluttered and dried up. And along the emperor's smooth face, tiny fissures began to appear under the intense sunshine.

'My arms are killing me,' said the emperor, whose real name was Viviano when he wasn't dressing up. Gradually, he broke his disciplined pose to shake out his limbs. In the process, a dolphin became detached and crashed to the ground, revealing his tanned hand clasped around a Super Soaker.

'Damn.'

It wasn't every day that a child decided to hang off his costume, but Viviano was pleased to have been considered so realistic. Anyway, he'd been stationary for hours, and despite his relative youth – twenty-seven – he still needed a break in the shade. The plaster pillar encasing his body was solid and Viviano grappled with it, struggling to get free. Next to his spot, a flat cap was littered with shimmering coins.

Definitely enough for a cold beer and a slice of pizza, he thought with a smile, removing the ornamental cherub from the top of his head.

Viviano packed up and was about to leave when he remembered the thick clay caked on his face.

I'm currently half-man, half ruler of an empire, he thought. The idea didn't displease him. With a direct blast of water from the Super Soaker, the clay softened.

'My men! I must depart, but you shall do battle!' he said, issuing a final order to his loyal and make-believe troops, before rubbing his face with a towel and wiping the ruler from existence.

The sun was still beating down as Viviano began to roam, dabbing the sweat from his forehead and hiding his green eyes behind a pair of sunglasses.

All along the street, he spotted fellow performers doing their best to entertain the tourists: a cowboy galloping on a stuffed steed, a grey ghoul haunting an alleyway and a genie levitating and granting wishes. They winked at him as he passed.

As Viviano rounded the corner – the taste of a beer already on the tip of his tongue – he stopped dead.

She was here.

He glimpsed her among the crowds, and just for a moment, her infinity eyes blinked in his direction. Then, in a heartbeat, she was gone.

THE STARLING DANCE

A MIDSUMMER ROME-ANCE

BY

LUCY ELENA

For you Ellie, my muffin

First published in 2025 by Rolling Wave Books
ISBN 978-1-8382119-4-3

CHAPTER TWO
La bella vita?

'*C'est pas vrai,*' Laure groaned as her alarm wailed like a siren. 'It can't be morning already.'

In her dream, she had been on a bouncy castle, leaping higher and higher until the world below slowly fell away.

Now Laure half-opened one eye and immediately scrunched it shut, startled by the sunshine which streamed through the open window.

'Not yet,' she whispered, silencing the alarm and burying her face into the clammy pillow once again.

It felt like everything in the room was sweating, as if, overnight, her flat had been transformed into a tent in the heart of the rainforest where even tropical birds would struggle to fly through the soupy air.

Another forty-degree day in Rome.

Il faut que tu te lèves, it's time to move, said her brain, speaking as it always did in Laure's native French so its points would resonate.

'I know,' said Laure, her voice muffled in the pillow, 'but those bastards next door have only just let me get to sleep!'

As Laure turned and searched once again for her peaceful dream, the malicious cries of her neighbours began to rattle around her brain. It was no exaggeration to say that the couple next door had hit a rough patch. Everything had started small – the odd disagreement in the evening, a disgruntled reproach – but little by little, the looming storm had hit. Their fights became louder and longer, the accusations more hurtful, until every night was a shouting match. All the noise came screaming through the wall, assaulting Laure's eardrums and ripping her from the depths of sleep whenever she managed to drift off.

It had been like that for weeks.

Laure had never actually come face to face with the struggling lovers, but the more she lay awake at night, silently drowning in their vicious gripes, the more detailed her plots to violently assassinate them had become. On particularly rough nights, she'd even made preliminary plans to follow through, but it had all begun to feel rather unhealthy.

Unhealthy, but not unenjoyable, Laure thought, as she rubbed her sleepy face.

Her brain raised a nervous eyebrow.

A second attempt at eye opening proved more successful and Laure's surroundings gradually came into focus: the neat pile of folded clothes on her desk, an undrunk glass of water by her bed, the rickety fan peddling lukewarm air around the room … and her phone. A knot formed in her stomach. The lack of sleep and warring neighbours might be easier to bear if her own love life wasn't such a mess, but without a hint of warning, the man she was just beginning to call her boyfriend had evaporated into thin air, taking their blossoming relationship with him and leaving Laure feeling increasingly hollow.

Don't despair, mon amour, her brain said. *He might still get in touch.*

Maybe, Laure thought, scrunching up her eyes and feeling the beads of sweat on her forehead slide into her hair.

With a tentative arm, she retrieved her phone. Davide was last online at 2 a.m., but there was still no reply to her messages. The first she had sent three days ago, just after their last date:

> *Ciao bello,* I had so much fun tonight.
> I looked up that exhibition you were
> talking about and there are still some tickets
> available. Would you like to go together?
> Good luck with tomorrow's busy day. x

After much deliberation, she had sent a follow-up yesterday morning, feeling half-desperate, half-justified and half-hopeful:

> Is everything OK, Da'?
> I haven't heard from you.
> Are you free sometime in the week?
> Hope you're alright. x

Laure could see that he had seen both messages, but he hadn't deigned to reply.

'*Quel connard,* what a bastard,' she whispered, trying to ignore the stab of pain spreading through her chest.

Searching for a distraction, Laure felt around for her mysteriously disappearing earplugs, eventually pulling one out from under her back. Since the fighting next door had begun, she had tried a variety of brands, shapes and sizes, spending a small fortune on little foamy dots, gel balls and even super-duper top-range ear plugs, so advanced they looked like a tech guru might soon launch them into orbit, but over the course of a night, they all seemed to vanish, lost somewhere among sheet-folds. With a sigh, Laure rolled out of bed and shuffled towards the shower.

The shower knob of destiny. Kind and cruel in equal measures. Laure flinched as she gave it a short sharp turn, then wailed as icy water cascaded onto her hot and bothered body. Slowly, as she adjusted to the glacial temperature, her mind wandered back to Davide. Had he really just ditched her? It wouldn't be the first time she'd been ghosted. Still, Laure had believed, perhaps naively, that an advantage of being twenty-nine years old – and very nearly thirty – was leaving situations like this in the past.

'Stop this,' she said with a shake of her head that sent thousands of water droplets whizzing through the air.

What did she always tell her friends when they were in the miserable clutches of heartache? 'If someone you're dating is capable of doing that, then they really don't deserve you.' But now it was her turn, it wasn't so simple. In just two short months, Davide had managed to spark her imagination. He was witty and spontaneous, and for the first time in a while, it had felt right.

'You need to be stronger than this,' she tutted while over-squeezing the shower gel. 'If he's a bastard, it's better to know sooner rather than later.'

Another classic consolation, but in the back of her mind there was still that irritating glimmer of hope that he would get in touch.

As she dried off, Laure paused to appreciate the one fleeting moment in the day where she actually felt fresh. In a matter of seconds, the humidity would announce its presence again, covering her skin with a thin film of sweat. Moment appreciated, she walked back into the living space and began to lightly perspire.

In Rome, Laure's salary didn't go very far, but she had managed to rent a little studio. The minimal furniture – a sofa-bed, a small desk, a wardrobe and a large bright window nestled next to the kitchenette – gave at least the illusion of space. Although a downgrade from her previous flat in Paris, it had turned out to be the anonymous refuge she needed.

With robotic rhythm, Laure dressed for work, selecting a black pencil skirt and pulling a white blouse over her head.

I still have a bit of time, she thought, glancing over at the 'oven clock of truth' which, in reality, ran two minutes fast.

A dull headache pulsed at her temples and the puffy bags underneath her dark eyes stared back from the mirror. Hastily, she attempted to disguise them with concealer. Any more make up than that tended to drip down your face over the day.

It was August – the height of summer and almost exactly one year since she had arrived in Rome.

'My Italian anniversary,' she said to the tired reflection.

All things considered, the Eternal City had started to feel like home. Laure had found routine, a handful of friends, and had learned to navigate the quirks of Roman society: She could replace the correct words with the right hand gesture, discern exactly what was and wasn't allowed on a pizza, and she no longer batted an eyelid when a seemingly trivial traffic dispute between two taxi drivers ended up coming to blows over whose whore mum had given birth to the more deplorable bastard.

But recently, things seemed to be moving backwards.

It's just a rough patch, said her brain. *Think how far you've come.*

'Have I?' Laure asked, shrugging at the mirror.

Mais bien sûr, said her brain. *Of course you have. Just look at your hair. It's growing back, isn't it?*

With fingertips, Laure felt around her thick mass of black curls and located a few shorter patches – they were now a couple of inches long. Luckily, she had so much hair, it wasn't that noticeable when it had started to fall out.

'You're right,' she told her brain with a sigh. 'I'm making progress ... I'm just so tired.'

The concealer had had little effect and Laure took a moment to blend more of the smooth liquid into her olive skin. Finally, she did her best to pull her curls into a professional-looking bun, accepting that a few coils had a life of their own.

'Today, it's not going to get any better than this,' she admitted.

Grabbing her bag, and a banana for a snack, Laure let the front door slam behind her.

CHAPTER THREE

I've been watching you

At this hour the normally buzzing neighbourhood was just starting to show glimmers of life. Trastevere lay south of the river, over the bridge from Rome's Centro Storico. Visitors were enamoured by the narrow, cobblestone streets, dotted with cute cafés and restaurants that came out of hiding behind every twist and turn. Tangles of vines crept up buildings, which were painted the colours of autumn leaves, to windows where the few original residents that remained still hung out their washing. Over the years it had gentrified, filling up with the trendiest hangouts and attracting tourists, students and Roman up-comers alike. They thronged the streets, packed out pizzerias and gathered in the ancient piazzas to smoke and drink with friends into the early hours. Laure could tolerate the crowds in exchange for the freedom that she felt here. It was different from Paris, where the lines of grey buildings had started to close in, until her only option was to escape.

The mornings, at least, were peaceful, and Laure navigated the uneven cobbles on the way to Da Antonio, her local coffee shop. Only a small, beeping rubbish truck disturbed the quiet as it reversed at pace around a corner and almost knocked Laure over. Even though it wasn't her fault, Laure waved in apology to the driver and hopped out of the way.

'*Bonjour* salvation,' she said, as the café's cream veranda came into view and the aroma of freshly ground coffee hit her nostrils.

Da Antonio wasn't a fancy nor particularly personable place, but Laure had come to feel comfortable there. Antonio, the owner – sixty-odd, with bright white hair and a dark tan – spotted Laure as she slipped in behind the row of elegantly dressed customers at the bar.

Some were gawking at newspapers, still stunned by the results of the weekend's General Election, while others pleaded ignorance, choosing instead to stare at football highlights on the mounted screens. Most, however, were silently savouring their first coffee of the day – a sacred moment in Italian culture. Then, one by one, they would head off, dropping a few coins on the counter, slipping on their sunglasses and nodding to Antonio before making way for the next early riser.

Laure no longer needed to order. No sooner had she perched on the swivelly bar stool, than Antonio slid a macchiato her way. Laure quickly read through the news headlines that flashed along the bottom of the TV screen. She liked to be informed at the office, even if no one actually asked for her opinion. Finally, she lifted the petite cup to her lips. As the rich, dark liquid slid down her throat, she closed her eyes and savoured it circulating around her body, turning on a few more lights in her head.

Some much-needed energy, she thought, *which could be put towards something useful, such as work or making weekend plans, but certainly not,* she told herself, *to be expended pining over Davide.*

'I'll just see if he's online,' she said, pulling out her phone.

Her brain tutted its disapproval.

7.50 a.m. Davide Damiano is online! Great! Laure thought, staring fixatedly at the screen. *And now, Davide Damiano is offline, too bad.*

'Well, what a fun game,' Laure muttered to herself, as she sipped down the last mouthful and made for the door.

She flashed a half-hearted smile towards Antonio, who wasn't looking, but would have been mortally offended if she'd left without at least trying to say goodbye.

As she walked, Laure couldn't help running over her last date with Davide. Had there been any signs that he was planning to ditch her? Anything she had missed or something she might have said? Could she have done something differently?

Lost to obsession, she failed to notice a pair of eyes shining out of the shadows. They tracked her every step, right until the moment she disappeared around the corner and out of sight.

CHAPTER FOUR

Mother, I'm fine

At the bridge, Laure's hurried footsteps and lovesick daydreams sent her colliding straight into the back of a tall, lanky, man.

'Oh, *scusi,* excuse me,' she said, immediately recoiling.

The man barely seemed to notice. He remained stationary, staring up at the sky. Laure followed his gaze and saw thousands of starlings soaring above. Like a Roman army, they conquered the skies, gliding in an ever-changing cloud of tiny black dots. They fanned out, creating huge swirls in the air which rippled like waves, before drifting apart, only to reform seconds later with a new story.

Rome was famous for these murmurations. Laure had seen one on the day she arrived. On an evening as hot as the Sahara, she had been dragging her life – packed into three suitcases – towards a tram stop, while trying not to trip over her own feet. Every few steps, a wheel caught in the cobblestones, twisting her wrist and trying her patience. At that time, inside her, there were only sprouting weeds and anxiety: Was moving to Italy the right decision? Would she always feel this heavy weight in her chest? Is that who she was now?

Amid the maze of thoughts and wearisome suitcases, Laure had glanced up and found a cascade of starlings swooping across the sky. She didn't know how long she had stood there, lost in their tangle of pirouettes and twirls. Someone could have stolen the luggage from under her nose and she wouldn't have noticed. Something about the birds' graceful movements brought her close to tears, but there was also a sense of unease, as if at any moment, one of them might drift out of line, barrel into their neighbour and spark a colossal bird crash across the city.

Now, recalling the scene from one year ago, Laure shook her head.

Italian birds are so dramatic, she thought, as she tore her eyes away and crossed the bridge into the city centre.

Laure's offices lay just behind the Largo di Torre Argentina, an excavated area full of Roman ruins and the site where Julius Caesar was brutally assassinated in 44 BC. Like every other fascinating relic in this ancient city, the death spot of Rome's most famous figure was barely signposted. It sat in the middle of three heavily congested roads in the centre of the city, next to a shop that sold cheap household appliances and a 'Tiger' store. Nowadays, it was perhaps better known for the colony of stray cats that had made the ruins their home. As Laure passed, she saw at least ten of them sunbathing on the remains of statues of deities or talking a stroll through what was, once upon a time, Pompey's theatre. Laure had stopped briefly to admire a tiny grey kitten playing hide and seek among the grassy moss, when her phone rang.

'*Salut, maman,*' she said, greeting her mother.

'*Bonjour, ma puce. Comment vas-tu?* How are you doing today?'

'I'm good,' said Laure, not finding the energy to get into specifics. 'I'm nearly at work.'

'This early? I thought the Italian lifestyle was supposed to be relaxed.' There was a pause. 'You're not working too hard, are you?' The voice was trying to be casual, but sounded concerned.

'No, not at all, Mum,' Laure said in her habitual bid to calm the woes. 'How are you?'

'I'm glad, *ma chérie.* I'm good. I was on the phone for two hours with your grandma last night.'

'How is she?'

'Oh, same old same old: barking orders at grandad under the pretence that he's deaf, relaying all the gossip from her little book club, and complaining about the way people drive in Marrakesh, even though she's got the worst road rage I've ever seen.'

Laure laughed.

'And she wants to come and visit us in Paris,' her mother continued. 'Said our Christmas trip to Morocco is too far away.'

'When? I'll ask for some time off and come back for a few days,' Laure said, suddenly feeling a jolt of angst at the prospect of actually doing so.

'Oh, that would be wonderful, *ma puce,* if you're feeling up to it, of course, but no pressure. If not, we'd be happy to come and see you again. I just love Rome! Anyway, I told *lalla,* grandma, we'll get her ticket for after your sister has finished her exams, then we can all be a little more relaxed.'

Laure sensed the silent grimace of exasperation on the other end of the phone. Nayla was in the middle of her law finals, and her stress was smothering the entire household.

'I rang her to say good luck,' Laure said, eyeing the selection of pizza slices on display at the trattoria by her office. 'She'll do great.'

'Of course, she will, and she knows it deep down,' replied her mother. 'All my children are so clever.'

Laure smiled down the phone but felt the knot of unease tighten once again.

'It must be so busy at work at the moment, with all the election coverage,' her mother continued. 'Tell me, *mon cœur,* you're not overdoing it, are you?'

'Mum, honestly, you don't need to worry at all. It's actually the opposite. I'm barely lifting a finger,' said Laure. 'I'm just a secretarial assistant, so even if the company is crazy busy, my role hardly changes.'

'Good, *ma chérie.* I know what you're like.'

'I know,' Laure said, before falling silent.

'You'll get your spark back, I promise. Give it some time, and for now, enjoy that

12

beautiful city.'

'*Merci, maman,*' said Laure. 'I'm just getting to the office. I've got to go.'

'OK, *mon cœur.* Have a good day and don't work too hard.'

With that, Laure hung up and walked through a fancy courtyard with neatly sculpted hedges, to work.

CHAPTER FIVE

The perceived excitement of the election slog

FranceJournal was France's most respected news organisation. With offices across every continent, it took the world's pulse, followed global stories, and published its findings in print, video and photo. Laure's friend Mélanie was a big boss at the Paris HQ, and a little over a year ago, when Laure was struggling, she had sent her the ad for a job in Rome.

'I think it will be good for you,' Mélanie had said. 'It will be an adventure. A new city for a new start. Laure, the role is a breeze compared to what you've just left behind, I promise.'

'What about the Italian?' Laure had asked shyly, her head a ball of confusion.

'They'll pay for your classes. Haven't you always wanted to learn? Just think about it, OK?' And then she paused. 'I don't want you to get stuck in a rut of no-confidence.'

The conversation had gone something like that.

Now, a year later, standing at the entrance under the cool shade of an arch, Laure patted her face down, took a deep breath and tried to push Davide, the fatigue and the wailing neighbours from her mind.

'Let's count down from ten before going in,' she suggested to her brain.

Euh, meditation normally takes longer than that, tu sais, came the response.

Laure shrugged, counted down from three and then climbed the two flights of stone steps to the office.

A buzz like a hornet was zipping around the newsroom. On Sunday, Italy had voted, and despite months of election build-up, analysis pieces and opinion polls, no one had expected quite such a right-wing government to be handed power. Laure's colleagues were charging around, the majority, she suspected, hadn't been home since the results were announced. In great haste, they greeted her with a mix of two kisses starting from the right from her French compatriots, a double kiss but starting from the left from the Italians, and a shy smile and self-deprecating quip from her British friends from across the Channel. With fifteen minutes to spare before her working day officially began, Laure liaised briefly with her boss, made a list of tasks and read through the dozens of emails that had dropped in to her inbox – none of which directly concerned her, but she liked to be up to speed.

At 8.30, Paolo, the news editor, summoned everyone over for the daily meeting.

Paolo Roquet. Tall, serious, half French, half Italian. Paolo, the big dog, the news junkie, the if-it's-happening-he-knows-about-it kind of guy. On the ball, topping up the ball, inflating balls for his staff. He might have been a bit of a silver fox, Clooney-type, if he didn't look like he'd pulled one too many all-nighters chasing after breaking news. As he stood, lightly bouncing on his toes, his staff formed a semi-circle around him.

In the team, there was a bit of everything. The 'born to be journalists' echoing Paolo's angsty enthusiasm, growling like a pack of dogs and waiting for him to dangle the day's juicy news steak in front of them. The 'moderate-news junkies' – keen, but burnt out from the election coverage, stifling yawns and pushing through for the team. Then there were the others – there in presence, nodding and noting down every tenth word, while in their heads, calculating how long they had left until retirement, some doing a better job of hiding it than others. Wherever they stood on the spectrum between extreme over-enthusiasm and unapologetic dejection, the international spotlight was firmly on Italy and the pace in the office was a million miles a minute.

'Right, right, right, team,' Paolo said, clapping his hands, 'a busy day ahead of us, as we've come to expect.'

He turned and pointed at Marta, FranceJournal's star reporter.

'We've got Marta hounding the new Prime Minister's office to see how they plan to implement some of their more controversial plans. Let's not let them dodge the tough questions.'

Marta growled.

'Brussels is sending us reactions from EU politicians which Tom is weaving into a 'bigger picture' piece,' Paolo continued, nodding at Tom who nodded back. 'Elodie's on the ground already, and she's interviewing everyone – the old, the young, the rich, the poor, migrants, tourists, household pets, anything within reach basically. How do they feel? How did they vote? Are they shocked, pleased, scared, constipated? We want to know. Then there's Roberto …' Here Paolo paused and a sheepish look crept across his face. 'Well, Roberto has been standing outside Parliament since I can remember, frankly.'

'A whole week now, boss,' someone at the back chimed in, and the team stifled sniggers because, well, Roberto was a real *stronzo*.

'Yes', Paolo said, eyeballing them sternly. 'He's monitoring the situation down there, a very important task.' He paused again. 'We should probably bring him back … at some point … Anyway, moving on! To my favourite, the features.'

Feature pieces were where the company could differentiate itself from competitors. It was a chance to tell the human stories, sift through the mundane for that unique nugget of news, or locate the people vibrating on a different frequency to the ordinary folk.

'Renata,' Paolo said, turning towards Laure's colleague who looked like she'd been in the office for so long, she was contemplating jumping out of the window just for some fresh air. 'You're covering the ninety-eight-year-old woman who was moved to vote for the first time in her life.'

'Yes, boss, but we … er … just got confirmation that she died at the polling station,' Renata said, glancing up from her phone.

Paolo could barely contain himself. *'Mamma mia!'* he said. 'Tie it in! Find the daughter and make a beautiful piece. Go, go, go!'

Renata scuttled off to her desk, taking a route which passed a little too close to the open window for Laure's liking.

'Then,' Paolo said, still beaming and rubbing his hands together, 'the man who used his life savings to get the entire Italian Constitution tattooed on his body. He's now crowdfunding laser surgery as the populists have vowed amendments. Nick, that story is for you. And, of course,' Paolo's smile became nervous as he looked towards Pierre, a veteran journalist who, though pretending to listen, was actually working on his food blog. 'Pierre, as requested, you'll be at the Tuscan vineyards seeing how Italian wines tie into all this.'

The team held back eye rolls and disguised scoffs as yawns, while Pierre, a self-professed gift to journalism who felt he'd done his time on the newsbeat, stood a little straighter and stared everyone down, daring anyone to suggest that wine wasn't integral to the general election story.

As usual, Paolo finished by addressing the video team, doing his best – which was terrible – to hide the disdain for what, in his eyes, were a bunch of photogenic halfwits whose increasing importance in journalism made his blood boil.

Taking a deep breath, he brought his contempt under control and muttered, 'As for you all, just, try to keep up, OK.'

Giorgio, the head of video – or 'Gorgeous Giorgio' as he was informally known among colleagues – flashed a pearly white grin and nodded, the broadside lost on him as he admired his reflection in Paolo's glasses.

The meeting dispersed and Laure slipped back to her desk. Today's main task was to record staff holiday requests for the post-election period. Click, click, click. With dutiful precision, she began to fill in the spreadsheet, one box at a time.

What she had been allocated a day to do, was finished by lunch, and after double-checking and sending it over to her boss, Laure rose and wandered over to the kitchen. Here, she drank a coffee, chit-chatted, and sneakily devoured a lonely slice of pizza from the communal fridge. Left over from election night, she hoped. The lack of sleep was clouding her mind and a tension headache still prickled at her temples. Yawning, she returned to her desk and retrieved her phone from the drawer where, in the name of productivity, she had locked it away. As predicted, Davide was still MIA, but she did have several missed calls from her best friend, Eva.

She and Eva had met about six months ago when the bus they were travelling on had burst into flames in the middle of the street. During a panicked rush for the exit, Eva, a Roman native, had struck up a conversation with Laure, informing her that this seemingly terrifying experience was not actually uncommon in the city.

'It's the old fleet,' she had said with a casual shrug. 'They're always going up in flames. It's amazing that no one has ever been hurt. I don't know if it's because bus drivers are just on the lookout for it now … you know, in the same way you might

16

expect to be stuck in a traffic jam.'

Together, they had watched as bright scarlet flames licked up the sides of the bus. Firemen arrived, unleashing powerful water jets which doused the vehicle until it resembled nothing more than a sopping, burnt-out husk. As the drama subsided, Laure and Eva realised that they had missed their respective appointments and decided to get a coffee together instead. One espresso and two beers later, they had discovered that they were both twenty-nine and enjoyed each other's company.

Eva was a waitress, aspiring poet and artist who marched to the beat of her very own special drum, something Laure was quietly in awe of.

Now, sitting at her desk, Laure smiled as she contemplated the missed calls, knowing that Eva had either rung during a weed-soaked daytime bath or one of her 'romantic' bike rides with some random guy she'd spotted cycling at the Villa Borghese. Every week, she flagged down a handsome man and charmed him into taking her around the park on the back of his bike, an opportunity she used to yell out her latest poems into the wind and see how nature responded to them.

Laure stepped out into the corridor and rang back.

'Ciao, bella! Where on earth are you?' responded Eva's echoey voice amid the sound of sloshing bath water.

'Love, it's the middle of the day. I'm obviously at work. What about you?' asked Laure, knowing the answer.

'I'm in the bath, love! I'm on a late shift at the restaurant.' Weed toke. 'You sound a bit down, sweetie. Is everything OK?' Exhale. Bath water, weed toke.

Laure hesitated and felt her words jar against a lump in her throat. 'Davide still hasn't texted back,' she said. 'The blue ticks are there. He's online all the time but hasn't replied. I think it's over ... I feel quite shit.' Laure breathed out a shaky sigh, feeling some relief at actually voicing the sadness.

'Stronzo di merda, fucking piece of shit,' said Eva.

'I don't know,' Laure muttered, leaning her forehead against the cool corridor wall while trying to organise her thoughts. 'It's just, he seemed to really like me, that's all. He always made a big effort, and ... sometimes he would say little things that made it sound like he was thinking long-term. I just liked his company.' Laure scrunched up her eyes to head off the arrival of tears. 'God, sorry, I'm such a mess. He clearly doesn't care.'

'Don't apologise. You know, you're allowed to feel sad, amore,' said Eva, toking intensely in the background.

'I know,' Laure said, moving her head away from the wall and into a less grief-stricken position in case any of her colleagues were stepping out for lunch. 'I guess it's just the same story all over again, and I'm so tired of it. Tired of feeling disappointed and pulling myself apart. Tired of the questioning and insecurity. Tired of finding myself back at square one ... It just felt different this time.'

'Well ... I mean, it did sound as if he really liked you, from everything you told me. Did you try calling him?'

'I thought about it,' said Laure, 'but I can't bring myself to. I'm not sure I've got the guts.'

'Hmm,' said Eva, seemingly savouring her special marijuana blend and leading Laure to wonder just how high she was today. 'I would do it. To see where you stand. At least it ends the confusion. Hopefully, he will pick up and you can have some peace of mind, whatever the outcome may be.'

'I know,' said Laure. 'You're right, I know I should.'

'*Assolutamente,*' said Eva. 'You know, it might turn out he hasn't ditched you at all.' She paused for dramatic effect. 'Maybe he has died, Laure.'

'Ha!' said Laure.

'I want to cheer you up,' said Eva. 'Let me take you out for a glass of wine, to-night, at around 2 a.m., when my shift ends. I've got a new poem in the works and I think you'll really enjoy it.'

Silently, Laure disagreed. Eva's poems were always of a sexual nature and often mildly disturbing.

'You know, Laure, I love this one,' Eva continued. 'It recounts the sexual experiences of an extremely elderly woman I've been chatting to at theatre group. Sex has changed so much, and yet, her memories are graphic, sensuous and relevant. I think people would be fascinated.'

'A sex poem about Grandma,' Laure remarked. 'Thank God Italy isn't a socially conservative country.'

Eva laughed. 'Anyway, I'll need your approval before I give it a whirl at the park.'

'Thanks for the early morning drinks offer,' Laure said, knowing Eva's concept of time was upside down, 'but I'm exhausted. My neighbours are still screaming at each other. I just want to go home and crash.'

'Still fighting?' said Eva. 'I'm so sorry, dear. It sounds miserable.'

'*Grazie, bella.* Let's rain check on the drinks. I should get back to work now.'

'Go. Get some rest tonight,' said Eva, as green fumes began to trickle through Laure's receiver. 'And let me know what happens with Davide, OK. I love you.'

With that, Eva hung up. Laure could picture her tossing the phone across the room and plunging her head under the soapy water, the dying spliff still firmly wedged between her lips. Eva always liked to finish her baths with flair.

Resisting the urge to see what time Davide was last online, Laure returned to her desk and tried to find more work.

Davide was last online at 11 a.m.

I'm so weak, she thought.

The rest of the afternoon ticked by in a mix of random admin, sweat and Paracetamol. At around six, Laure's line manager left, along with the rest of her team, and Laure was just gathering her things when Paolo ambled over, looking somewhat timid – very unusual for the big boss.

'Laure, I know you're heading off,' he said, his voice quiet, 'but I wanted to ask … This election has really thrown us, budget-wise.' He cleared his throat. 'You know, HQ demand extensive coverage but have denied every request I have sent for an increased budget. I'm really under the pump.'

Laure had never seen Paolo quite so uncomfortable.

'I know, I mean,' he stuttered. 'I remember reading your CV when you applied for

18

this job … Very impressive stuff.'

Laure smiled politely, wondering where this was going.

'Would you be able to stay this evening?' he asked. 'And help me balance the books. We've got some great coverage planned, and I'd hate to disappoint.'

Without really having time to consider, Laure nodded, and Paolo seemed to come ten notches down the panic scale.

'If you could keep this between us,' he hastened to add. 'The team have been flat out for months. I don't want them to be disheartened by these spats with the higher-ups.'

Laure glanced around. The office had come to resemble something of an animal kingdom. Journalists were camped out like plotting lions, waiting to pounce on an unsuspecting piece of breaking news. Behind them, cameramen were running like gazelles to ensure video equipment reached the latest hotspot. Economic forecasters stood tall as giraffes, gazing into the distance, trying to predict what the future might hold. All around, there were newspapers, phones, unfinished drafts and photos scattered like wild Savannah grass. Even veteran Pierre was still around, sipping Grappa and soaking in the blood, sweat and excitement.

Why don't you set some boundaries? her brain asked. *If you're going to stay, ask if you'll be paid overtime. Remember, there's no food in your house and you need to get to the supermarket, so you can't stay too late. Tell him that. Can I remind you that you are extremely sleep deprived and were hoping to rest a bit this evening?*

Laure looked at Paolo.

'I'd be happy to help,' she announced with a reassuring smile, but inside her heart sank. Here she was, one year later, and still unable to say 'no'.

'Just don't make this a habit again, Laure,' she whispered under her breath, nervously pawing at a hidden stump of hair around the back of her head.

19

CHAPTER SIX

The business of being a tree

It was past midnight when Laure finally stepped out of the office. From underneath a mound of paperwork, Paolo had sincerely thanked her for the help. During the hours spent poring over spreadsheets, they had managed to salvage most of the coverage and still send Pierre to Tuscany.

While retracing the familiar route home – over the river and down the winding side streets of Trastevere – Laure's brain switched off. The argument with herself over whether she should or shouldn't have stayed this late and where this landed her on the path to self-progress had destroyed any sense of pride she might actually have felt in helping her boss out.

The sun had long since set, but the neighbourhood still purred with life. Couples were finishing dinner under the warm glow of restaurant fairy lights, and groups of friends were gathered outside bars, clinking glasses and attempting to ward off the aggressive serenading of city buskers. Laure wandered past it all, home finally within her sights, aching for bed.

Viviano looked up and his tree costume rustled with the sudden movement. Slowly, he unfurled, detaching his body from the wall's crawling vines, and stared down the street at the place where she had just faded from view. With a few timid steps, he drifted in her direction, but she was gone and he knew it.

'I guess today is not the day … again,' he said with a sigh, before turning back.

This was his preferred spot for the evenings. He liked the way his willowy silhouette caught the light of street lamps, and the element of surprise, combined with his fluid movements, often earned shrieks or gasps from night revellers, especially if they'd had a few. People would stop and stare at the human tree swaying gently in the breeze, and he could always count on a group of Americans to try and distract him. They would wave their arms in front of his eyes, or offer sips of beer and tell jokes to see if he would crack a smile. Whatever it was, they always tipped heavily for the entertainment, which he appreciated.

With painted hands, he removed the leafy gauze from his hair and unravelled the vines around his olive T-shirt. The cascading water at a nearby fountain helped clean the paint from his face until only remnants of faded green remained around the edges of his chin and temples, creating a rather ghoulish look. Viviano caught his reflection in a shop window and smiled. He enjoyed the days when he was a tree, liked the idea of slipping into nature for a while. The muscles in his neck were stiff, and with a low sigh, he stretched them out. The exact time was a mystery to him, but now she had appeared, he could head home.

In no rush, Viviano followed the streets that were floodlit by the moon. It was a shame, he thought, that he was not still in costume. He would have liked to see the sewn-on leaves glisten in the shimmering light. From cobblestone to cobblestone he leapt, stretching his limbs out into the air, casting shadows on the ground which resembled gigantic night birds. Whenever a passer-by appeared unexpectedly, Viviano came to an abrupt halt and his bashful smile assured them there was no cause for concern.

Around the next corner, a couple strolled towards him, hand in hand and just for a second, Viviano's green eyes flickered over them.

That woman's smile is hiding sadness, he thought, his mind ticking away as it always did, independent of his will. *I bet this holiday is a final bid to save their relationship, but deep down, she already knows it won't work out. She is searching for the right moment to tell him.*

The man's hand was clasping his girlfriend's tightly. Viviano could see he was giving it everything.

Time is ticking away and he desperately wants a family, Viviano thought. *But there's a secret … she can't have children.* The story clicked into place in his mind. *She doesn't want to tell him, though. She's waiting to share her story with the person she's meant to be with.*

'Listen, we need to talk,' Viviano heard the woman say to her boyfriend, as he slipped by and left them behind.

Alone once again, Viviano sprinted at full pelt towards a wall and sprang into the air, just managing to curl his fingertips around some holes in the tired brickwork. Feeling for chinks, he began to climb, almost reaching the top before dropping stealthily back down to where he had started, pretending to be a spy as he landed. From across the road, Mickey spotted these antics, and despite shaking his head, was unable to stifle a laugh which caused his oversized sunglasses to fall from his nose.

'You're an idiot,' he mouthed at his tree-clad friend before resuming a phone conversation with family back home.

Just like Viviano, Mickey was also partial to a night-time stroll. It helped him put his thoughts in order. Also, the squat where he had lived since arriving in Rome eight months ago was most crowded at night – the less time spent there the better. After crossing paths again and again on the empty streets, long after the people with more normal schedules had returned home, Viviano and Mickey had struck up a conversation, and then a close friendship.

Mickey was from Senegal. He was one of the many Africans who had become stuck in the Italian capital after finding the pathway to Europe's rich north blocked by hardening politics and sharp border fences. Dreams of the promised land where anything was possible had immediately faded upon arrival, replaced with a reality of poverty, destitution and prejudice. He had ended up squatting in an abandoned building, moonlighting illegally as a cleaner or pot-washer here and there, and selling trinkets on the streets. All in a bid to make the money his loved ones in Senegal were counting on. His best, and often only, sellers were pairs of supersized sunglasses with chunky fluorescent frames, which he donned during his sales pitch. Every day, Mickey waited for news of the government papers that would allow him to settle and start a dignified life in Italy, so that a time might come when the scars etched into his body and soul at the cruel hands of human smugglers might begin to fade. Until then, he just had to get by.

As Viviano meandered past, Mickey nodded and tipped his gigantic sunglasses towards him, while chatting animatedly into a phone nestled in the crook of his neck.

After a few more twists and turns, Viviano reached the door of his building, crept along a dark corridor and up one flight of stairs to his flat.

CHAPTER SEVEN

If you could get a life, son, I'd really appreciate it

Quiet as a mouse, Viviano tiptoed in and closed the door. Then he turned and came face to face with his mother, a pile of folded laundry in her hands.

'My son,' Isabella said, giving him a kiss. 'Do I dare ask where you've been?'

'I'm not your son, I'm a tree,' he said, waving his arms.

With (semi) mock despair, his mother sank her face into her hands and Viviano put a branch-like arm around her. It always wound her up when he did the 'I'm a tree' bit.

'Do you want some dinner, Viv? I've left some lasagne out for you,' she said, ushering him towards a dining room chair before bustling off to the kitchen. Twenty-seven years old and she still treated him like a child.

Sitting at the small wooden table, Viviano leant his head against the wall and extended his arms out in front of him, trying to ease the stiffness that comes from holding a tree pose for hours on end. His mother returned with a plate of piping lasagne and sat down opposite.

'So, go on then, tell me, *tesoro,* what did you get up to today?' she asked, opening a beer and pouring two glasses.

The point had passed where she expected anything normal to come out of her son's mouth in response to that question. They had always been close, she and Viviano, in truth, because they hadn't had a choice.

'It was good,' said Viviano. 'I didn't see any of the other tree statues, maybe because of climate change.'

Isabella shot him a withering look and he grinned.

'On my break, I went to Piazza Navona and caught Venezuelan Michael Jackson's performance.'

'Oh, *mi piace,* I like him!' said Isabella. 'Is his mum still his business manager?'

'Yes. She was there, of course, aggressively handing out flyers and haggling with other performers to try and secure him the prime-time slot.'

'Classic. If that boy becomes a star one day, it will be down to her tenacity.'

Viviano nodded. 'In the afternoon a man came and wrote a sonnet in my shade.'

His mother raised her eyebrows.

'And later, this guy thought I was so authentic, he almost took a piss up against me. You should have seen the look on his face when I dived out of the way. The highest form of flattery for my costume, I believe.'

'All in the day of a tree, eh,' Isabella said with a soft laugh. 'You know, I bumped into your friend Camilla today. She spotted me while I was waiting at the tram stop. Honestly, she's such a lovely girl.'

'She is,' Viviano said. 'And she's doing so well too. Been assigned some important human-rights cases recently. People are really starting to recognise her talent.'

'Yes, she mentioned a few, briefly. It all sounded fascinating, well, gut-wrenching too. So many difficult stories. She's very courageous. I hadn't seen her since the two of you were at law school together … I'm convinced, you would have had a similar career path, *tesoro*.' Isabella beamed at her son and a hint of wistfulness tinged her eyes.

By now, Viviano was used to these comments, but he still didn't know what to say.

'Anyway,' Isabella pressed on, 'Camilla said you still volunteer together sometimes, down at the homeless foundation. Neither of you have ever compromised on your morals. I'm proud of you, *tesoro*.'

Viviano smiled. 'Yes, we often overlap there. It's a nice group.'

For a moment, Isabella was quiet, contemplating her son. Then, after a long pause, she spoke again. '*Tesoro*, tell me, have you thought anymore about coming to *Signora* Solari's funeral?'

'Ma, you know I wish I could, but I promised a friend I would help them move house that day. I can't let them down now,' Viviano responded without hesitation.

'*Lo so, lo so,* I know,' said his mother. 'You said. It's just … she looked after you so much when you were little. She's like family. I thought you would want to say good-bye properly. You don't get those opportunities twice, son.'

'It's just bad timing,' said Viviano. 'I wish they were on different days. I'll go and pay my respects at her resting place one day.'

Isabella ruffled her son's dark curls. 'I understand, *tesoro*,' she said.

Viviano could see the disappointment on his mother's face and she was right. There was no house move he had to attend, but unfortunately, he was incapable of giving a different answer.

CHAPTER EIGHT

The woman without a story

'What's that?' Viviano asked, grabbing a white tube from the corner of the table. 'Ma, you've been to see that foot doctor again, haven't you?'

'I might have been with your aunty after work today,' Isabella replied in a casual tone. 'She has a nascent rash.'

'That man always diagnoses you with a nascent something,' Viviano said. 'He's a complete fraud, Ma. Tell me, why did *you* need to buy this cream if you were just accompanying Aunty Rosa.'

'Doctor Carlo recommended it to avoid future nascent issues,' Isabella responded, dodging her son's incredulous stare. 'That man really knows what he's talking about. You know, he helped your grandma a lot.'

'Grandma too?' said Viviano with a grimace. *'Cazzo,* fuck. I expected better from Grandma.'

His mother slapped him lightly on the wrist.

'You can't keep giving him your money just 'cause you think he's handsome, Mother.'

'Yes, he has got nice eyes and strong hands,' said Isabella, seeming to ignore her son's tone as she leant her head back against the wall. 'But he's also doing excellent work.'

'Well, I can see it's too late for you,' said Viviano. 'You're beyond saving.'

'You know, he could take a look at your feet too, son,' Isabella said, a twinkle flashing across her eyes.

'I want no part in this, Ma … You're not selling me out to your foot-cult leader. My feet are fine.'

'Peccato, shame,' she said, her lips just curling at the corners. 'I would have liked to be the one to tell him I had found a new client.'

Viviano snorted, but inside, his heart felt suddenly light and he took a second to appreciate the scene: His mother sitting with this relaxed demeanour while she joked with him. He never tired of seeing her happy: there had been a time when it was unimaginable.

'I'm going to bed, Ma,' Viviano said, having tucked the image away somewhere safe. 'Lay off that cream, OK. If I find your feet in the corridor tomorrow, I'll know where to start my investigations.' Rising from his chair, he kissed his mother on the cheek and took his empty plate to the kitchen.

'Viv, thank you for cleaning this morning,' he heard Isabella say. 'It was so nice to come home after a busy day and find it so tidy.'

'*Figurati*, no problem. *Buona notte*,' Viviano said before heading down the cramped hallway to his room.

As usual, the door jarred sharply and Viviano threaded his hand through the tiny gap and shifted his costume rack before entering.

The walls had always been dark blue, like the Roman night sky, but the boyhood posters of football legends had disappeared long ago, replaced by photos with friends and a random array of artwork. Some he had bought, others he had drawn himself – impressions from the streets or of people whose faces had left an impression.

Viviano dodged around his sewing machine, laden with its carefully stitched, half-finished garments, and selected some music, an album by a Brazilian busker whose voice he had fallen for a few weeks before. As her set had drawn to a close, Viviano had broken his statuesque pose and rushed over to buy an album before she disappeared from the city and continued her worldly travels. The singer from Rio had noticed the sketch book by his spot and, in the end, she had gifted him the album in exchange for a drawing of her performing.

Now, jaunty notes began to drift across his room, meandering out of the open window onto the streets below, as the woman's deep voice sang in Portuguese about love, life and sorrow. He should have felt calm, but instead, Viviano began to pace up and down at the foot of his bed, staring at his marching feet.

Is Signora Solari's death my fault? he wondered, his thoughts steering him somewhere dark, as they often did.

Don't do this, Viv. That's Impossible. She died of cancer. She was ill for years, his brain fought back, attempting to stop the intrusive thought from spiralling.

'But maybe I did something and I didn't realise …' he said, yanking at a tuft of hair behind his ear. All of a sudden, his head hurt and breathing was harder.

Stop it. Stay in reality. You know you. Do you hurt people? his brain asked, trying to be a rational voice and calm him down.

'No,' Viviano whimpered. 'I don't think so.'

Right, and you studied law. Where is the evidence for your supposed brutal take down of kind Signora Solari? his brain continued. Humour was another technique to steer him back on track. *You know, your ungodly, Viking-esque, no-mercy assassination.*

'I don't have any …' Viviano admitted. 'It's just a feeling, just a feeling I have.'

You know you do this – it's just your thoughts.

Viviano sat down at his desk and pulled a sketch book towards him, letting it fall open on the page it always did. With a black biro, he turned his attention to a pair of eyes, accentuating the lashes with light pen strokes and pressing down into the paper to fill the onyx irises. They stared back, pulling him in. The woman without a story, and the only clarity he'd ever felt. Who was she? And why was she a mystery when he could read everyone else?

As he stared into the lullaby gaze, Viviano's breathing calmed and his eyes closed.

26

An image of *Signora* Solari crept across his mind – her warm smile as she collected him from primary school, the little high-five she would give him before asking about his day.

'I'm just sad she's dead,' he said aloud, finding some lucidity amid his chaotic thoughts. 'It's really hard.'

The sudden admission of sadness translated into a burning, bubbling ball of lava in his stomach. Viviano leapt up and jumped onto a strip of slackline stretched across a corner of the room.

I need to work on a new costume, he thought, bouncing up and down, trying to distract himself. *I have to focus on a fresh idea … Maybe a mythical creature with feathers and horns, something that will make people smile … a unicorn … or maybe a dead person … a rotting corpse lying in the street.*

Viviano shook his head violently. 'Stop it! No, nothing to do with that … I can't think right now.'

The lucidity had vanished and Viviano now turned to his other trusted remedy – escape. Springing off the slackline, he landed like a cat on the floor and looked around.

'I have to go back out for a bit. I need to breathe.'

He tiptoed down the corridor, past the bedroom where his mother was sound asleep, and felt in the dark for the cold metal handle.

'I feel like I've done something wrong,' he murmured as the door closed behind him.

CHAPTER NINE

Sleep? I don't believe in it, personally

'You're a selfish bastard!'

Laure's eyes flew open as her neighbour's words cut through the night's silence.

'No, no, no, no,' she said, burying her head under a pillow, tears of exhaustion flooding her eyes.

'A selfish bastard?' a deep voice, dripping with incredulity, retorted on the other side of the wall. 'How can you call me that?'

Suddenly, a burning rage seared Laure's spine and she sat bolt upright. 'I can't take this anymore!' she yelled, pounding her fist into the mattress. 'You shut up, you assholes. You absolute fucking pieces of shit! Shut the fuck up!'

You could do that against the wall, tu sais. It might make more of an impact, her brain suggested.

'That was the plan,' Laure said, shaking her head, 'but the last thing I need is to get involved in their madness.'

Anyway, it was a lost cause. The war next door was back on and Laure crumpled into the foetal position, preparing to be annihilated.

Oh wait! she thought as a lightbulb switched on in her foggy mind. *There's a grenade in the kitchen. I know there is. I've seen it!*

The room was like the inside a boiled kettle, and Laure slid across the sweaty floorboards to the cupboard above the sink. With anticipation, she peered inside. There it was, nestled behind the washing powder, the moonlight catching its tortoiseshell metal.

'Parfait,' she said, reaching out a greedy hand.

At that moment, a heartfelt expletive came soaring through the wall, knocking Laure squarely on the head and sending her stumbling sideways.

'Oh, you bastards,' she said, rubbing the sore spot and feeling a lump form. 'So, you heard about my grenade, did you?'

She spun around, tossing the weapon into the air and feeling its satisfying weight sink back into her palm. At the open window, she took aim and prepared to pull the pin.

Wait, dear, her brain piped up in a gentle voice, *I'm not sure you're thinking straight … I'm not sure you're awake.*

Laure's eyes snapped open and she found herself in the darkness, still curled up in bed in a little ball.

Next door, the anger was mounting.

'You know how much I've got on at the moment!' the woman shouted, her Roman accent so strong, it could almost be dialect. 'Yet here you are traipsing through the door at 2 a.m. again.'

Now fully awake, Laure clambered out of bed and began to pace.

This just can't keep happening, she thought as her fingertips found their pre-made dents in her aching temples. *I really should go over there and say something.*

But a glimpse in the mirror suggested otherwise. She was giving off 'girl from The Ring' energy and Medusa wanted her hair back.

It's not good to go over in the middle of the night. I'll knock and speak to them calmly tomorrow, she resolved, just as she had a hundred times before, convinced in the moment that, this time, she wouldn't chicken out when the sun rose.

In the kitchen, Laure poured a glass of water and scraped her fingers down into the dregs of a cereal box. The dry honey oats scratched her groggy tongue, and, in the dimness, work began to flicker across her mind. She had Paolo's spreadsheets in her emails. The ones they had worked on together just hours before.

I bet I can find a more efficient system for the budget, she thought. The idea had started playing on her mind while she was helping him, when for the first time, she had caught a glimpse of the big picture, the budget breakdown for the Rome office. 'There's so much unnecessary waste,' she muttered, as now, in the shadowy room, her desk came into view and her ticking mind began to drown out the neighbours' cries. 'I could work from here, but it would be easier to go into the office. I'd have more headspace. I think my badge would still get me in at this time. That's how it was at my old company back in Paris anyway.'

Laure, it's 2.30 in the morning, qu'est-ce que tu fais? her brain asked. *What are you doing?*

'I can't sleep, and I can't bear this shouting, so I might as well make myself useful.'

Aren't you tired?

'Exhausted, actually,' she admitted, placing a hand on her forehead. 'I don't feel very good.'

Right, her brain said. *And, dis-moi, tell me, is that your job? To streamline the budget for the office? Maybe you'd be stepping on someone's toes. The accountancy department, perhaps? Do you think they'd find it weird that you're going to the office in the middle of the night to do their job? Don't you find it weird?*

'I didn't used to.'

And how did that work out?

Suddenly, Laure stopped.

'You're right,' she said, her hands starting to tremble. 'I can't do this anymore.'

For as long as she could remember, work had been Laure's point of reference, a way to define herself. When she reflected, she thought it was probably because of her parents. Both had emigrated to France in their early twenties, her mum from Marrakesh and her dad from a small village lost in the dry and rolling fields of central

Portugal. From a young age, Laure had absorbed their passing anecdotes, the ones about scarcity, dead-ends and unequal opportunity in their native lands. She had seen them work tirelessly day and night to build a life in France and provide their children with the opportunities they themselves had never known. 'You kids are so lucky,' they used to say, to her and her siblings. 'Go and grab life with both hands.' Laure had a yearning in her bones to make them proud.

After putting her head down, Laure had graduated from one of Paris' most renowned universities and walked straight into a top accountancy firm, ready to give her all. And for five years, she had, until she couldn't anymore. Climbing the ladder came at a cost: deadline after deadline, relentless and unforgiving clients, the pressure falling on your head like a ton of bricks. At first, working through the night had seemed like a novelty, but after a while it was the norm, along with the 2 a.m. business calls. She had constantly told herself to keep it together, had fought through the lonely sadness. She was the go-to girl, the 'yes' woman. 'You can handle this, just keep pushing,' she would tell herself, over and over, as her health deteriorated before her eyes.

Now, in her room, Laure shuddered at the memory. 'It's such a ridiculous idea to go to the office at this time,' she whispered. 'I don't want to go back down that path.'

As she looked around, her eyes fell upon the bed. It was almost trembling from the thunderous noise next door. An image of her and Davide lying there together filled her mind. On a few occasions, she had confided in him about her burnout, increasingly opening up as the trust between them had grown. One night, wrapped together in the sheets, she had told him about the anxiety dreams, the painful cramps that had begun to kill her appetite and the clumps of hair that had fallen from her head.

He had wanted to know what the final straw had been.

'My boss found me crying and hyperventilating on the floor in the supply cupboard,' she had replied. Anytime she had to articulate the words, Laure still felt a hole of shame in the pit of her stomach. 'She put me on sick leave the same day.'

In truth, it wasn't the first time it had happened, just the first time anyone had seen.

In the darkness, Davide had held her close.

Maybe that's why this hurts so much, Laure thought, as she limped back towards bed and the neighbour's shouting grew louder again. *I showed myself to Davide – the good and the bad – and he rejected it, rejected me.* She fell back onto the mattress where the sheets still smelled of his warm skin and cologne. *What happened to you, Da? Will I see your face again?*

Just as her head hit the pillow, Eva's suggestion of ringing Davide came to mind and Laure felt a sudden urge to do so, even just to hear his voice again, but she shut it down immediately.

My mum didn't raise me to grovel before a man, she thought.

CHAPTER TEN

Priorities

On the other side of the wall, the fight showed no sign of abating.

'I can't believe you're behaving like this after everything we've been talking about!' the woman cried.

From her bed, Laure tried to recall mindful techniques such as sheep counting.

'*Talking?* You mean while you've been screaming at me?' the man's voice answered.

'I'm screaming because I'm exhausted! I'm working insane hours, and when I finally get home, you're not here. I stay up because I want to see you, to spend some time together, but you'd rather be out with your mates.' It sounded like she was holding back tears. 'I texted you tonight and you didn't even answer, for God's sake.'

There were loud footsteps.

'*Amore,* I told you I was going out. It was a work event, you knew that, and my phone died. I'm sorry ... I didn't think I needed to message.'

'Yes, of course, you don't *need* to text me,' she snapped. 'You don't even need to be here at all apparently. You know, when I got offered this promotion, you're the one that encouraged me. You promised to be supportive, but all you do is think about yourself. I should be in bed right now. Do you know how debilitating it is to be constantly sleep deprived?'

Am I listening to another couple drowning in the rat race? Laure wondered as she turned onto her side and tried to unhear the comment about sleep deprivation.

'*Amore,*' the man's voice came next door. 'I know you're under pressure and you're incredibly busy, but you've been in this role for a year now. You're getting sucked into the success. It seems like nothing is ever enough. At every opportunity, you take on more, and on the one hand, that's great, but ... there has to be some relief from work too. For you, for us, *sometimes* ... You weren't always like this, living and breathing your career. We used to go out *together,* switch off from the job. We said we would work to live, *remember?*'

'Oh, you are so patronising! You clearly have no idea how much responsibility I have on my shoulders,' the woman spat back.

This comment seemed to particularly irk the man.

'Ha!' he said, with a high-pitched laugh. 'I have no idea? Believe me, your stressful life is *all* I ever hear about. In fact, I don't think we talk about anything else! You come in, everything is about work, and then we go to bed. Valeria, we're thirty-two years old but we've got less of a life than an elderly couple.'

'Oh, listen to yourself!' the woman shouted back. 'Remember before you were self-employed? All the hours you sacrificed, slaving away to build your CV until you could go at it alone? That must have slipped your mind. But now it's *my* turn to progress my career, and suddenly, I'm no fun anymore! Honestly,' she said, her voice cracking, 'I just don't know how much more of this I can take. I-I find myself wondering if it's even worth it.'

A heavy silence blanketed the air, and in the apartment next door, Laure stared up at the wall. This was new territory for the couple, even she could sense it.

Indeed, when the man spoke again, his voice was a shadow.

'What?' he said. 'What do you mean by that? You wonder if we are worth it?'

'Well, yeah … don't you?' the woman replied. 'I mean, should it be this much of a struggle?'

'I don't know how you can say that,' the man said. 'It's been rough. It's a tough period for us, but I have never questioned you and me.'

'Wow,' Laure whispered from her bed. 'I guess everyone is struggling … even these wankers.'

CHAPTER ELEVEN
Yes, I'm late. Are you as proud of me as me?

Laure awoke in a crumpled heap. Her limbs were splayed like a swatted mosquito and the stifling heat was an invisible assassin, pushing down on her windpipe.

'*Merde,*' she said, glancing at her phone. She must have snoozed the alarm.

Over the past weeks, Laure had become accustomed to the headache that felt like a stiletto lodged in her skull, and the neighbours' fighting was the new soundtrack to her life.

In a zombie-like state, she fell under the shower, stumbled into some clothes, and left the house without even bothering to look in the mirror. What would have been the point? Even breakfast was off the cards – there was no milk or much of anything in the house, thanks to her late night with Paolo.

After pelting down the first two flights of stairs, Laure rounded the corner and stopped abruptly. An elderly man was standing immobile, halfway down the next flight. His feet were together, seemingly glued to one step, and his frail hands clung to the banister as if it were a matter of life and death.

Slowly, Laure approached until she was standing next to him. The man's stiff pose reminded her of a lost hiker who had been petrified for decades on a mountain until an ice thaw revealed their presence. His knuckles were white and his terrified eyes stared unflinchingly ahead.

'Are you alright, *signore?*' Laure asked, speaking gently so as not to startle him. The man didn't move.

'I-I almost tripped,' he finally stuttered. 'That's never happened to me before … I've been coming down these stairs for over sixty years, and I've always felt completely secure.' Gingerly, his head turned towards Laure and he fixed her with a frightened gaze. 'What do you think that means?' he asked.

Laure looked back at the man and tried to understand the situation.

I think he's OK, she thought to herself. *He just seems scared. The stumble has made him panic. Still, I should check it's not something more serious.*

'Are you feeling well generally, *signore?*' she asked. 'Can you maybe tell me what happened?'

'I feel fine,' the man said defiantly, his tone incongruous with his current predicament of clinging to the handrail. 'I came out of my flat just here, like I do every day, to go walking in the city with my friends. You know, my doctors say I'm in amazing shape,' he continued. 'I may have just turned eighty-four but I walk 10,000 steps a day, I can still hike up the Gianicolo Hill and I can win a debate with anyone, I'm telling you.'

Laure nodded, and confirmed in her mind that this gentleman was just rattled. *He probably felt his age catch up with him for a second,* she thought. *Saw his own mortality. It must be scary.*

'Wow,' Laure responded to the man with a smile. 'It sounds like you've got more energy than me.'

Visibly pleased with the acknowledgement, Laure saw his grip on the banister loosen.

'You know,' she went on, 'I tripped down these stairs myself, just a few weeks ago. Easily done when we're used to flying down them. I had to remind myself to take care.' She stepped down until they were facing each other. The man's eyes were lively. They looked like they were once a dark mahogany, but had gone slightly grey with age. Here and there, a reddening at the rims had crept in across the pale white irises.

'I hope you didn't hurt yourself when you tripped,' the man said, and Laure could sense his desire to be seen in the dignified light he was accustomed to.

'Luckily not,' she replied, and after a moment's hesitation, added, 'Can I accompany you down this time?' She expected he might protest, but instead, the man looked grateful.

'*Grazie,* just this time. I feel a bit shaken up in truth.'

'I think you just panicked, didn't you?' Laure said, taking great care as she wrapped his bony arm around her shoulder, while supporting his slim frame with her own.

Together, they descended. After one flight, Laure noticed she wasn't really helping anymore and by the time they reached the ground, the man had detached himself and regained a certain spring in his stride.

'Do you live alone?' Laure asked as they stepped out into the morning sunshine.

'No, with my wife. I won't tell her about this, though,' he said. 'She's been calling me an old man for decades.' His tone changed from lighthearted to serious. 'She'd only worry anyway.'

Laure nodded.

'Well, *signorina,* my walking group will be wondering where I've got to. We always meet early, before the heat hits and turns us into snails.' He took her hand. 'I want to thank you for your kindness. You didn't tell me your name.'

'It's Laure. And yours, *signore?*'

'Laure, *la bella* Laure. I'm Ernesto. Nice to meet you. Come and knock sometime. We're on the second floor, just next to the stairwell. I make wonderful cannoli – my family is Sicilian, originally,' he said, his voice suddenly warm with pride. 'Anyway, *ti giuro,* I promise you won't find me on the stairs like that again.'

'*Lo so, lo so,* I know,' said Laure.

With that, they parted ways. The man strolled off and Laure began to beeline to work, with one look back to make sure that Ernesto was still sprightly.

He's fine, she thought, as her power walk turned into a light jog.

'Faster, faster, faster, *allez!*'

As she passed Da Antonio and the aromas of freshly ground coffee and warm pastry perfumed the air, a pang hit Laure's heart. At the bridge, she looked up, as was customary, to see the starlings. Unlike her mood, their swoops were calm and, under her gaze, they flocked together, forming the shape of a giant espresso cup in the air. It pulsed enthusiastically in the bright sunshine. For the first time that morning, Laure stopped. Her head was hurting, legs as heavy as lead, and she was sweating through her flowery blouse.

'I'm not going to last the day,' she admitted, closing her eyes. 'I need a coffee.'

What about work? her brain asked.

Laure shook her head. *'Je sais,* I know, but I'll just have to be a little late.'

Turning on her heel, she skulked the path back towards Da Antonio, too tired even to marvel at what she'd just said. She had never been late a day in her life.

The café was busier than usual. Laure slipped in among the customers and shuffled towards a free nook at the counter. Rather than the sleek business crowd with their tailored suits and 'deal-making' energy that normally inhabited the space, today the vibe was different. Hipsters with laptops had set up in the veranda's shade, sipping coffee and listening to podcasts as they worked. Stay-at-home dads rocked babies and pushed buggies while drinking lattes and, along the counter, the stiff white shirts and steamed dresses had been replaced with an array of colourful clothing worn by customers who had left conventional working schedules behind.

What a difference half an hour makes, Laure thought, glancing nervously at her watch.

As he spotted the dishevelled figure down the end of the bar, Antonio shook his head and immediately prepared her order.

In a daze, Laure picked up the coffee in front of her and took a deep sip.

'Oh, *scusami,* I think that's mine,' a stranger's voice said next to her.

CHAPTER TWELVE

Why would I care whose croissant this is?

From her position, hunched over the coffee, Laure's head jolted up to see a pair of dark, almond-shaped eyes contemplating her with a perplexed expression.

Feeling confused, she glanced down at what was clearly not her order and then back at the eyes. 'Oh, I'm so sorry,' she said, immediately relinquishing her grip on the mug.

'No worries! Easy mistake,' the man said with a laugh. 'This place is packed today! Did you also order a cappuccino?'

'No,' said Laure. 'A macchiato.'

The man's smile grew into a grin and two dimples carved his stubbled cheeks. 'Long week?' he asked.

'You don't even want to know,' said Laure, unable to muster the energy to match the jokey charm of this stranger. 'I'm so sorry about your coffee, though. Please let me buy you another one.'

The man cocked his head to one side and evaluated Laure's distressed state. 'Out of the question,' he said. 'I've already forgotten about it. In fact, I'm going to get you some marmalade cake.'

Laure attempted a polite smile, knowing this man's intentions were good but hoping to be left alone soon. 'No, no,' she said with a light wave of her hand. 'Honestly, please don't. It's not necessary.'

But at the mention of cake, her stomach grumbled and the be-dimpled man sensed her conflicting thoughts on his offer.

'Eh, come on, it's only cake,' he said, moving his hands up and down in a classic Italian prayer-like position, meaning, 'you don't need to think so hard about cake'. 'Anyway,' he said, suddenly serious, 'I feel I have to cheer you up because … well, it seems like something just *terrible* has happened to you.'

He flung his arms out for dramatic effect, and Laure couldn't help but laugh at his outlandish manner, which was turning a few heads either side of them.

'Oh, *mon Dieu*,' she said, placing her face in her hands.

Buoyed by the reaction, he continued. 'I mean, it really seems like you're going through the worst of the worst! Antonio!' he bellowed, twisting to look back over the counter, arms still outstretched. 'This woman needs cake!'

For a brief moment, Antonio observed his customer, before turning and going out for a cigarette break.

'Stop it!' said Laure, fully laughing now.

'Eh, a smile!' the man said. 'That's better. So, tell me … who died?'

'It's my grandma,' Laure said, meeting his gaze.

The friendly stranger froze, his cheeks ashen as shame flooded his face. '*O mio Dio*, I'm so sorry,' he began.

'I'm kidding,' Laure interjected rapidly. 'I'm sorry, that's not funny.' She shook her head. 'I'm just exhausted. I'm not sleeping properly, and as is apparently obvious, it's taking a toll.'

His legs like jelly, the man clung to the chair. 'I nearly just died on the spot,' he said. 'In Italy, you NEVER make jokes about the *nonna*, especially not death jokes, for God's sake!' He made the sign of the cross on his chest. 'The *nonna* is sacred.'

Laure rolled her eyes.

'Rolling your eyes at the *nonna*,' the man tutted. 'Shame on you.' But his frown twitched at the edges.

As the waiter cut a slice of apricot marmalade tart, and the smell of buttery pastry reached her nose, Laure contemplated her apparent new friend.

'That's really kind of you,' she said, pulling the plate towards her. The golden jam tasted sweet and delicious, and after the first bite, Laure shut her eyes and felt some of the tension that had built up inside melt away – a combination of the much-needed calories and this man's easy manner.

He grinned at her. 'Where are you from?'

'*Francia.*'

'*Mamma mia*, now I really do understand why you're so miserable,' he said. 'Get this woman another piece of cake!' he hollered at Antonio.

After sweeping a stray strand of white hair back into its perfectly coiffed position, Antonio opened a large newspaper and blocked them both from view.

'Eh, *calmati!* Calm down!' Laure said, in fits of giggles as she brushed the man's hand out of the air with her fingertips.

'I'm joking, of course,' he said. 'I love *la belle* France. But what on earth are you doing here in this chaos?'

'I live here,' said Laure, savouring the last mouthful of tart. 'Actually, it's pretty much my one-year anniversary.'

'Wow' he exclaimed. '*Auguri!* Congratulations! And, why Rome?'

Laure shrugged, and tried to ward off the prickles of anxiety in her throat. 'I just needed a change, I guess,' she replied, swallowing hard.

'Well, let me say, you seem to be really loving it.'

This comment caused a snort to spill from Laure's mouth which she hastened to control, lest pastry crumbs should be sprayed all over the counter.

I'm having fun here, she thought.

'How about you? Where are you from?' Laure asked.

'Ah, I'm a little ashamed,' the man said. 'I haven't moved much. I'm from here … the beautiful Eternal City, complete with its garbage pile ups, pot holes and rampant traffic jams. Roman born and raised. Actually, I grew up in the outskirts, near the beach, but now I live just around the corner with my girlfriend.'

Laure felt a small jolt in her stomach, but she nodded enthusiastically at the man, hoping he hadn't caught the glimpse of her disappointment. 'Oh, that's great!' she said, still nodding.

'Ha, apparently you think so!' he laughed, fervently nodding in imitation until they both looked like toy dogs on a dashboard.

S'il te plaît, please don't be that person, her brain said as Laure calmed her head movements and brushed aside the remnants of disillusion. *You don't need to fall in love with everyone you meet.*

'I'm sorry,' said the stranger. 'It's not kind to make fun of you when you're so tired. To be honest, I'm quite sleep-deprived myself.'

'Really?' said Laure. 'It's horrible, isn't it? I feel like a zombie all the time. What's been keeping you up?'

'Just restless, I suppose,' he replied, suddenly looking a bit miserable. 'Dealing with some stuff at the moment … but hey, I guess everyone is.'

There was silence between them for the first time since they'd met and the man glanced up at the TV screen.

'Fuck,' he said. 'My poor Lazio was humiliated last night.'

'Oh, you like football,' said Laure. 'I guess I'm a Roma fan.'

A guttural noise like a wounded boxer came from her companion as he choked on his coffee before turning to stare at Laure. She kept her eyes fixed on the screen, pretending she hadn't noticed the over-reaction, and then casually turned and said, 'What?'

'Oh, you're good,' the man muttered, his eyes narrowing, and Laure shot him a winner's grin.

I'm not crazy, she thought. *There is chemistry between us.*

'I hope you know,' the man said, 'that being a Roma fan is actually immoral. They're all fascists.'

'That can't be true!' said Laure, laughing. 'Anyway, they're just the first team I came to know when I moved here. They're named after the city after all. And actually,' she said with a shy smile, 'I have heard the same thing about Lazio fans.'

'Not possible,' the man said, clicking his tongue in disapproval. 'Lazio fans are the total opposite. They're always risking their lives to *save* people … Some of them have even died in truly selfless acts.'

'I see,' said Laure.

'A non-believer,' said the man. 'Well, I have a reconversion therapy to propose. Lazio is playing Roma next week and we always watch the derby with friends. This time, my partner and I are hosting and you should come. We cook, we drink, we have fun … and we *all* support Lazio,' he said. 'Give me your number, if you fancy it, and I'll send you the details. A Roma fan, for crying out loud,' he mumbled.

Laure passed over her phone with her number displayed on the screen. One year in Rome and she still hadn't managed to memorise it.

'I don't actually know your name,' the stranger said.

'It's Laure.'

'Laure, I'm Marco. *Enchanté,*' he said in a pretentious voice, kissing his own hand. Laure laughed.

'But seriously,' Marco continued, handing the phone back, 'you're welcome to join us. We always have fun. Our place isn't far, either, just around the corner – Sant'Angelo Street. Got a nice view up the Gianicolo Hill.'

Laure smiled absentmindedly as she slipped the phone back into her bag, and then the words passed through her head again. 'Sant'Angelo Street?' she repeated.

Marco nodded.

'You're kidding! That's my ...' Laure began to say, but the words dried up on the tip of her tongue and a huddle of seamstresses started stitching in her head.

Sleep deprived. Dealing with some things ... The words echoed in her mind. *Sant'Angelo Street. Just around the corner. Sleep deprived. Dealing with things. Partner. I live with my Partner ... Dealing with things.*

From all these words, the needle workers weaved together an intricate tapestry onto which the form of a man with a fresh trim and long dark eyelashes appeared.

Oh my God, it's him! her brain shrieked, reaching the epiphany.

The seamstresses applauded.

This charming guy is the source of all the misery in my life!

CHAPTER THIRTEEN

Lies, oh lies!

It appeared to Marco that the woman in front of him might be having a small stroke. He glanced around, wondering whether to intervene. 'You were saying something?' he prompted nervously.

'Oh, yes!' said Laure, springing back to life. She stared at Marco, still processing the information. 'Sant'Angelo,' she said. 'Angelo.'

Marco refamiliarised himself with the numbers for the emergency services under his breath.

'That's my ... that's my favourite name for a boy,' Laure finally said, even to her own surprise.

'Oh, right!' Marco said with a relieved laugh, opting to write off Laure's behaviour as a 'French quirk'. 'Well, good! A fine name, for sure.'

Just outside the café, a large man in a red bucket hat was strolling past at the head of a group of tourists. 'And then I said, you've really let the rabbit outta the hat there,' he howled in a US drawl. It must have been an entertaining story because his friends were in stitches.

Marco and Laure observed them through the window as they strolled on.

'Trastevere is always packed with people from everywhere,' said Marco, glancing away from the group and back at Laure. 'Do you live around here?'

'Ha,' Laure laughed, her mind whirring. 'Do I live near here?' She thought hard. 'Well, yes ... well, kind of ... yes,' she nodded, confirming her flat's fake location in her mind. Laure cleared her throat and announced, 'I live about ten minutes away, near the river ... down by the Piazza Trilussa, really. But I love Da Antonio, so I always make the effort to come.' Relieved to have finally put together a coherent sentence, Laure took a breath, but was unsure as to why she had scrambled to lie.

'Che bello, so nice,' Marco said. 'I love it around there. Though, I bet its unbearably noisy at night. No wonder you're not sleeping!'

'Ah, OK,' said Laure, feeling her jaw clench and willing Marco, for his own good, to stop talking about the night-time noise.

But he pressed on, leaning in closer, as if sharing a secret. 'We're lucky where we are, tucked away down a little cul-de-sac. There's nothing to see, so generally people just walk straight by. It's a coup, really, so central but peaceful.' He leant in again.

40

'Mostly only those of us from the neighbourhood know about it. I'm giving you an inside scoop in case you ever move.' Sitting upright, he winked at Laure. 'Me and the missus are very happy there, anyway.'

In that moment, it took all of Laure's strength not to launch herself at Marco, knock him backwards onto the scuffed floor tiles and kick him until Antonio had to come and drag her away.

Oh, yes, she thought. You and your wonderful missus, with your divine relationship, living happily in your quiet street, are you? You winky asshole. It doesn't matter that you're ruining my peace, does it? You patronising son of a …

'Thanks for the tip,' Laure said aloud, a placid expression on her face and her eyes fixed on his. She paused for a moment, and then suddenly, more words tumbled from her mouth. 'I know some people, especially when they're getting older, want a quiet life, but I personally would find that so boring. I just love being able to go out and enjoy myself.' She beamed at Marco and her heart thumped against her ribcage.

Marco nodded and Laure caught the stirrings of a wistful look.

'But then,' she continued, 'I'm sure it's different for you and your missus. You probably love those cosy nights in, probably got tired of the night scene a long time ago.'

For a moment, Marco shifted around on the spot before looking up and finding his affable smile once again. 'Ha, of course we do enjoy nights in, we do,' he said. 'Well, she more than I, to be honest … ha ha. But we do also like to go out, and you know, we used to love making the most of everything Trastevere has to offer …' He trailed off.

'Oh, that's great!' said Laure, unable to stop the weeks of sleepless nights from carrying the conversation. 'I think it's so wonderful when couples still have fun together. It's so important.'

This time, Marco avoided Laure's eyes. 'That's true,' he said, somewhat distantly. 'Hey, is that why you were so sad this morning? Were you nursing a hangover?' he asked with a chuckle, recovering some of his good humour. 'And here was me thinking you were in a world of pain.'

'Guilty,' Laure said, with a coy shrug. 'It's worth it, I guess. Anything to avoid getting stuck in a cycle of misery, you know?' And she flashed a smile which bore fangs.

Um, excusez-moi, what ze fuck are you doing? her brain enquired.

In front of Laure, Marco's manner had become fidgety. He ran an anxious hand through his hair and rubbed his neat stubble. 'You know,' he said after a while, 'I actually couldn't agree more. Anyway, Laure, I've got to do some work. Are you heading out as well?'

A long queue was forming at the front of the café as Laure passed Antonio, who was busy making magic at the humming machine. Before leaving, she smiled at the back of his head, a gesture he saw reflected in the milk jug's shiny metal, and noted.

Back in the sweltering heat, the pair faced each other – Laure and the handsome hostage holder of her sleep.

'Well, *mademoiselle*, it was a real pleasure, your fascist tendencies aside. I'll text you about the football. I hope your day picks up.'

'Grazie,' said Laure. 'É stato un piacere anche per me, it was nice to meet you too. I'll make sure my Roma T-shirt is freshly pressed for the match.'

With a wave, Laure turned and began wandering towards the bridge. Along the way, various street artists were setting up for the day. To the right, a life-sized pigeon, who still had a human head, was polishing the beady eyes of his costume's feathery headpiece. Further along, two flautists were practising scales as a would-be snake charmer attached invisible cords to his wrists, ensuring his toy serpents would dance for those passing.

As she walked by, Laure's brain was swirling around the surprise encounter with her neighbour.

Your behaviour was a bit strange back there, her brain said. *Why did you lie? You had the chance to confront Marco there and then. You could have even done it in a jokey way, if you think he's a nice guy.*

'I know,' said Laure as she walked on auto-pilot to the office. 'Rationally, that would have been better. But the fake 'relationship bliss' just made me so angry. You know, I'm a human too. I understand that life isn't always great – God knows I understand work-related stress. Who is he helping by pretending that *his* life is perfect? It's a big lie and he's making other people feel like shit.' Her face turned red. 'Well, you know what, I can lie too, and then *he* can feel like shit. See how easy that is!'

Je vois, I get it, you're tired and he was being irritating. I'm just wondering, is there any other reason you didn't tell the truth? her brain asked, as Marco's dark eyes sparkled in Laure's mind.

Laure shrugged and crossed the bridge.

CHAPTER FOURTEEN

Loose change

From Da Antonio, Marco strolled in the opposite direction, sticking close to the wall where the shop fronts provided a meagre strip of respite from the bright sunshine. After a few steps, his arm brushed against a cluster of vines. It was only when the leaves recoiled, that Marco turned to see if he had hit something, but there was nothing there. He was about to continue, when a pair of dark brown shiny shoes caught his attention. Slowly, Marco traced a line upwards and drew level with two bright green eyes peeping out. With a cry like a startled yeti, he leapt backwards and glared at the leafy wall, until feeling very foolish, he realised he was face to face with a street performer.

'Mi scusi!' he said breathlessly. 'I didn't see you there! Great outfit, man. You scared the life out of me.'

The large eyes, surrounded by dense green paint, gave no indication that they had seen Marco, but a pair of arms, cloaked in vines, glided upwards until they rested like gnarly bark tentacles above the tree man's head.

Marco smiled and felt his pockets, searching for some loose change to give the statue. Finding nothing, he walked on, forgetting about the interaction almost as soon as it had happened.

Slowly, Viviano's head turned to the right and his eyes searched for the woman without a story.

CHAPTER FIFTEEN

Heroics make the world go round

At around 1 p.m., Laure was unsticking her legs from the syrupy leather office chair, when her phone buzzed. She glanced up, and for the thousandth time, dabbed away small beads of sweat from her forehead with the edge of her sleeve. By now, her stomach had stopped doing its anxious flutter every time her phone made a noise and the nervous anticipation that it might be Davide had dissipated. All that remained were the lingering feelings of bitterness, insecurity and disappointment at the way he had left things.

Searching for closure, she had tried to get some of her feelings onto paper during a lull in the morning's work. But what was meant to be poetry for the soul had quickly turned sour. Her last attempt read:

Davide, I hate you, you unfathomable wanker. Die.

She had run it by Eva, who had kindly informed her that it wasn't poetry. Laure knew that, but thought it could be avant-garde.

As she looked towards her phone, a vision of Davide, his shoulder-length, shiny brown hair, pale-blue eyes and angular features, appeared across her desk. Laure frowned and jammed a pencil into his right cornea, snapping it cleanly in half. This action happened to coincide with the moment star-reporter Marta was heading out for lunch and she shot Laure a worried side glance.

Sensing someone had witnessed her aggressive pencil therapy, Laure's head snapped up and her eyes met Marta's.

'I just couldn't get it to work anymore!' she said with a flustered laugh, gesturing at the pencil and shrugging her shoulders in a what-else-was-I-supposed-to-do? kind of way.

Marta nodded, decided Laure was crazy and walked off.

Whatever, Laure thought, wiping the dopey smile from her face. She would get over Davide in her own time and using her own methods. With one swift movement, she brushed the pencil end into the bin, and laid the small tip in front of her. That would still work fine.

The text she had received was from an unknown number, and when Laure opened it, the frontpage of a newspaper filled the screen.

'Eh …?' she said aloud, taking a closer look at the main photograph – an adorable golden retriever was yomping around on a rainy day and a headline had been haphazardly cropped over the top.

LAZIO FAN SAVES DROWNING DOG FROM DEEPEST PUDDLE

Laure snorted and zoomed in on the soggy puppy. 'I didn't think you'd actually get in touch,' she muttered under her breath. She texted back.

> What a hero

The response came quickly.

> Preach, Laure. That dog never misses a match now.

'Alright,' Laure said aloud, fighting a smile, then responded tentatively.

> I see you're having a very busy day. To be honest, I wasn't expecting to hear from you

'Well, not until my eyes are about to close,' she murmured.

> Come on, Laure, I am a man of my word! I wanted to formally invite you for football next Friday, 7 p.m. Also, I left as you were walking towards the bridge, and to be honest, I wanted to make sure you hadn't jumped off it.

Laure raised an eyebrow. It wasn't out of the question.

> I'm OK, thank you.
> Just struggling through the day

> I hear that. Get some rest tonight,
> resist the night temptress.

'Oh, fuck you,' Laure blurted out just as Marta was passing by again.

Jesus, what are the chances? thought Laure, as with her kindest eyes, Marta communicated that she would be talking to HR about her behaviour.

Resisting the urge to reply to Marco, Laure instead opted to focus on work and began to draft an email informing staff of available timeslots to book the meeting room.

But then the phone buzzed again.

'*Ça suffit!* Give me a bit of peace!' she said.

It seemed like everyone in the office was striving for calm. In one corner, an impromptu lunch-time yoga class was taking place for those who still hadn't glimpsed the outside world since election night. Various dishevelled figures were participating: some recited interview questions in downward-facing dog, others napped in child's pose, a few were eating McDonald's while balancing in tree.

Not far from them, however, Marcello, the photo editor, was losing his shit. 'What do you mean, you don't have a suit?' he barked at Domenico, a photographer with a penchant for wild nights and Gothic tattoos. 'The Prime Minister's inauguration is obviously a formal event, for ALL those attending, *idiota!* You won't be let in like this! ... Louis!' he bellowed over to the other side of the room.

Louis, an impeccably coiffed reporter, dressed in a shirt and silk waistcoat, strolled over.

'Go and change clothes with Domenico, now! It's an emergency. *Ti prego,* I'm begging you!'

Looking as if he had been asked to pet a maggot, Louis contemplated Domenico's ripped black jeans and tank top, emblazoned with a bleeding heart, before trudging off to the toilets to change.

What a relaxing environment, Laure thought as a chorus of flailing 'omms' rang out across the room.

From behind the desk, she let out a bear yawn that stretched her jaw to its extremities, inviting in the lethargic office flies. Midway through, she could feel Marta watching, as if she had bought a ticket for the wild animal enclosure at the zoo. Laure snapped her mouth shut, turned away from the over-curious Marta, and picked up her phone. The text she had received was from Eva.

> *Amica,* my shift has been cancelled
> tonight. Let's meet at our usual place
> for a catch-up and well-deserved drink.
> *Aperitivo* at 6.30 p.m.?

Laure looked at the message. *Honestly, I'd really just like a night in,* she thought. *To curl up in bed and put on a funny series, or maybe finally, read a few chapters of my book. I could order a pizza and get a proper sleep.*

Do you think that's going to be possible? asked her brain.

Laure imagined herself cosy at home, a typical weekday evening before the arguing had begun. But the flat was no longer her little safe haven. If she tried to have a relaxing night in, even the expectation that, at any moment, the racket next door might begin would put her on edge.

With a sigh, Laure sent a thumbs up to Eva.

Maybe a glass of wine will make everything feel easier, she thought.

At the stroke of six, Laure slipped out of the office and strolled towards Piazza Navona, one of the city's most famous landmarks. The vast oval space had been an athletics stadium in ancient Rome, commissioned by the powerful Emperor Domitian. Now, many centuries later, it was a treasure chest of Baroque architecture, filled with towering churches and grand fountains. It had always been one of Laure's favourite places and she glided through, passing the sculpted marble statues of river Gods perched above pools of crystalline water. Piazza Navona was forever popular with tourists, whose babel of languages added to the culture and history humming in the air. Some visitors stayed for dinner, lounging under parasols with a crisp glass of wine. Others stopped to have their futures told by tarot readers whose foldable tables were dotted over the black cobblestones. In the centre was an art market where a tangle of painters sat depicting the city's landscapes or sketching caricatures of ever-changing subjects. Their works hung from chairs and easels or lay across the floor, drenching the square in colour.

Mega Bar – Laure and Eva's regular spot – was just a few minutes away, and even though she had stood in that square a thousand times, Laure couldn't help but pause and let it transport her back through Roman history one more time. It made her moderate headache and lurking heartache seem rather insignificant.

CHAPTER SIXTEEN

Pressure, pushing down on me

Viviano was making his way to Piazza Navona, dressed in full tree minus a few branches. It was time for a break and he wanted to sketch a man he had seen before his face disappeared into forgottenness.

Bored of the same old route, he spun through the crowds, imagining he was among the clouds instead of the everyday buzz of Roman heads bobbing along.

Inside, his mind was bursting and his body felt as if an electric current was pulsing through it. From experience, Viviano knew this ceaseless agitation could go one of two ways: would it inspire creativity or feed his anxiety? Drawing was a good idea – it should calm him down.

As he moved, he jostled a passer-by. Immediately, Viviano apologised and continued on, but suddenly he felt worried.

Did I hurt him? he wondered, turning to check that the man had not fallen and injured himself.

You saw that he was fine, Viv, when you apologised.

'Yes, I think I know that,' said Viviano. 'But I'll just check again.'

You barely touched him, Viv. Check again if you have to, but you're being silly, his brain said in reassuring tones.

Viviano craned his neck and managed to spot the now distant stranger. He was walking quite normally, just as he had before. Viviano stared, checking, checking, checking until he faded from view.

Is that better? asked his brain.

The lack of sleep hadn't helped his mental clarity, and Viviano could feel the anxiety bully starting to gain ground. He looked around and tried to slow his mind. Despite the heat, it was a beautiful sunny day.

'I have so many good things in my life,' he said, taking deep breaths to stem the angst. He noted how people, no matter how serious looking, cracked a smile when they saw his whimsical costume. A tree 'come to life' and roaming the city.

'I make people happy. I'm not bad,' he repeated.

A family passed by – a mother, father and three children. At the sight of his outfit, the children shrieked with delight and pointed.

'Take a picture with us, Mr Tree man!' a boy, no older than a toddler in tiny denim dungarees and a yellow cap, said.

'Ma certo, of course,' said Viviano.

Instantly, he launched into his best 'tree in stormy weather', as the kids danced around him and the two, tired-looking, parents snapped away.

'Thank you so much,' the father said to Viviano in a polite British accent. 'They've been in a terrible mood all day, bickering and complaining. This is the first time we've seen their grins! The heat is intense, especially for them.'

Viviano smiled and felt some happiness return to his own body. 'My pleasure,' he said.

The smile remained on his face until the family were a few metres away. Then, before his eyes, his brain transformed the scene: an explosion nearby, destruction everywhere, the children covered in blood as their parents wept and screamed.

'Please stop this,' Viviano pleaded with himself. 'That's not what's happening. Look! Everyone is fine. Why are you taking something so nice and making it bad?'

Go and draw, his brain said. Breathe.

Viviano walked quickly until he reached Piazza Navona and sank down in the shade of an easel. He often dropped by here and the artists considered him one of their own. From his rucksack, he produced a sketch book and a black biro, and with long pen strokes, began to draw the man he had seen in the early hours that morning as he returned home.

With a slight hunch in his back, the elderly gentleman had been hobbling down a deserted street at dawn, before even the early risers came to life. It was his expression that had caught Viviano's attention. Despite the effort of each step, his face was bright and his eyes clear.

He has seen a lot in his life, Viviano thought, now seated on the piazza floor. He peppered the man's cheeks with fine lines and began to take shelter in someone else's story, rather than his own. Perhaps he was conscripted in his youth. Every day, he relives the horrors of the war, the innocent victims and friends left behind on the battlefield. That silent walk as the sun rises is a sacred moment in his routine. A time when he can appreciate the acceptance found in old age and the peace in the skies above him.

Viviano had just began depicting the curve of the old man's moustache when, suddenly, he sensed her presence – the woman without a story was nearby, in Piazza Navona.

CHAPTER SEVENTEEN

Please, blow my mind

From among the toing and froing crowds, she emerged.

With her every step, a light breeze blew, taking some of the heat out of the air. It whistled through Viviano's ears, humming an unknown melody, and without any rush or bother, began to soothe his thoughts. The breeze dared to venture right down into the darkest depths of his mind where his most intimate fears lurked like shadowy monsters. Instead of being frightened or shocked by what it found, the tranquil guest acknowledged Viviano's anxieties, chuckling at some and tenderly embracing others, as if soothing the woes of a crying child. Then, it swept everything up among its swirls.

As the woman without a story passed by, the breeze sailed away, taking with it the slimy darkness of intrusive thoughts and leaving in Viviano's head an island of peace. Sitting among the artists in the bustling Piazza Navona, Viviano leant back against a chair and basked in the glow of a calm mind.

It had happened to him for the first time last August.

Viviano had wanted to speak to her ever since that morning exactly a year ago, when a summer storm sent thick silvery ropes cascading from the sky which amassed in a river on the floor.

A lone red umbrella bobbed along the street, fighting against the deluge, and Viviano caught a glimpse of two deep, soulful eyes which dipped in and out of view from under the umbrella's sopping rim. He noted the woman's inability to navigate the cobbled stones without stumbling every couple of steps, which made him laugh.

Expectantly, Viviano had waited for his intuition to come out to play, to reveal her name, an element of her history or, perhaps, a funny anecdote from her past, but he was met with absolute silence. It caught him off guard. The woman glanced around for somewhere to shelter and Viviano stared at her, scouring the expanse of his imagination for a scrap of insight. As his impatience grew for the answers that were always at his beck and call to materialise, a cool wind brushed the tips of his fingers, rustled his T-shirt and tousled his hair. Then, without warning or explanation, the calm of an ocean washed over him. He had never experienced anything like it.

For the rest of the day and late into the night, Viviano had wandered around the city, but everything felt different – the sky was bluer, he could hear the birds chirping to one another, and he could see clearly. He could see how, when he wasn't fighting himself, there was a chance to live, a day that was worth seizing, without the need to hide away. The joyful moments he experienced stayed that way, instead of being churned up and spat out by his mind. In this reality, life was not frantic and sad, and he, Viviano, was not the perpetrator of hurt – that burning hurt that persisted in his invented scenarios, but whose real source evaded him, constantly.

This must be happiness, Viviano thought as his heart floated. *Is this how life could be?*

He ran up to the top of the Gianicolo Hill and shouted to the city below. Shouted out for all to hear that he was happy, that he was normal, that no one needed to worry. There he stayed for hours, lying under a tree and staring at the stars, marvelling at how brightly they shone.

Little by little, as the sun rose, the chaos began to trickle back in. He could feel it happening. One dark thought, and then another, a dull ache in his mind, until eventually, he was reacquainted with the frenzied tinnitus which had plagued him since he was a child.

But the experience had left an indelible mark.

At first, he didn't think the anonymous woman with the soulful eyes and red umbrella could be responsible – that wouldn't make any sense. If it had happened once, it would happen again, he told himself, his heart fluttering at the thought.

Viviano waited and waited. Whenever the wind blew, his eyes lit up and he held his breath, willing nature to work its magic. But it never did. He stopped eating and sleeping, couldn't focus. The pursuit of that fleeting paradise began to consume him. It was only when his mother referred him for an appointment with Doctor Carlo that Viviano heard alarm bells.

'*Basta,* enough, Viv. This can't go on,' he said one afternoon while dangling upside down from a tree near the Vatican, dressed as a ripe pear. 'It was a freak coincidence, and it might never happen again … I must learn to live with myself, just as I am, like I have my whole life.'

Over time, things returned to normal and the vividness of the emotion he had felt that day lost its edges. Then, one day, as summer gave way to autumn and the city filled with golden leaves, she appeared again, strolling towards Da Antonio with the same shy and uneven approach.

For the first time, he saw her properly. She had dark curls which escaped their bun forming a coily crown around her head, a warm, rounded face and poetic eyes – the ones he had first seen peeping out from under the umbrella.

At that moment, he knew that she was the reason. The mystery woman's gaze wandered over, and the walls of his prison cell began to fade. Viviano had wanted to take a few steps forward, to get closer, but he hadn't dared, worried that even the slightest movement might shatter the perfect tranquillity that was making him float.

'That was almost exactly a year ago,' Viviano said, as now, back in Piazza Navona, four paws landed with a light thud on his shoulder, jogging him from the reverie.

'Prrrrrrrrrrrrr.'

'*Buona sera, Signor* Bigoli,' Viviano said, shifting his head to see the candyfloss tail of a ginger cat slinking around his neck.

Signor Bigoli nuzzled his face into Viviano's cheek, asking as he always did, for some affection, and Viviano caressed the soft mass of hair around his neck. To him, the feline's snow-white breast always looked like a nobleman's ruffle, which was fitting for his background.

The fluff ball belonged to an aristocratic family that lived nearby, and every day, he waltzed through his ruby-encrusted cat flap to come for a stroll. Although humble, he did appreciate the odd salute or bow from other neighbourhood cats as he paraded around the square. Those who really knew him, though, were aware of his main *raison d'être:* to get himself in as many tourist photos and paintings as possible. For almost two decades, *Signor* Bigoli had unexpectedly popped up in holiday snaps, videos and even postcards. And of course, the piazza's artists had immortalised him in oil paintings – *Signor* Bigoli had a particular penchant for caricatures that transformed him into a fierce lion which he found whimsical.

After stretching out his limbs, the cat hopped down onto Viviano's lap and purred.

'Who is that woman?' Viviano asked, stroking *Signor* Bigoli's fluffy coat. 'Will I ever be able to talk to her?'

The feline's topaz eyes flickered towards Viviano, but he wasn't listening. A few metres away, the enticing flash of a camera had caught his attention. He offered a disinterested shrug to his human friend before sprinting off for an Instagram cameo.

Alone again, Viviano closed his eyes and watched the woman walk through the calm plains she had just created in his mind, left right, left right, like a metronome.

She's beautiful, he thought, envisaging her smiling face. *I bet ... I bet she's funny too.*

But, in reality, his thoughts were a stab in the dark. When it came to her, for the first time ever, his brain drew a blank.

CHAPTER EIGHTEEN

How does it look when you fall in love?

Laure and Eva always met in the same little bar tucked behind Piazza Navona, away from the crowds. As Laure walked, a swirl of starlings flew above, warming up for their evening performances.

Mega Bar was old but maintained with love. Its sturdy walls were lined from top to bottom with antique bottles of wine and all through the interior, hundreds of misshapen mirrors dangled from the ceiling or were tiled into the floor, making the customer feel as if they had entered an optical illusion. To get the evening started, the owner liked to play electronic remixes of classical music. The pulsing melodies drifted out of the door and down the winding streets.

As soon as Laure arrived, she spotted Eva floating over, her long henna-tinted hair and shiny silver piercings catching the evening light.

'Belllaaaaa,' Eva said, wrapping Laure in a tight embrace.

Eva smelt of weed and fresh lavender, as if she'd spent the day skipping through fields, as high as a kite.

'I'm happy to see you,' she continued, beaming and taking Laure's face in her hands. Most days, Eva changed her contact lenses to reflect her mood – today, her eyes were lilac. 'Let's get some food, I'm so hungry,' she said.

The two women had come for '*aperitivo*', an Italian custom where buying a drink gives access to a large Italian buffet, filled with pasta salads, mini pizzas and cured meats. After ordering a bottle of rosé, they proceeded to stack their plates with everything on offer, dipping large spoons into one bowl and then the next. Dinner and drinks in hand, they shuffled back outside.

The bar was packed. Dozens of customers were seated at tables which sprawled across the cobblestones, and Laure and Eva beelined towards a free spot among the chatty crowds. Once seated, Eva lit a cigarette and gazed at the plume of smoke she sent floating into the even air.

'I've started swimming lessons,' she declared.

'Interesting,' said Laure. 'I didn't know you couldn't swim.'

'I can keep afloat and do a good doggy paddle, but I've never felt comfortable out of the shallow end. Water is so calming. I want to enjoy it without stress,' Eva said, raising her arms high in the air and letting her head fall back.

'And how are the lessons?'

'Hmm, I'd say alternative,' said Eva, gradually re-adopting a socially acceptable posture. 'The teacher has a really soft voice and the pool is loud, so she just mimes the movements over and over again in slow motion, and we have to copy as best we can. The only thing I've ever heard her say is, "You can't teach the butterfly. You either have it or you don't".'

'That can't be right,' said Laure, biting into a mini pizza.

Eva shrugged. 'I tried it once, on her suggestion, and immediately sunk to the bottom.'

'Maybe it's not the right teaching style for you, or for anyone,' Laure suggested, sipping her wine.

'I'll keep it for now. I quite like that she doesn't talk. We all just make shapes in the water – it's very freeing.'

'*Va bene*, OK,' said Laure. 'I'd like to come and watch one day.'

Eva laughed. '*Mamma mia*, that would be a sight. Like watching dolphins on acid. Anyway, how are you, *bella*? Any news from Davide?'

'None,' said Laure, feeling a dull pain in her heart.

'Are you OK?' her friend asked.

'I mean, what else can I be?' said Laure with a shrug. 'I hate that sinking feeling in the morning … That's when it's worst, when you wake up and remember, and feel that dead weight in the pit of your stomach. In the daytime, I feel better.'

'I'm sorry,' said Eva, stroking her friend's hand with fingernails painted a deep shiny red. 'You know,' she said, reflecting while replacing oxygen with nicotine, 'I saw that the police have intercepted a convict in the mountains. Escaped from Rome up north a few days ago. Diamond thief apparently. About our age. They're not releasing his name.'

Laure raised an eyebrow. 'Right.'

'Well …' Eva said, 'do you think it might be Davide? I mean, the dates match up …' She fixed Laure with a probing look. 'Did he seem like a convict to you?'

Laure burst out laughing. 'Oh *mon Dieu*, I don't think so.' She paused for a moment and took a sip of wine. 'Is there a photo?'

'I checked, but not yet. You could make some enquiries, but if it is him, you might have to bail him out.'

'Hmm, I don't have any money,' said Laure, giggling. 'I could visit him in jail, though.'

'Did he ever give you any diamonds? Or any other gifts? Something that looked like it once belonged to something or someone else, for example?'

Laure thought about it. 'He did give me a ring that said *"On our 50th anniversary"* and said that it already felt like we'd spent a lifetime together.'

'Really?' Eva shrieked.

'Ha, no!' said Laure. '*Ma dai*, come on.'

The two burst into fits of giggles and Eva reached out and took Laure's hand. 'I'm here for you whenever you need,' she said, suddenly serious. 'I'm sorry this guy got into your heart. You didn't think he was the one, did you?'

Laure sat back in her chair and looked at the merriment around them – the buzz of chatter, the laughter and clinking of glasses that filled the warm evening air. 'When I look past the feeling of humiliation, I can't really say if he was the one. We weren't together for very long, even though it felt quite intense. I think I was just ready to believe it, and that's what hurts the most.'

'What do you mean?' Eva asked, pulling another cigarette out of the packet and lighting it with the dying embers of the one in her mouth.

'I haven't always been open to relationships,' Laure said. 'But I let myself be this time. I was ready to believe his words, that he thought I was special and that, just maybe, he was thinking, "Wow, *ça y est*, I can stop looking now." It was the promise of building something with someone. I feel like I'm ready to do that.'

'It's disappointing,' said Eva, shaking her head. 'I don't think it matters how long you've known someone for, an abrupt ending is painful, especially when your hopes are up. But I think, all in all, the fact you were being open and honest is really positive.'

'Yeah, I just have to battle the feeling that I wasn't good enough, or worth the effort in the end.'

'*Amica*, of course, that's not true. It was just the wrong guy, my love,' Eva said, as she wrote 'RIP Davide' with cigarette smoke and watched the words hang in the air.

Laure nodded and absentmindedly moped up the sauce on her plate with some focaccia. 'Is that something that you want?' she asked Eva, timidly. 'To build something with someone?'

'*Assolutamente*, fucking, no,' said Eva, shovelling more fusilli into her mouth. 'I like being free. I literally have no desire to build something stable. I mean, I only get to be on this earth once. I want my life to be an adventure.' She looked at Laure, and her lilac eyes sparkled. 'Maybe one day those feelings might change, but at the moment, it's something I feel so strongly in my bones.'

'I'd love to feel that sure about anything right now,' said Laure, taking a gulp of wine.

'It's partly experience based,' said Eva, sipping and smoking. 'The last time I was in a relationship, I felt trapped. I wanted to end it for ages, but I felt so guilty and he was a nice guy. Every time I think about getting stuck there again, I have this visceral reaction, and I have to smoke at least two spliffs to calm down.'

'That doesn't sound like a huge chore for you,' Laure laughed. 'Gosh ... it's crazy how we are shaped by our scars, isn't it?'

'*Ma certo*, of course,' said Eva. 'They're everywhere. We can't let them overwhelm us, but they can teach us, and I've learnt that I like being free.'

As Eva blew out a plume of smoke, Laure could swear she saw the dagger tattoo on her friend's wrist quiver.

'ARE YOU READYYYY FOR A GOOD TIME TONIGHT, PEOPLE?'

The customers at the bar jumped out of their seats as a desperately energetic voice came booming through a megaphone. Laure and Eva had forgotten about the weekly

DJ set. It had supposedly been introduced to 'add a new dimension to the bar's atmosphere', but in reality, the young DJ was the owner's nephew, and his mother had forced her brother's hand.

Across the street, a group of Erasmus students, wearing hot pants and chugging margarita slushies, let out whoops of encouragement.

'I SEE YOU LADIES. COME ON OVER!' bellowed the DJ, winking at the unenthusiastic Mega Bar customers, many of whom shook their heads at him.

Giggling, the girls looked like they had every intention of coming over to raise the roof, and the DJ's self-esteem. But, as they paraded towards the bar, one of the young women's whoops turned into margarita-slushie vomit, which she then hurled down the leg of her unsuspecting friend.

Shrieks of, 'Ewww' rang out and the puker was quickly carted away down a side road by her crew.

'OKAY, OKAY, LADIES, NO PROBLEM. I'LL CATCH YOU NEXT WEEK THEN. STAY HOT, LADIES,' boomed the DJ, turning his hands into guns and doing a little dance towards the disappearing girls. 'NOW LET'S PARTY, ROMA!'

Everyone groaned.

Eva laughed. 'Honestly, I don't know how he can bear to come back and put himself through this every week,' she said. 'But his ability to shake off humiliation is somehow inspiring. I sometimes think of him when I have nightmares about nobody turning up at my shows.'

'*CHE,* WHAT?' mouthed Laure, straining to hear over the latest Reggaetón hit which was now blasting out of the speakers.

'I said his humiliation is inspiring,' Eva shouted.

'Oh, right,' yelled Laure, with a perplexed nod. 'If you say so.'

All of a sudden, Mega Bar's owner came rushing out and charged at the DJ. After a brief back and forth involving aggressive hand gestures and matching facial expressions, the volume of the music was taken down, much to the DJ's obvious dismay.

Collectively, his audience breathed a sigh of relief.

'For the love of *Dio,* this kid thinks he's fucking Daddy Yankee,' the boss could be heard saying as he went back inside.

The mood calmed as the young man begrudgingly selected some mellow tunes and the conversations resumed – only occasionally interrupted by a melodramatic sigh or groan over the megaphone when a new song that the DJ hated came on.

'I'm writing a new theatre piece,' said Eva.

'Is this the ninety-year-old top shagger you were telling me about yesterday?' Laure asked.

'Irma? No, that's a spoken word,' Eva grinned. 'Anyway, this isn't part of the sex series.'

Internally, Laure breathed a sigh of relief that there was something more on the cards than the sex series.

'It's a choreography depicting the female orgasm.'

Laure nodded. 'That really sounds like it's still part of the sex series.'

'*Ma certo,* of course, it is. I was joking before. There isn't a different series, but you need to be less old fashioned.'

'To be fair, I would watch it,' Laure said. 'You're so creative, I'm sure you'll bring "the orgasm" to life in a beautiful way.'

'You *will* watch it,' said Eva. 'How's your work going? It's been a year now, hasn't it? A year since I dragged you from that burning Roman bus.'

'And I'm still hashtag grateful every day,' said Laure, bowing to her friend. 'Work's OK.' After saying the words, she took a moment to consider whether it was the truth. 'In reality, it's exactly what I wanted when I first came to Rome. It's so easy and I'm good at it. It's hard not to be, in truth. It's zero stress, regular hours and it stops me from going broke.' Laure polished off her glass of wine and stared at the cork which had fallen into one the table's wooden grooves. 'Recently ... just recently, I've started to miss being challenged. I don't want to go back to what I had before,' she hastened to add, 'but maybe I could be challenged in a different way.'

'What would inspire you, my dear?' Eva asked.

'Well,' Laure said, feeling suddenly nervous. It was the first time she'd had the discussion with anyone. 'I've looked up nursing courses a few times now. I thought about retraining as a doctor too,' she said, almost in a whisper.

'Wow, *amica, fantastico!*' said Eva, beaming. 'You'd be really good at that.'

'I don't know,' said Laure. 'Do you think so? I keep coming back to the idea that if I'm going to give something my all, I want it to have a purpose, to help people ... but then, I'm also scared. It's a lot of responsibility and I don't want to fall back into a dark place.'

'You could do it, Laure,' Eva said, nodding decisively at her friend.

'Thanks, my dear. Gosh, my parents would be so proud if I did that.'

'Your parents?' asked Eva, raising an inquisitive eyebrow. 'Is that important to you?'

'*Oui*,' said Laure, the wine and Eva's company making her open up. 'It definitely factors. You know, it wasn't easy for them to leave their home countries and start over in France. They sacrificed a lot. I don't want it to have been in vain.'

'But, Laure, I've met your parents. They're so sweet. Have they ever put that kind of pressure on you?' asked Eva.

'No,' said Laure. 'They always say they just want us to be happy.' She shrugged. 'You know, funnily enough, my parents met during a swim class. They were teachers at a holiday camp. To get the job, my dad pretended he could speak English. So,' and she pointed at Eva, 'I'm guessing he was a disciple of the miming method too.'

'Well, I am a fan of the miming method,' said Eva, with a drunken giggle. 'Let's get another bottle, Laure.' Swaying like a scarecrow in the wind, Eva rose and began a mimed backstroke through the crowded tables to the bar.

With a hazy smile, and feeling the wine meander through her bloodstream, Laure looked at her phone for the first time since she'd arrived.

A photo of an over-sized squirrel perched atop a tall oak appeared before her eyes. The headline:

Lazio fan saves scared squirrel from tall tree nightmare

'Mon Dieu,' said Laure. Marco had sent it a few hours ago. As she contemplated the dodgy Photoshop, another message arrived.

> *Ciao* Laure. Sorry for the silly messages,
> I got carried away with my love for Lazio.
> I'm done now, I promise!
> Anyway, your night is probably only just
> getting started!
> Enjoy it! *Buona serata*

'So silly,' Laure said, tossing the phone back into her bag and recalling Marco from the café and her chaotic morning. It now seemed like an eternity ago.

'E dai, come on, what are you smiling about?' Eva said, reappearing with a new bottle of wine.

'It's a long story.'

'Laure, spills the beans!'

'I can't really,' Laure laughed. 'To be honest, I have no idea what's going on. It's all a bit weird.'

'Oh, good,' said Eva, leaning closer.

'Well, you know about my neighbours?'

'The miserable night fighters? Of course!' Eva said, filling Laure's glass.

'Exactly. So, last night it was the same story, just like the night before, and every night for the past few weeks. They were fighting and I got barely any sleep,' Laure said.

Eva tutted. 'What a nightmare.'

'Then, this morning, I got chatting with a random guy at my local coffee place, and half way through the conversation, I realised it was him. My neighbour! But he didn't know who I was, obviously.'

'Assurdo, no way!' said Eva. 'So, did you tell him off?'

'No,' said Laure. 'I wanted to say something, but it was just so unexpected. It caught me off guard and I really didn't know what to do.'

'So ... what happened?'

'Well ...' Laure said, shifting her eyes away from Eva's. 'I'm not sure I handled it great. I told him I was so tired because I was out partying all night, I lied about where I live and, in the end, he invited me to watch a football match at his place with his girlfriend next week.'

Eva snorted wine onto the table and placed her head in her hands, leaving a small gap between her fingers for her cigarette to poke through. 'Ha, Laure!' she said. 'Well, what a lovely way to spend your free time! I think you'll enjoy that. Will you be climbing down the side of your building and then taking the stairs back up for the full visitor effect?'

'Oh *mon Dieu*, I hadn't even thought about that!' said Laure. 'I think I was experiencing delirium through exhaustion. I was sure we'd never actually speak again, but now he's texting me.'

'Texting you?' said Eva, her eyes narrowing. 'Texting you how? Like flirty texting?'

'I don't really know. He's been texting me these little jokes. I think he thinks I'm depressed and wants to befriend me.'

'Oh, right,' said Eva, trying to hide her amusement but not managing. 'I wasn't personally aware of your depressed state.'

Laure rolled her eyes. 'Don't. I was just knackered this morning. It was a whole thing, you had to be there … Anyway, I don't get it, to be honest. He was really nice and quite funny and I think there was a spark between us, but then he invited me to watch football with his girlfriend. And now he's texting me these odd jokes involving Photoshop and pets, so I'm at a loss really.'

'Fascinating,' said Eva, and Laure could tell she was resisting the urge to spin the story into a wacky fantasy and offer wildly inappropriate advice. Instead, she saw Eva begrudgingly opt for her more sensible self. Despite hailing from another planet, when it came to friendship Eva was solid as a rock. 'Maybe your lack of sleep is clouding your vision, Laure,' she said, visibly disappointed to pass up the opportunity for high drama. 'He doesn't sound like a catch to me.' Eva blew out a dancing plume of smoke. 'I think, just don't reply, and if you bump into him again, deny you've ever met him. He must have mixed you up with someone else. You are not his depressed friend from the café but his angry neighbour. I mean, the last thing you need is to get involved with another man who doesn't know what he wants, right? Especially one who incorporates Photoshop into his jokes.'

Laure nodded. 'Yeah, you're right. It was just so weird, bumping into him like that …'

At the decks, the DJ was wrapping up his set. Everyone always knew it was the last song because, each week, he threw caution to the wind, cranked up the volume and blasted out 'one for his fans' before signing off for the night.

'AS ALWAYS, YOU'VE BEEN THE WORST! I'LL SEE YOU NEXT WEEK, YOU BORING BASTARDS!' he yelled through the megaphone, before sprinting into the distance to avoid a good *schiaffo* or slap from his uncle.

Suddenly, a pigeon hurtled into the wall with a loud smack, fell to the floor and died instantly by the decks. It seemed to spell either the end of the night or the death of the DJ's career, Laure wasn't sure which.

'Let's finish this off and get an Amaro before we go,' Laure said, as a group of concerned citizens attempted pigeon resuscitation. 'It might just knock me out and I'll sleep through the fighting tonight.'

'*Buona idea,*' Eva said. '*Personalmente*, I don't even feel that drunk.'

One bottle of wine and a final nightcap later, the two ladies tottered to their feet and Eva did front crawl towards a cab. Only after she had gone did Laure spot her cigarettes lying on the table. Dutifully, she tucked them into her bag and began to meander down the web of streets back home.

The moon was high in the sky, casting an uneven light ahead. It bathed leafy vines, shop signs and sleeping Vespas in pools of shimmering pearl, while leaving other patches of the route in complete darkness. Somewhere along the way, Laure flopped against a wall to shake a stone from her shoe. At the same time, her phone buzzed, and while trying to multitask, she slid straight down onto the dusty cobblestones.

God, I'm drunk, she thought.

The message was from Eva, asking if she was home safely. By way of reply, Laure nodded, before flicking over to re-read Marco's texts.

He is funny, she thought. *Maybe I've been overthinking everything. Does this have to be a big deal? I met a guy and we had a nice chat. He's been open about having a girlfriend and wants to be friends. Is that so weird? I miss my guy friends in France. It would be nice to have some here.*

'*Oui*,' she said aloud, Eva's cautionary words temporarily banished. 'Let's be friends. Maybe I'll tell him I live next door and we'll laugh about it.'

Shifting her bum up to a small ledge behind her, Laure hunched over the phone and tried to concentrate.

> Don't worry, it made me laugh

Then she added more.

> but maybe that's because I'm a bit drunk! Hopefully I'll see you soon. It was fun chatting this morning.

That's nice, she thought, and concluded with:

> I'll try and get some sleep if you do. We're all in this together.

That last part would sound strange, but to those in the know, it made sense. Laure winked at herself, before hoisting her body up and continuing home.

Couples were still dotted along the bridge, gazing out across the water towards the Vatican's illuminated cupola, as Laure ambled by. Every so often, a beam of light from the nearby Fori Imperiali picked up a swooping starling which glided through the air, then disappeared among the shadows.

Back into Trastevere, there was immediately more life. A guitarist was strumming Bob Marley's *Three Little Birds* on the steps of a fountain, and around him, a crowd swayed in unison. A few had broken rank with the group, spinning and dancing across the square as if communicating with higher spirits. Laure noted a scent of weed hanging in the air. Night-time vendors were hard at work, churning out pizza slices for tipsy tourists, while street sellers dived in and out of the crowds, touting anything from red roses for 'the beautiful lady' to flashing lighters shaped like toilets.

Laure left the scenes behind. As she passed Da Antonio, now locked up for the night, it occurred to her that she would be back there in just a few hours. She sped up. The last part of her journey was always the most tedious.

CHAPTER NINETEEN

Il giorno in cui sei partito – the day you left

Isabella was awake. Viviano hadn't come home again. She tried to focus on a shopping list for a picnic that Sunday, rather than feel the heavy weight in her chest that threatened to pull her through the bed.

Two or three times a week she heard him slip out. If Isabella was lucky, he'd be there again by morning, but more often than not, his bed lay empty and her son would only resurface hours later. On a few occasions he had gone for longer – one or two nights. Nights where Isabella sank into a pit of worry. When he finally returned, Viviano always brushed off her concern with smiles and jokes. Now, she didn't even bother to ask. After all, he was an adult. He didn't need to justify himself.

With a sigh like a felled tree on the forest floor, Isabella turned her head away from the side of the pillow where the tear stains had begun to chap her face.

It hadn't always been like this. For years Isabella had allowed herself to believe that Viviano remembered nothing of his father leaving, but only a fool would keep up that lie now. She just didn't know how worried to be.

'It's strange, I can recall every detail of the day Gianni left like it was yesterday, even though twenty years have passed,' she had once remarked to her sister.

It was true.

He had come through the door at 5.08 p.m. one sunny June evening. Isabella knew the exact time because she had glanced down at her watch. He was home earlier than usual and was holding flowers which she had found strange. Viviano was playing at a friend's house. Gianni had asked her to sit down, handed her the pink roses and then broken down in tears. He had met someone else on a business trip and fallen in love. She was from the north of Italy and he wanted to be with her. He was so sorry.

Her husband left the house shortly after having made his confession, and before Isabella really had time to process any of it. At the door, he had begged her to tell their son that he loved him and promised to be in touch. But time passed and they never heard from him again.

It was just before Viviano's eighth birthday.

By all accounts, her son had dealt with the news like a champion. Isabella hadn't wanted to patronise him, so, when Viviano came home, through her tears she had told him the truth.

For a little while, he had cried with her and asked some questions: Was his dad coming back? When might they hear from him? Who was this other lady and how could she possibly be better than their family? Then he had looked at her with his green eyes, identical to Gianni's, and said that they were going to be fine together, without him.

From that moment, Viviano seemed to put it all behind him. At school, his teachers noticed no change in behaviour.

'They're keeping an eye on him, of course,' Signora Solari told her after picking Viviano up one day, 'but they say he's still the same kind, sociable little boy he's always been. He's very bright, Isa. You should be so proud.'

'I don't know how he manages it,' she had replied at the time. 'It's some kind of miracle.'

Now, as she lay in bed wishing to hear the key turn in the front door, Isabella felt the familiar whip of guilt lash her chest. 'I should have pulled myself together. I should have been there for him,' she whispered.

Years later, after the dust of Gianni's departure had settled, Isabella had tried to speak to her son about everything that had happened. Maybe it would help them both, but she always came up against a brick wall. Viviano was adamant that he did not want to talk about Gianni. Either he would change the subject or flash an irresistible grin and say, 'Who is this 'Dad' that you're mentioning? I don't recall him.' The topic was closed.

One day, while cleaning, when Viviano was thirteen, Isabella had stumbled upon a diary tucked under his bed, and with a pang of shame, she opened it.

The whole thing was covered in her son's unmistakeable scrawl – not a millimetre was blank. As she flicked hungrily through the pages, desperate for an insight into Viviano's mind, her jaw slowly dropped. It contained stories, hundreds of them, each offering a different ending to his father's departure, every one more elaborate than the last.

On page five, the secret services had called upon Gianni to undertake important business, a request that he could not refuse. 'Your family will be provided for,' they promised, while stamping his fake passport. By page fifty, the State had discovered that her husband possessed a special gene making him capable of metamorphosis. They wanted to perform tests, forcing him to go on the run. In between, there was everything from mobsters and mistaken identities to a tragic bungee jumping accident.

Her heart breaking, Isabella noted that in every single story, including the most fantastical, Gianni had found a way to say goodbye to Viviano. Even during the devastating bungee crash, he had yelled, 'Goodbye, figlio mio, my son. I love you', while plummeting through the air.

After finding the diary, Isabella had sat for hours on the floor of Viviano's darkblue room until the sun, which streamed through the window highlighting the small lint particles floating in the air, transformed into a pinkish tinge on the far wall and then finally disappeared. Still, she stayed, in the shadows, tears rolling down her face. Viviano's tales were so outlandish, yet he had put so much detail into them, they could almost be true. Isabella was amazed at the imagination swirling in his head.

When he came home, she had shoved the diary under the bed, wiped her eyes and switched the hoover on, smiling casually as his head popped around the door.

Not once did she mention the diary or go looking for it again, but in her mind, Isabella decided that her son was destined for a career in the creative arts: Viviano would be an actor, or a great author, and success and personal fulfilment would make him forget all about his Godforsaken father. Immediately, she enrolled him in drama classes.

'*Tutto andrà bene,* everything will be all right,' she told a puzzled Viviano out of the blue one day.

But, over time, it became clear that something was not quite right. Although he could have had the world at his feet, her son didn't want it. Viviano's teachers began to lament his wasted potential and poor attendance. His signature relaxed demeanour went hand in hand with a non-committal attitude and, even at times when he needed to knuckle down, Viviano quickly lost focus and squandered opportunities. It didn't seem like the future was on his mind.

One day, on a summer's afternoon at the end of high school, Viviano had made her the happiest mother alive when, in his usual chaotic manner, he had come bursting into the living room, a shiny brochure rolled loosely in his hand. Standing tall, he announced that he was going to enrol in law school to study human rights. Viviano said he wanted to give a voice to the people that he had met on his adventures around the city who were down on their luck and had been abandoned by society.

'The law forgets about the people it thinks don't matter, and it's not fair,' he said.

As the bright sunshine poured through the window, Isabella had hugged her son so tightly and felt the anchor of guilt fall away for the first time since Gianni's departure.

It had all lasted a few sweet months. Viviano was transformed into a dedicated and motivated student, intent on making a change in society. But as the year ticked by, that too slipped away. After emphatically failing his university exams, Viviano spent the night in his room fashioning various props. For want of something to do, he and a few friends began to put on street performances, dressing up and entertaining tourists with amusing skits. Isabella had been to see them a handful of times and was quite impressed, but she had no doubt in her mind that amateur theatrics was not a career.

'Don't you ever think about finding something more secure, *tesoro*? These are the years to work hard and build your future. I'm worried.'

'Come on, Ma, there are more serious things in life,' Viviano would always answer, with a wave of his arm.

The response always infuriated Isabella because nothing, without exception, was ever serious to her son. He confronted every situation with the same jokey aloofness.

In the end, she had given in. Viviano was, after all, a kind boy, and at least he wasn't on drugs. Perhaps one day he would dedicate himself to something which didn't involve sewing octopus tentacles into his shirts before breakfast or cartwheeling over rooftops. If he was happy, she was happy, she thought. But then, the nighttime disappearances had begun.

CHAPTER TWENTY

This time, it doesn't bother me so much

Laure let herself into the flat. One a.m. and blissful silence. It hadn't been this way since she could remember. Although the room was gently spinning, walking home had helped to sober her up. Now, she just felt sleepy, contented and slightly off balance. With the grace of a one-legged flamingo, she yanked off her heels and collapsed into bed.

'I know I have to get up again,' she murmured, 'but I'm so comfortable and my flat hasn't been this quiet for so long. I just want to enjoy it for a few more minutes.'

Staring up at the ceiling, Laure's eyes glazed over as she caught the first glimpses of sleep. Only the gentle hum of her fridge and the far-off cry of an adventuring night bird disturbed the silence. A light breeze drifted in through the window, cutting through the block of festering heat that had accumulated during the day.

It would be so perfect to pass out right now, Laure thought. *Let them be sleeping next door and then I can sleep.*

Just as she abandoned reality, a noise from through the wall jogged her slumber. Staying deathly quiet, halfway to dreaming, Laure waited.

'Come on, baby,' a man purred, inches from her head.

It's Marco, Laure thought. His voice was unmistakeable. The same one she had been hearing for weeks, only now she could picture its owner, the tousled hair, the big brown eyes.

'*S'il te plait,* please, don't do this,' Laure whispered. 'Be that lovely man I met today. Let me get some rest.'

'Marco, not tonight. I'm exhausted,' the woman's voice responded next door.

Mon Dieu, what am I listening to? thought Laure, pulling the sheet over her head.

'Come on, *amore,* it's been ages since we've ...'

'Marco, things haven't exactly been great between us, have they? We've been at each other's throats most days.'

'I know, but tonight was really good. I just want to be close to you again, Valeria. I miss you, I miss your body, I miss kissing you ...'

'I'm really tired, Marco, I just want to go to bed. Can't we just sleep together, you know, next to each other? I have to be up again in a couple of hours.'

'But I want you, baby.' His voice was silky and seductive.

'I know, *amore,* I want you too, and we will soon ... just not tonight. Please don't push this anymore. Isn't it enough that we've had a nice evening together?'

'Yeah, I guess,' Marco said. 'I just thought it would be the perfect way to finish the night, that's all. You know, have some fun together. Get back to you and me. I can think of a thousand ways to make you happy.'

'I know, sweetie, and of course, that all sounds wonderful,' Valeria replied, and Laure detected her exasperation. 'We will soon, I promise. Let me get through to the weekend and we can relax together.'

'All weekend, just for us?' Marco said, sounding excited.

'Ouch!' His girlfriend let out a playful shriek, causing Laure to flinch on the other side of the wall.

'Marco, calm down!' Valeria giggled.

With an eye roll, Laure turned, burrowed her head deep under the pillow and tried to lose consciousness.

'Oh, by the way,' she heard Valeria add in a clear bid to distract Marco from his amorous intentions, 'I forgot to tell you, Alice and Francesco invited us for lunch on Sunday.'

'You know, I actually meant to tell you that too,' Marco said, his tone now conversational, in acknowledgement that he wasn't getting lucky. 'I bumped into Francesco at Da Antonio a few days ago. You know, that café is always packed nowadays. I've met a few people in there.'

Suddenly wide awake, Laure looked up at the wall. Was he going to mention her?

'Really, Da Antonio? God, that used to be our little place. I've been so busy, we haven't been together in so long,' Valeria sighed. 'Who else have you bumped into?'

'Oh, no one really,' Marco said. 'But today I got chatting to this woman when she drank my coffee by mistake. She was funny. Well, she was completely out of it, to be honest!' He laughed, perhaps recalling Laure's crippling hangover.

Through the wall, Laure's ears were burning. The niggling doubt in the back of her mind that the morning's strange affair was merely a figment of her imagination disappeared in an instant. She inched her head closer to the wall.

'Oh, that's funny,' Valeria said, without any indication in her voice that she thought it was. 'So, who is this woman?'

'She's a French expat, about our age, I guess. At first, I thought something awful had happened because she was so down, but it turns out she had just been partying all night. And actually, when we started chatting, she was really nice.'

Laure's body had frozen. Now so close to the wall, she was worried they might sense her presence.

'I see,' Valeria said. 'Did you two chat together for a while then?'

'Yeah, I guess a little while, while I waited for another coffee!' Marco joked, apparently unaware of his girlfriend's stiff tone. 'She lives down by Piazza Trilussa. I thought it would be too full on living around there, but it sounds like she really loves ...'

Valeria cut him off. 'Why do you keep saying how much fun this woman is?'

'I don't know, I just thought ...' said Marco. 'I was just telling you about—'

Valeria interrupted again. 'Yes, I know, you were just telling me about this girl who loves going out. 'Cause we both know that's what you'd like to do, but you never get a chance anymore because of boring old me. I mean, honestly,' she continued, the pitch of her voice rising. 'Did you bring her up just to spite me, because I didn't want to have sex?'

There was silence and Laure tried not to breathe.

'*Amore*,' Marco said. 'I'm just telling you about my day. I'm answering a question that you asked. It was honestly such a non-event, I don't know why we're still talking about it. I even told her about you. I said we would invite her round to watch the football. I think you'd like her, too, so stop trying to bite my head off, OK?'

Laure pursed her lips. She didn't know how she felt about being described as a 'non-event'.

'Oh well, *bravo*. At least you remembered to mention your girlfriend of seven years,' the woman's voice spat back.

'Jesus,' said Marco, his patience seeming to fray. 'Look, dear, with all due respect, I think we both know that I'm not the one that has that issue.'

'Oh,' Laure whispered on the other side of the wall, unable to stifle her surprise.

'And what is that supposed to mean, Marco?' Valeria asked, her words slow and deliberate, as if daring him to respond.

Yes, wondered Laure. *What does that mean?*

Sorry, can I get you some popcorn? her brain enquired with a tut.

'Shhhh,' Laure said, focusing back on the argument.

'As if you have to ask, Valeria,' Marco muttered.

They must have been right next to the wall because, for Laure, every word was crystal clear. Suddenly, all was quiet, and Laure scrunched her ear against the white paint, straining for the next scoop. Immediately, she regretted it.

'ARE YOU HONESTLY DRAGGING THAT BACK UP AGAIN?' Valeria exploded next door, her reaction so forceful it sent Laure's head jolting backwards.

Laure heard a flurry of thundering footsteps, and for the next minute, she stayed glued to the wall, listening, but Marco and Valeria had moved elsewhere.

I'm a bit thirsty, she thought, still feeling tipsy as she peeled herself away, tiptoed to the kitchen and began scanning the shelves: *water, orange juice, wine … that gin bottle up there … yesss*, Laure thought, reaching for the top shelf.

Now that it's quieter, wouldn't you like to go to sleep? her brain asked.

'*Oui, oui, bientôt*, soon,' Laure replied, pouring an over-sized shot of the clear liquid into a glass and returning to the wall theatre.

Her brain muttered disapprovingly in French.

Marco and Valeria were still arguing, but Laure couldn't tell where they were. Squatting down on the bed, she shuffled left towards the bathroom, tracing her ear along the wall.

No, even fainter, she thought.

As if in an Olympic gymnastics event for deranged people, Laure did a neat 180 pivot without spilling her drink, and began the shuffle back. At the tricky dismount off the bed, she dropped to her bottom, freed her legs and landed with beautifully parallel feet on the floor.

'Stunning!' she heard the commentators applaud in her head.

The neighbours' voices were growing louder.

'They're by the window!' Laure said, pumping her first in the air.

Oh putain mais quel loser, what an absolute loser, her brain bemoaned.

With precisely zero poise, Laure hoisted herself up onto the desk, swept her legs through some neatly organised documents and tuned back towards the wall.

'Marco, we can't go down that road again. Is that really what you want for this relationship?!' Valeria was asking, desperation in her voice. 'It was four years ago. We've put that behind us.'

'I'm just pointing out that it's a bit rich of you to jump to conclusions after what you did.'

'Oh, for God's sake, you know it was a mistake,' Valeria said. 'It meant nothing to me. Less than nothing. It makes me feel sick that I did that to you, but we worked so hard to overcome it.'

'Well, it still hurts me sometimes, OK!' Marco shouted. '"Just one time! Some random guy!" I obviously still think about it, Valeria. You *slept* with someone else!'

'*Ouh la la, c'est compliqué ça,*' Laure whispered, sipping her gin.

'But, of course,' Marco continued, 'I'm not allowed to talk about it because it upsets *you!* How selfish of me!'

'Wow,' Valeria said, her tone now glacial. 'Tell me, Marco, do you get to bring this up whenever we argue to get the upper hand? 'Cause the last I'd heard, you'd forgiven me.' She hesitated and her voice softened. 'You even said that you understood … that you knew you weren't behaving like a caring partner at the time, and how alone I felt. I know what I did was wrong, but we both agreed, it takes two people to make a relationship work.'

Marco scoffed. 'Well, look at you talking about making a relationship work. Yesterday you said you didn't know if you wanted to be in one anymore.'

'Oh, fuck you, Marco,' Valeria spat.

Close to where Laure was sitting, there was a loud clatter. It was a sound she recognised instantly: one of them had flung the windows open too quickly next door, sending the shutters hurtling into the building's façade.

'*Cazzo,* fuck!' she heard Marco curse at the accidental racket.

. . .

On the other side of the wall, Marco was glaring out at the sky, trying to control his temper. Humidity was thickening the air. It wouldn't be too long before the sun rose.

Were they really arguing through another night? he wondered, in disbelief. *Am I trapped in this never-ending fight?*

Like claws, his large hands gripped the window sill, as if at any moment, he might rip it cleanly from the brickwork. Anyone looking up could have mistaken him for a gargoyle, his long neck protruding out and face contorted in anger.

After a few minutes of stillness, Marco dropped down to his knees and began rummaging in a cardboard box which propped up the internet router. Hidden at the bottom, his fingers found a crumpled cigarette packet with a lighter tucked inside.

He straightened up, lit one and inhaled deeply, holding the smoke in his lungs before blowing out a billowing spiral into the darkness. The rush of nicotine calmed his nerves. For a moment, he kept his eyes shut and mentally prepared for the consequences of his actions.

Just metres away, a drunken Laure was passing out. The first hints of dawn were beginning to creep through the window, along with an unpleasant smell of cigarette smoke which piqued her nostrils. Everything had been quiet on the other side for a little while now.

'Are you smoking, Marco?' Valeria's voice, dripping with disgust, swirled over to Laure's ears.

'Smoking, and I can smell smoke. I get it now.' Laure yawned, her eyelids sagging.

Next door, Marco's girlfriend strode towards him.

Valeria was petite with shiny, poker-straight black hair which stopped abruptly above her shoulders, and freckles that were concentrated around her nose and fanned out across her cheeks. In happier times, Marco used to trace his lips lightly along them, choosing a different path every time to kiss her on the nose. It was his way of being affectionate, but recently any playfulness between them had been lost.

At the window, Valeria stopped right beside her partner who was staring, nonchalantly, out into the sky.

'Why are there cigarettes in the apartment and since when did you start smoking again?'

Marco took another long drag. Only when he had finished, did he turn. 'It's a cigarette, OK. You used to smoke yourself, remember? Lighten the fuck up.'

'Well, why don't you come and talk to me when you've decided not to behave like a complete asshole,' Valeria said, her body shaking with rage. Slowly, she turned and disappeared into the bedroom, slamming the door with a bang.

Marco stubbed out his cigarette and flicked the butt down onto the street, before immediately drawing another from the packet.

This is shit, he thought.

Retrieving his phone from his pocket, he let out a smoky exhale as he saw the text message from Laure.

> Don't worry, it made me laugh
> but maybe that's because I'm a bit drunk!
> Hopefully I'll see you soon.
> It was fun chatting this morning.
> I'll try and get some sleep if you do.
> We're all in this together.

The clumsiness of her message and the little Italian errors made him smile. She was obviously tipsy when she wrote it. 'At least someone is having a good time,' he muttered.

After some more cigarette therapy, he replied.

> Oh, *che fortuna*, lucky you. You have no idea how much I would have loved to be out having fun

Marco paused, added a winky face and pressed send, before slipping the phone back into his pocket and heading over to the sofa where he knew he would be spending what was left of the night.

CHAPTER TWENTY-ONE

As a child, I always wanted to be a smoker

Laure awoke on her desk. It felt as though a boxer was pummelling her head and somewhere in the room, an alarm was bleating incessantly.

What on earth is going on? her brain screamed.

Slowly, she untangled her limbs and brushed a waterfall of knotted hair from her eyes. Among the blurry surroundings, she spied an empty shot glass and chaos scattered across the floor. It all came back to her: the night out with Eva, the argument and her final resting place on top of her desk.

'Oh, Laure,' she sighed heavily.

With an 'do or die' movement, she rolled, crashed onto the floor and crawled over to silence the noise devil coming from her phone.

'A shower,' Laure mumbled, shuffling towards the bathroom, peeling off last night's clothes on the way and trying not to see the disorder in her normally clean and tidy flat.

Standing was too ambitious for now and so she sat on the floor of the enamel cubicle and reached, tentatively, to twist the tap with her fingertips, a decision she instantly regretted.

'Putaaaaaain.' The freezing water hit her body and she recoiled into a tight ball. 'Fuck!'

Because of your antics, this is how it has to be, voilà, her brain said.

Gradually, under the warming jets, Laure re-enacted the story of evolution, and emerged on two feet out of the shower.

I need to speed up.

Fifteen minutes later, dressed and looking somewhere between life and death, she grabbed her bag and headed for the door, but just before opening it, she stopped.

Marco might be at the café, her brain said.

'So?' Laure asked.

So, do you want to look shit?

'I don't care,' Laure responded.

Don't you?

Laure paused. *Maybe some mascara, she thought. And some concealer, just so I don't look so tired.*

She slipped back into the bathroom and reappeared shortly afterwards looking almost the same, but with a flattering filter.

You might also want to check he isn't leaving the flat at the same time as you, her brain suggested. *Now, that would be awkward, tu imagines, can you imagine?*

'I want him to see me,' Laure responded. 'Get this situation cleaned up once and for all.'

Do you?

Laure pressed her ear to the front door.

Silence.

'There,' she said to her brain, before slamming the door and descending the stairs. 'Are you happy now, you bitch?'

Trastevere could tell that Laure had had a rough night and it took pity.

'Prego cara, here you go, my dear,' said a passing *nonna,* handing Laure a custard-filled croissant from a paper bag.

A gardener who was tending to some nearby roses, spritzed Laure with a refreshing mist of water, and even the cobblestones seemed to even themselves out under her feet. Antonio, however, wasn't playing ball. Catching Laure's eye as she entered the café, he raised a disapproving brow.

What could he possibly know? Laure thought, taking a seat in her usual spot.

The café was quieter this morning and Laure covertly scanned the room, but there was no sign of the almond-eyed man from yesterday.

'Definitely for the best,' she said with a nod.

But upon taking out her phone, Laure did a little double take when a message from Marco appeared on the screen. He had sent it at 4 a.m.

> Oh, *che fortuna,* lucky you. You have no idea how much I would have loved to be out having fun ;)

She stared down at the words and the winky face at the end.

He must have sent it during the argument.

He was thinking of me, she thought, her stomach doing an involuntary flip.

Or, maybe he'd only just seen the message you sent him, her brain reasoned.

Tentatively, Laure scrolled back up the conversation to assess the quality of her drunken banter, and with a frown, returned the phone to her bag.

I'm funnier in French, she thought, glancing at her watch.

In lion-sized bites, Laure devoured the *nonna* croissant and made for the door, brushing away loose pastry flakes from her mouth as she went.

Antonio shook his head.

This is ludicrous! Laure thought. *He just likes winding me up.* She narrowed her eyes suspiciously at Antonio and left the premises.

'Hey Laurrre,' a voice called out in a heavy Italian accent as she stepped out from under the veranda into the blistering heat.

Through squinted eyes, she spotted Marco hurrying over. He was dressed entirely in black and sporting aviator sunglasses which Laure knew were hiding a pair of very tired eyes. When he removed them to greet her, Laure saw that he did, indeed, look as bad as she felt.

'Oh, *ciao*,' she said, giving him a clumsy wave, her heart beating a little faster.

'*Come stai*, how are you?' he asked.

'*Ça va*, I'm OK,' said Laure. 'I'm actually running a bit late for work.'

'You might have got a message from me very late last night … or very early this morning, you could say,' Marco said, looking sheepish. 'I'm sorry I texted you at that time.'

'That's OK,' said Laure, breezing past the remark.

A silence fell between them.

'Four a.m.,' Marco said. 'I checked this morning.' He smiled, but Laure could see the strain behind his eyes.

'What were you doing up so late?' Laure asked, curious to hear the response.

'Arguing, actually,' he responded, dryly. 'With my girlfriend.' He hesitated. 'We've been having some problems recently.' Marco looked down at the ground and then appeared to shake it off. 'Anyway,' he said, 'never mind about that. How was your night? You were out again it seems!' He found a smile and poked Laure lightly in the ribs.

'Ha, sure,' Laure said, caught off guard and bending awkwardly where he had touched her. She returned his gesture with a jokey arm punch to compensate for her confused emotions and stammered over the words, 'You know me.'

Marco nodded and his dark eyes caught hers, just for a second. 'Actually, I feel like I do,' he said.

At the moment their gaze met, Laure noticed a shimmer behind Marco's eyes. It transported her back to university and the way her boyfriend – her first and only proper one – used to looked at her when they had just begun dating.

Wow. It's been a really long time since anyone has looked at me like that, she thought.

Suddenly flustered, Laure looked into the distance. 'Um … I really have to go to work,' she said. 'But you seem like you're having a bit of a hard time. You were so kind to me yesterday, your coffee is on me today.'

She opened her bag just as Lorenzo, a rotund waiter, came barrelling backwards out of the door, yelling the punchline of a joke at an unamused Antonio. As he turned, he collided with Laure, sending her staggering sideways and her bag flying into the air.

'Oh, Laure! *Scusami tanto!* I'm so sorry!' he exclaimed, rushing to her side.

'I'm fine, *non ti preoccupare*, don't worry,' Laure said as she straightened up.

'Let me get your things,' Lorenzo insisted.

'I'll sort this out,' said Marco, waving Lorenzo off and squatting down. After gathering the scattered items, he looked up at Laure 'You smoke?' he asked, holding up Eva's forgotten Marlboro Lights.

'What?' said Laure, catching her breath and giving the cigarettes a perplexed look. 'Oh …'

She was about to explain but Marco was beaming at her, every inch of his expression willing Laure to say 'yes'. She looked at the cigarettes and then back at Marco, and thought how nice it would be if he gazed at her with shiny eyes again.

'Sure,' she replied, giving in.

Marco cackled with giddy excitement and his dimples carved deep valleys into his cheeks. 'I knew you would smoke,' he said. 'Let's have one together. Why not?'

He handed Laure a cigarette, sparked the lighter and tended it towards her.

Laure felt bewildered. She hated cigarettes at the best of times, and was even less keen on ones that had been scooped off the floor. But she put the cancer stick to her mouth and tried to look happy about it.

Euh, this is your own fault, her brain said, even though no one had asked.

Marco lit Laure's cigarette and then his own, taking a blissful inhale and seemingly breathing out all his problems. 'This is nice, I feel relaxed,' he said.

'I didn't know you smoked,' Laure said, still only posing.

'I used to. I gave up a couple of years ago, but to be honest, I miss it. Especially smoking with other people. It's so sociable, you know?'

Laure nodded absentmindedly, entirely focused on the task at hand.

Maybe I could be someone who smokes, she thought.

Why? her brain asked.

Ready to try, Laure inhaled a fraction, immediately blew out and repeated, wondering when she was supposed to actually breathe.

All the while, Marco was exhaling another plume of happiness. '*Allora, dimmi,* so, tell me, where did you go out last night?' he asked.

Laure felt herself relax a little. Finally, something she didn't have to lie about.

'To this little bar near Piazza Navona,' she said.

'Mega Bar?' Marco asked.

'Yes!' said Laure.

'I know it, of course,' said Marco. 'I used to go all the time when I worked nearby.'

'Did they have the DJ when you went?' Laure asked, struggling to stifle a growing bubble of laughter as nicotine flooded her body and her head started to spin.

Even her brain was experiencing the dizziness. '*Desolée,* sorry,' it stuttered, unable to form a coherent opinion or even a cutting remark.

'Yes! He was there!' said Marco, joining in the fun.

'He's so ...' they both began to say.

'Shit!' Laure said.

'Amazing!' said Marco at the same time.

Laure exploded with tobacco-filled mirth. 'Amazing?' she asked, staring at him.

'Laure!' Marco shook his head. '*Dai,* come on. I'm joking. He's shit, of course! The bar is famous for that!'

Laure laughed, her head now spinning uncontrollably. In a stroke of lucidity, she stubbed out the cigarette.

'You barely smoked it!' said Marco.

'I know,' said Laure. 'But I really am going to be late for work.'

'OK, Laurrre,' Marco said. 'I don't want you to get into trouble. *Buona giornata.* Take care of yourself OK.' He grinned before furiously sucking once more on the yellowing stub.

Laure wandered towards work, feeling as though her head might fly away. On the way, she passed a beautiful tree with abundant blooms of pink blossom.

Viviano watched her sweep by. His face, which was covered in dark gnarled bark, bore a bemused look, and a blossom dangled in front of his eye.

Well, that was different, he thought. He had never witnessed anyone smoking quite like that.

CHAPTER TWENTY-TWO

Holy cow! You must hear about this!

As soon as Laure reached the bridge, she retched violently and spat charred saliva onto the floor, much to the disgust of some tourists who were about to take their 'dream Rome selfie' next to the Vatican.

'That's so gross,' one lady in a large summer hat said, contemplating Laure as if she were something unsanitary on her shoe.

Unfortunately, Laure had to agree. Swiftly, she continued walking, but in her mind, the rude woman went tumbling off the side of the bridge.

Everything is weird at the moment, Laure thought.

At this point in her journey, she usually looked up to see the dancing starlings, whose presence had become a reliable constant in her life. But today, even they were out of sync. Instead of seamless routines, the birds were in a muddle, sprawled unevenly across the sky, trying and failing to make recognisable shapes.

'It's not just me,' she sighed. 'You guys are acting strangely too.'

At the entrance to her office, Laure took a few deep breaths. 'Thank God it's Friday,' she muttered, before pushing on the dark-red door.

Amen, her brain chimed in, re-announcing its presence after the unexpected nicotine injection.

Today, the newsroom represented a sauna for the battered and bruised. Everyone was languishing at their desks, sweating out the exhaustion and political overkill, and hoping to be reborn.

Laure was checking her to-do list, which consisted of a handful of hotel bookings, when a colleague, Jan, sidled up, leant in close and whispered, 'It's terrifying, isn't it? I can't stop staring!'

'What are you talking about?' Laure asked.

In a bid to communicate with her eyebrows, Jan tipped her head back, and indicated to the other side of the office, before turning and walking away.

Laure looked over at the team of hardworking journos who were busy typing, and immediately spotted what Jan was referring to. She let out a yelp which she tried to disguise as several sneezes. Rob, a veteran journalist of the Rome bureau, was wearing a gas mask.

As on any other day, the tall, slim news reporter was sitting in front of the computer, but today, his face was entirely covered by an imposing black mask. Two air filters jutted out of the sides like stark mountains and his eyes were only just visible through large oval lenses.

Laure stood up and hurried over to the kitchen where she found Jan wetting herself with laughter.

'What the fuck?' Laure said.

'I know!' replied Jan, bouncing up and down like a pogo stick. 'He came into work like that! Didn't make any reference to it at all! He just sat down and started working. We've got the meeting in ten minutes, Laure. How is anyone going to keep it together?'

'But why?' asked Laure. Personally, she had always liked Rob. He was one of the few people in the office who interacted with everyone, and unlike some of the others, he never lost his good manners when the pressure was on.

'Has anyone spoken to him about it?'

'Apparently someone asked, and he told them it was PTSD. *PTSD!'* Jan said. 'Laure, I've worked here with that man for years and I've never seen him go anywhere!' she said, laughing in disbelief. 'Anyway, I heard that PTSD story from Luigi, so I'm not even sure it's true.'

The two women poked their heads around the kitchen door and stared down the corridor. There was Rob, looking like he had been parachuted into the desk chair.

'Are you two watching Rob?' asked Amélie, a photographer who had appeared behind them.

Laure and Jan turned sheepishly.

'It's PTSD apparently,' Amélie whispered, shaking her head before going to switch the kettle on.

'He must be boiling,' said Laure. 'In this weather!'

'You know what trauma's like,' Amélie replied, her expression sombre. 'He probably can't even feel the heat.'

'But what trauma?' asked Jan, waving her arms wildly in the air.

Amélie shrugged. 'No idea. Luigi told me.'

Laure sat back at her desk and tried to concentrate, but her eyes kept sliding towards Rob. She glanced around. The whole office had transformed into a silent disco of rhythmic head bobs and eye shuffles in his direction, peppered with some impatient foot tapping. Everybody was counting down to the morning meeting. Tucked away at the back of the room and out of Rob's view, the broadcast team were having a field day.

Laure received an email entitled, 'Meet the Rome team' from Katie, a TV reporter. It contained a photo of Laure and her colleagues, taken from JournalFrance's website, except a gigantic gas mask had been cropped onto Rob and the company motto had been changed from 'JournalFrance: Bringing you the news since 1910' to 'Rob: scaring the shit out of you since 7am.'

'Right, everyone ready?' said Paolo, pasting a confident smile on his face while scanning the room with a 'don't make this harder for me than it already is' look in his eyes.

Laure had never seen the entire office spring up with so much enthusiasm. Rob ambled over in his own time.

'Right,' Paolo repeated, clearing his throat.

'I just have a question before we start,' said Marta, never one to shy away from an uncomfortable situation. She was, after all, a journalist.

Paolo gave her a pleading look, but it was to no avail.

'Rob, why are you wearing a gas mask?' she asked.

Everyone's gaze swung from Marta to Rob.

'I don't have to answer that,' replied Rob through his mask. He turned back to face the boss. 'Can we stick to work-related questions, please?'

'I have an urgent email,' Paul, a reporter, suddenly announced.

'Yes, I also have an urgent email,' Michel, a photographer, blurted out.

'Please excuse me briefly,' said Susanna from the accountancy team as a flurry of voices making excuses rang out in unison.

In a flash, they all left the meeting, sprinting in different directions and trying, unsuccessfully, to hide the whimpers spilling from their mouths. After a few seconds, shrieking laughter erupted from the kitchen. Those still in the room either stared intensely down at the floor, or very distinctly, not at Rob.

The meeting continued in this way, no one looking up as Paolo went through the usual 'blah blah blah' and Rob nodding in his gas mask. Things took a turn for the worse when Paolo, who was co-starring alongside Rob in the 'everything is normal' delirium, directly addressed his subordinate to get an update on a story and Rob asked him to repeat four times, straining to hear through the mask.

'No, I'm afraid I'm still not getting it,' he said, even after Paolo had gone up several decibels and slowed his speech almost to a halt.

The meeting drew to a close without anyone getting fired by Paolo for mentioning the unmentionable, and everyone trailed back to their desks. Laure sat down and checked her phone, as whispering colleagues slipped past her, the gossip of the day on the tip of their tongues.

Two messages. The first from Eva.

> *Ciao bella!* I loved seeing you last night.
> Good luck with your noisy neighbour.
> Let me know how it goes! *Un bacio,* kiss!

The second was from her noisy neighbour.

> *Ciao* Laure. Just a little message to
> say thank you, you really cheered me
> up this morning. *Grazie.*

Laure blushed and without hesitation wrote back, dying to share her scoop with someone.

No problem. I'm glad I could help. Guess what, I think I can cheer you up even more … One of my colleagues is wearing a gas mask!

Um, Laure, I'm not sure what impression I gave you. But just to clarify, I'm not really into that stuff.
People in gas masks don't lift my mood.

Laure could imagine the wry smile on his face. Giggling, she eagerly clarified the situation.

Mais non!
We're all so confused. He came in wearing it this morning. No one knows why! He's just sitting there in it, working like normal.

You're kidding

No!

Photo, or I can't believe it

I can't, obviously!

Well then, I guess it didn't happen. Nice story though

Laure sighed and turned her head towards Rob, the dark-haired, gas-masked journalist in his mid-fifties. Currently, he was conducting a phone interview with the Italian Minister of Education, guiding the receiver from his ear, around the protruding air filters to his mouth and then back to his ear.

'Right, I see,' he said, the mask distorting his voice.

'Oh, this is frankly ridiculous!' Marta tutted loudly, earning herself a dark look from Paolo. 'I can see from here that he's not taking notes! He's …' Marta got up and walked behind Rob. 'He's sketching a picture of himself wearing the mask! Rob, what is going on with you?'

'Marta, please,' said Paolo, trying to maintain the calm. 'Just focus on your own work, OK.'

Rob acted as if he had heard nothing. 'Right, I see,' he repeated down the phone.

Laure looked back at her messages and made Marco a promise.

> **I'll do my best to get the photo**

The pledge had been made, but pulling it off was a different matter. Laure tried simply raising her phone in Rob's general direction and pretending to read something on it, but it was too obvious. Paolo was on the lookout for such behaviours. Back to the drawing board.

I can't be the only one who wants this photo, she thought. *The broadcast team must be keen.*

She emailed Katie.

> **Any chance of a photo?**

Instantly, a reply dropped into her inbox.

> **We're on it – your role could be key. Stay alert, be prepared to act.**

Hurrah! thought Laure, content that Rob's bizarre behaviour would not go undocumented – this was, first and foremost, a news organisation, after all. She began her patient wait for further instructions, the hotels bookings on her list completely forgotten.

The plan arrived twenty minutes later via an email entitled: **'Gas Mask Rob's Media Moment.'** Inside was a list of precise instructions.

Laure, go to the right-hand window, parallel to the general news desk, and look outside. In exactly two minutes a small protest group of Pickle Conspiracists is due to pass by. Express an interest in their cause, take out your phone to 'get a few snaps'. We will create a scene behind you. Swing around with your camera STILL raised and BOOM, you should be directly in line with Rob for the pic.

Get ready. The time is NOW.

Laure reread the email carefully, feeling unenthused about her task. Generally, she was serious in the office, and even acknowledging the existence of the Pickle Conspiracy movement was far more attention than she cared to give the weirdos.

'Pickleists' were convinced that the world was run by a select group of powerful men who were slowly turning the population into green, slimy gherkins – eventually everyone would be bottled and sold for the capitalist cause. They swore that with a special pair of glasses costing only $1000 on their website, you could perceive the moist lime pimples creeping across the skin of your loved ones. During protests, they solicited the *real* whereabouts of several A-list celebrities who they insisted were locked in bottling factories in Minnesota, replaced in Hollywood by cornichons in wigs.

Laure was considering backing out, but then a message from Marco arrived.

So, you just gave up? You forgot about me?

Laure groaned.

'What's that noise I hear?' she said loudly, forcing herself up and wandering over to the specified window. 'Some kind of protest going on?'

'Laure, you *know* it's the Pickle Conspiracists,' Marta sighed, shaking her head as if she couldn't quite believe the level of incompetence on display today. 'They pass by here every week.'

'Oh, wow,' said Laure, gazing down at the street, as about twenty angry 'Pickleists' appeared. Colourful placards in hand, they hollered personal truths about fermented brine and the master plan of the nefarious 'Pickle Kings', while hurling buckets of pickling liquid against the walls as they marched. 'God they're *just* the worst aren't they,' Laure mused aloud, to everyone and no one. 'You know, with their kooky conspiracies.' She laughed. '… ah ha ha.'

Unfortunately, that was where her improv ended. Unable to think of anything else to say about the swarm of idiots below, Laure's cheeks turned crimson and she began to panic.

'However!' she heard herself add in an unusually high voice, 'you know, *some* people say their views are increasingly being considered.' Laure raised her eyebrows and looked around, as if to say, 'Can you believe that?'

Silence.

'I mean ...' she stuttered on. 'One wonders, therefore, if one is missing something by not feeling an affiliation with them ... you know?'

Good Lord! her brain said. *Wrap this up tout de suite, right now, Laure.*

'I'm just going to get a few pics,' Laure announced, raising her phone to the open window. 'Some of my friends are really keen on this stuff and they'll just love this.' She emitted a strained laugh once again. 'You know, I remember this one time ... in Minnesota ...'

Laure glanced around, realised no one was listening, and with great relief, parked whatever nonsense was about to come out of her mouth there and then.

Paolo raised his eyebrows but didn't look up from his work.

'*Oh, mamma mia!!! Mamma mia!!!* BREAKING NEWS, BREAKING NEWS!' cried Alessandro, a video reporter, as he thundered into the centre of the room.

The whole office jumped to attention – for a press agency there is no sentence more powerful than 'Breaking News'. As planned, Laure swung around, her phone still raised, and pointed it directly at the general news desk. Click. Click. Click. Rob was perfectly framed. Gas mask on, sitting among his peers while they all gawked expectantly at Alessandro, a mixture of fear and excitement in their eyes.

'The Pope ... has *quit!*' Alessandro declared, staring at his colleagues and enjoying every second of the attention. 'Just look at this!'

He brandished his phone high in the air.

Among the staff, this outrageous declaration was met with general panic and be-wilderment. Immediately, Katie scrambled over and took his phone.

'Alessandro!' she said, lightly shoving his shoulder. 'You idiot! You read it wrong! *"Pope SITS with peace activists at the Vatican"'* she read aloud. 'It's a story published by our own newsroom an hour ago!' Like an ape, she gaped at him and Laure noted her considerable acting skills, far superior she also noted, to Alessandro's.

'Oh!' said Alessandro, planting his forehead firmly into his palms. 'Silly me! I haven't got my contacts in today. False alarm, guys.'

Paolo had had it. 'Team!' he bellowed, throwing down his pen and standing up with so much force his chair went somersaulting backwards. But just as the monster within prepared to roar, he stopped in his tracks. Paolo had been going to therapy. Slowly, he massaged the inner corners of his eyes with a thumb and forefinger and took several deep breaths. This, he had been told, was good practice. 'I just have one question,' he continued, staring up to the ceiling, seemingly appealing to God for inner calm. Finally, he drew his hands into a prayer-like position and sized up the whole team. 'What the fuck is going on here today? Have you all lost your fucking minds?'

God must have been napping because the boss had lost it.

'I mean first, *first!* For crying out loud!' He flung his arms in the direction of Rob. It was clear that Paolo wanted nothing more than to let loose and tell his subordinate exactly what he thought of the ridiculous mask. But as his eyes fell upon his long-time colleague, Paolo faltered.

Through Perspex bug lenses, Rob stared back, daring him to go on.

Paolo shook his head, and everyone knew he couldn't do it. 'Well, we have whatever is going on here,' he mumbled, flapping his hands vaguely towards the news desk. The rage unsated, Paolo swung around and found Laure. 'Then! *Then* we have Laure,' he said, 'who, for *some reason,* wants to wander around the office and loudly document her sudden fascination with the Pickle Conspiracists!' Paolo's eyeballs looked as if they might pop out of his head. 'While I have been patiently waiting for a hotel confirmation from her for two hours! The Pickle Conspiracists!' he yelled again, his face turning purple. 'The fucking Pickle Conspiracists, Laure! And let me tell you,' he said, as if unable to believe that he was having to make this clear, 'one does not *"wonder"* if one is missing something by not feeling an affiliation with them, *OK?* Jesus! But that's not enough for one day, is it?' he snarled, searching among the herd for the innocent face of Alessandro. *'Now,'* he yelled, 'the Pope has *quit!'* This last declaration reverberated around the walls and even Paolo fell silent. 'The Pope has quit,' he repeated more calmly, visibly trying to comprehend the circus in his office. 'I don't know if you've met Coralie, our Vatican correspondent?' Paolo said, gesturing forcefully towards the bespectacled redhead behind him. 'But I *think* she would know if the Pope had announced his resignation!'

Alessandro's expression was solemn. He held in the remark that print journalists were so behind on modern technology, he imagined Coralie received papal updates via local pigeon post.

That's a good one, he thought, making a mental note to share it with the broadcast team later.

'But you think it's OK,' Paolo continued, with a sneer, 'to come blustering into the middle of the room and announce that the Pope has quit. When you haven't even taken the time to read the headline properly! "Quits" and "sits"? "Quits"? *Really?* Not "resigns", not "steps down". No, no, *"quits"?'* he thundered, propelling his arms so wildly it looked like he might take off. 'Do you really think it would be written like that? As if he worked at the fucking supermarket? He's the head of the Catholic Church, for God's sake! He's not ditching a part-time gig at McDonald's to pursue an acting career!' It was all too much for the big man. He stopped and shut both eyes, all his dark thoughts about the broadcast team appearing to have been confirmed. 'Sit down all of you,' he said, shepherding them away. 'Shoo. Shoo. For the love of *God,* everyone go and do some proper work. This is a newsroom, not a clown school!' With this comment, Paolo shot a particularly disdainful look at broadcast boss, Gorgeous Giorgio. Gorgeous Giorgio had tuned out a while ago, but he smiled and gave Paolo a thumbs up anyway.

All in all, there were definitely easier ways to get the photo, Laure reflected, as she scuttled back to her desk, but Alessandro had always had a flare for the theatrical. She sent the image to Marco, a dizzy grin plastered on her face.

> I hope you know, this wasn't easy to get

CHAPTER TWENTY-THREE

Butterflies and ambiguity

The response from Marco came straight away.

> What the ...

> I know! It's just mad!

> You succeeded in your task! You
> have to tell me how you managed ...

> It's a good story!

> With you, it seems everything
> is a good story.

Laure's toes scrunched back and forth in her shoes and she wrote back.

> Really?

> Of course! You're a riot, Laure.
> Your boyfriend is very lucky to have you

Laure's heart skipped a beat. *Why is he bringing up a boyfriend?*
Feeling suddenly self-aware, she cast her eyes around the office then typed back.

> I don't actually have a boyfriend

> *Ma scherzi,* you're joking!
> Now, that does surprise me. Well, I guess
> you are very picky :)

> Ha, I guess so

> So, tell me, what are you looking for in a
> man, that you are not finding?

A breathless laugh escaped from Laure's lips.

Laure, her brain said, *don't get carried away. Marco is not your new boyfriend, d'accord, OK?*

'I know he isn't,' Laure replied. 'He is the one acting that way.'

It doesn't matter. You know he's in a relationship.

But Laure's body was fizzing like champagne and she couldn't stop herself from pulling on a pair of rose-tinted spectacles – they really suited her.

Her brain cleared its throat.

'OK, *tu as raison,* you're right,' Laure said. 'I'll remind him of the situation and see what happens.'

> That's a hard question … I don't know.
> What does your girlfriend find in you?

There was a pause in the conversation and Laure's eyes stayed fixed on the phone. The reply eventually came.

> I thought we were talking about you!
> Well, honestly, I guess we find security in
> each other. Good company and support.
> That is the idea anyway. OK, enough! Your
> turn now, *mademoiselle*

As Laure read the message she felt a sharp stab of humiliation pierce her chest.

Look, are you flirting with me or not? she thought, her face turning red.

Paolo peered over.

'Oh, *mon Dieu,*' Laure murmured. 'I have to do his hotel reservation.'

With a tense smile, she grabbed an invoice and wafted it around in Paolo's direction, but her mind was elsewhere.

I don't understand you, thought Laure, as she reread Marco's message. *If you feel that way, then why are you texting me all the time? And what about the cheating? Does that make you feel secure?*

Seeing that his reservation was once again forgotten, Paolo heaved a heavy sigh and muttered that he deserved the Nobel Peace Prize for the amount of shit he was putting up with today.

Laure wrote back, her fingers burning.

> Well, sincere guys are hard to find these days. To be honest, I just want someone who makes me laugh and who I can trust, that's really important to me.

She pressed send and exhaled frustration through flared nostrils. Marco responded quickly.

> It's nice to hear someone say that.
> Trust is very important to me too

'Yeah. I know,' Laure said aloud with a curt nod.

Laure, what are you doing? her brain asked, as little by little Laure's heart rate lowered and her bruised ego began to fade. *What are you trying to achieve here?*

'I don't know,' she admitted.

But there was little time to dwell as Paolo was striding over. With a panicked yelp, Laure dived into the open filing cabinet and simultaneously picked up the office phone. The boss diverted towards the kitchen and Laure typed quickly.

> *Ciao* Marco. I'm sorry but I have to get back to work

She parked her phone in the drawer and got on with Paolo's booking.

...

As the long day dragged on, Laure felt increasingly closer to death than life. After the morning's excitement had worn off, feelings of shame and self-consciousness about her behaviour had flooded in. At work, Laure had always prided herself on her professionalism, but today, she had been anything but. In a frantic bid to remedy her guilt, she had asked her line manager for extra tasks. Gleefully, Marie-Fleur had handed over a pile of shit that no one else wanted, and despite the exhaustion, Laure had got through it all. It was penance and hopefully word would get back to Paolo.

I let my feelings for Marco cloud my judgement, Laure thought. *I got caught up in the circus and portrayed myself badly.*

Tu es fatiguée, said her brain. *You're just tired.*

But what will my colleagues think of me? she continued. *Marta, Paolo …*

Laure glanced around the room at all the hard-working professionals, and her gaze fell upon Rob, sitting at his desk in his mask, pools of sweat dripping from his skin. He looked like he'd just exited a kinky steam room.

I'm not sure you're the story today, ma chérie, her brain said.

Suddenly, it dawned on Laure that however much her *own* reputation had taken a hit, the man in the gas mask, whose real face was starting to fade from her memory, had stolen the show.

Merci, Rob, you are a good man, Laure thought. *You have raised us up by plummeting yourself through the ground.*

Overcome with appreciation for her masked colleague, Laure gave him a little thumbs up.

Honestly, instead of 'Vive La France!', we should say, 'Vive le Rob!' she thought.

You're delirious, said her brain. *Rentre chez toi, go home and go straight to sleep.*

'You're right,' said Laure.

Just as she was about to log off, an email from Rob dropped into her inbox. It was only a sentence long.

'**You're the only one who understands me**,' it read, and then there was a large gas-mask selfie taken at his desk.

Laure froze and her eyes swung sideways. Rob was typing away, peering at the screen through bug eyes.

What could I possibly have done to warrant that? Laure wondered as she reread the email and tried to keep her heart rate down. *Was it the thumbs up?*

At that moment Rob rose from his desk, swung a grey rucksack over his shoulder and made for the door. Passing Laure, he gave her a little thumbs up.

'It was the fucking thumbs up,' Laure murmured with a grimace.

As soon as he was out of sight, she beelined over to Katie.

'Rob just sent me the strangest email,' she said in hushed tones. 'It was only addressed to me and it said: *"You're the only one who understands me."* And then a huge selfie!'

'Oh, Laure got one too!' Katie shrieked to the broadcast team. 'We've all had them! The same big gas-mask selfie and the worrying one-liner. Believe me, yours wasn't the worst,' she said, wiping tears of stupefaction from her eyes. 'Alessandro got: *"Your face is a saving grace,"* and I bloody got, *"When one feels they are sinking, one may drown."* She looked around. 'I think Aurelia also got, *"You're the only one who understands me."*'

Aurelia nodded.

'He must've run out of inspiration,' said Katie.

'Christ, what the fuck happened to Rob?' Laure said.

Everyone shrugged.

'And to think, all that effort we put into getting our photo this morning, only to be sent a gigantic selfie,' Katie said. 'Poor Paolo. I saw him meditating on the fire escape.'

On that note, Laure bid her colleagues farewell and ventured out into the city. Despite the late hour, the sun gods were dancing and Laure's sandals sunk into the softened tarmac as she crossed the road. Around her, traffic cones had been reduced to waxy orange pools, making patterns along the pavement.

With every step her mind was shutting down, until finally, she clambered up the stairs to the flat.

'Rob?' she whispered nervously at the door, pressing her ear against the wood. Easing it open, Laure quickly scanned around, worried her colleague might pop out from behind the shower curtain or swing round in a chair. But all that greeted her was the mess she had left behind in her drunken state.

'*Dieu merci*, thank God,' she murmured.

Next door everything was quiet. Laure drew the blinds and removed her sweat-soaked clothes, feeling like she had crossed the marathon finish line. Before closing her eyes, she reached for her phone and saw a message from Marco, sent just after she had signed off that morning.

> OK, hard worker

I'm going to switch it off for a while, Laure thought, sinking into the mattress. *No Marco, no nothing, just sleep.*

With a nudge of her elbow, her phone hit the floor.

Marco likes me, Laure thought, a smile tinging her face as she began to drift off. *Someone finally likes me.*

CHAPTER TWENTY-FOUR

Slacklining over the city

Viviano leapt high above the city skyline and landed on the thin elastic band. Up and down he bounced until the rush of adrenaline had worn off and a steady balance returned.

The scent of pine perfumed the air and, in the distance, Rome's jigsaw of buildings stretched for miles, shrouded in a golden pink light.

Viviano had spent the day dressed as a caramel-coloured cat, attaching his slackline between buildings and balancing for hours in various feline poses. Occasionally, he performed a trick or purred at passers-by – Leonardo the cat was always a crowd pleaser.

But work was over now. With three friends – Mickey, Juan Pablo and Elena – he had ventured up to the top of the Gianicolo Hill, a viewpoint over the whole city.

As was customary, they had tied the slackline daringly high between two large parasol pines. The concentration needed to maintain balance challenged Viviano, forcing his mind to focus. Today he was working on a backflip.

Although he had discarded the main cat-like features of the costume, the usual traces of make-up remained smudged down his cheeks, and his tanned skin had darkened in the beating sun.

The Gianicolo was their favourite spot for summer evenings. With a stash of beers and a good playlist, they would stay for hours, long after the stars appeared and the city gazers had wandered home. Occasionally, their night ended with a forbidden swim in the Acqua Paola Fountain, just a little further down. Under the ghostly lighting, its waters shone like an azure lagoon, and they could never resist taking a dip.

Once again, Viviano bounced high into the air and held out his arms to steady the landing.

'You know, I miss my neighbourhood sometimes,' said Mickey, who was perched on a tree branch. Cautiously, he placed a foot onto the slackline.

Elena and Juan Pablo, or 'JuanPa' as they called him, observed the pair from the safety of the ground, beers in hand.

'In my hometown, in Senegal, we could count on each other for everything. We were a real community.' Mickey let go of a branch, transferring his weight fully to the slackline. 'I feel completely left out of that here. People look at me like I don't belong to anything.' Sparring with the springy blue band, Mickey wobbled as he sought an equilibrium in the sky. The huge sunglasses perched on the tip of his nose made the balancing act more difficult. 'I'm not ashamed of my country and I don't want to be,' he said. 'You know, every time I meet someone new, I tell them something positive about Senegal, something they didn't know before, to give them a new perspective.' With baby steps, he tiptoed across the strip. The sunnies slanted dangerously to the right.

'That's what you did the first time we met. You told me about the pink lake and the surfing spots,' Viviano said.

'I know, but, Viv, you were something else!' Mickey said with a groan. 'You kept wanting to know more and more, and it was exhausting! In the end, I ran out of things to tell you. I had to invent unsettling *"facts"* so you wouldn't ask a follow up …' Finally stable, Mickey glided across the slackline towards Viviano, and with a grin, lowered the sunglasses to peer at his friend. '… which completely defeated the purpose of what I was trying to do.'

'Yes,' Viviano said, frowning. 'I remember. I was surprised when your beautiful tour of Senegal took a dark and frankly disturbing turn. You dick.' He dug his feet into the rope and Mickey swayed precariously.

'Ha,' said Mickey. 'That's the thing about coming from a country that people don't know too much about. You can say anything you want and everyone just nods and smiles politely.'

He flashed pearly whites at Viviano who rolled his eyes.

'Anyway, I'm glad I was persistent,' Viviano said. 'Because if I hadn't been, you would never have introduced me to all that music.'

'Good point,' Mickey replied. 'Let's get a tune on now. *Ragazzi*, guys, choose something from my playlist.'

He waved down to JuanPa and Elena who were eating pizza and soaking up the last light of the day. With a lazy nod, JuanPa reached for Mickey's phone.

A melody picked on the strings of an electric guitar began to weave through the warm evening air. Soon, it was accompanied by the beat of an African drum and a saxophonist's riff. In silence, the group listened as a hoarse voice sang poetry in a language only Mickey could understand.

'OK, I'm going for the flip,' announced Viviano, inspired by the music.

'You've got this,' said Mickey, jumping from the slackline and joining JuanPa and Elena on the ground. In unison, they stared up at Viviano.

Listening to the beat and trying to channel his inner cat, Viviano bounced on the slackline, each time a little higher, building momentum. He was nervous. With every jump, thoughts flashed through his mind: a scene from the day, a scrap of overheard conversation which echoed over and over. Faces from the streets merged into one and noisy chatter clouded his brain. Somewhere, something dark was lurking and his body faltered.

Concentrate! he thought.

Below, everyone held their breath.

Upping the stakes, Viviano bounced higher than ever before, trying to shock himself into a state of calm.

Bounce … bounce …. bounce ….. The landings became further apart.

On the fourth jump, her face appeared. It floated past him and their eyes met, just for a moment. On the fifth, he saw and heard nothing at all.

Now he was high in the air, head tipped back and hips launched towards the sky. It was happening. Viviano's eyes shone down at the earth like glowing moons, and just for a second, everything froze. Then, quick as a flash, his legs swung around and he landed on the strip.

Viviano's mouth fell open. After a few seconds, he punched a fist triumphantly in the air and roared 'Dajeeeeee! Come on!'

'Wow, amico, that was beautiful,' said Mickey, raising his beer in salute.

'Man, I love this fucking song,' said Viviano, leaping into the air again, his heart pounding.

Mickey jumped to his feet and scrambled up to rejoin his friend.

For a while, the quartet was calm, gazing out over Rome as the sun slopped off behind a distant hill. The music transported each of them somewhere different. The woman without a story enveloped Viviano's mind. She had come to his rescue today.

'You know in my region, on the Colombian coast, we have a song that is very dear to us,' said JuanPa, breaking the silence. 'We put it on at the end of parties and while it plays, everyone thinks about their mothers and the sacrifices they have made for us, and we all cry.'

Viviano and Mickey exchanged looks.

'Come on, JuanPa, you're joking!' said Viviano. 'If I came back from a party and told my mum I had spent the evening crying about her, she would start crying and tell me she didn't know how she had raised such a "sad boy".'

'That's because, in this country, you don't love your mothers like we do,' replied JuanPa.

'Ma che dici? What are you talking about?!' interjected Elena, the other Italian in the group. 'Are you seriously telling me that in Italy we don't love our mothers?' She gesticulated exaggeratedly at JuanPa. 'In Italy we love our mothers so much that we let them break our balls constantly,' she said. 'We let them do it, because that is how much we love them. But we are not going to cry about them at a party, because that, caro amico, is just really fucking weird.'

'Well, I guess you guys can just cry over your dance moves then,' JuanPa said through a smug smile. He jumped up, and demonstrating impressive strength, swung himself onto the slackline, sending Viviano and Mickey tumbling back to earth in the process. In the dimmer light, JuanPa's silhouette loomed large over his friends, and against the mauve sky, he began to demonstrate his best salsa moves, placing a whirlwind of light taps and bewitching steps along the stretchy band. 'You will never be able to do this, ragazzi,' he said, with limber hips swaying to and fro. 'Especially you, Viv.'

'Unnecessarily mean,' said Viviano. 'I've always liked to think that I move to the syncopated beat.'

'The syncopated beat, the imaginary beat, whatever makes you feel better,' JuanPa said, still shimmying to the music in his head.

'Such big talk now,' Viviano said. 'You didn't even know how to slackline until I taught you.'

'*É vero,* it's true, *amico,*' replied JuanPa. '*Grazie,* Slackline King, for teaching me such a useful skill.' He bowed and in doing so, lost his balance, and dived headfirst towards the dusty ground, landing with an embarrassing thud.

'You know,' Viviano said, lying on his back and gazing up at the darkening sky, 'I want to write a story about a king.'

'Oh, yeah?' said Elena, raising an eyebrow. 'Since when?'

'He's a king,' said Viviano, mapping it out in his head, 'but he's hiding something … a devastating drug addiction. Desperate for money, he secretly founds an anti-monarchy movement in the country. He uses donations to fund his meth habit. That way he can monitor the Republicans from the inside and have a steady supply of drugs.'

There was silence.

'That's a shit story, Viv,' said Elena. 'It makes absolutely no sense.'

They passed around more beers.

The group stayed on the hilltop until twinkling lights had appeared across the city and only a handful of people remained, dotted along the viewpoint.

'Want to stay at mine, Mickey?' Viviano said as they gathered their things.

'I thought you'd never ask.'

Elena and JuanPa sped off into the night on mopeds, while Mickey and Viviano ambled back down the hill.

'God, I'm exhausted,' Mickey yawned when they reached the flat.

Isabella was already in bed and everything was quiet. Viviano went to fetch some sheets and made up the sofa in his bedroom.

'Every time I come to your house, I forget what a trip your room is,' Mickey said, staring at the various outfits and props.

'My head is a trip,' Viviano said with a shrug.

'You know, in Senegal, if your room looked like this, we would hold a ceremony and everyone in the town would come and pray for your mental wellbeing.'

'Stop making things up,' Viviano said, tossing a pillow at Mickey, hitting him squarely in the face.

'*Buona notte,*' said Mickey, tucking it underneath his head.

Viviano turned out the light and flopped into bed.

'Mickey,' Viviano's voice sounded timid in the dark.

'Yes.'

'Have you ever seen me do anything bad?'

'What do you mean?' asked Mickey, his voice sleepy and confused.

'I don't know,' said Viviano. 'Just wondering. We're friends, you would tell me, right?'

'Viviano Conti,' said Mickey, using his full name and then yawning loudly, '*ascoltami,* listen to me. I have no idea what you are talking about, but no, I have never seen you do anything bad. Yes, we are friends and yes, I'd tell you.'

There was silence.

'Thanks,' said Viviano, but suddenly he felt panicked. He had never raised these fears with anyone, and his whole body began to squirm. *'Per favore,* please, Mickey, forget I asked, OK?'

'Asked what?' said Mickey, and Viviano could sense his grin, even in the dark.

'Viv,' Mickey said. 'I see you get stressed sometimes, all by yourself. All those brains in your head, *amico mio,* don't waste them on nonsense, OK. That's no life. *Buona notte.'*

'Buona notte,' said Viviano.

CHAPTER TWENTY-FIVE

Night owls

Viviano awoke a few hours later with a desire to sprint as far and fast as he could. Perhaps north all the way to Austria, or south, to the tip of Italy's boot, and catch a boat to Sicily.

I have to move, he thought as thousands of ants poured from his veins and began crawling over his body.

As quick as a city fox, Viviano slipped out bed and his mind scanned over the events of yesterday: the backflip, the music, fun with friends. His heart sank.

I felt happy then, so why am I like this now?

Without a sound, he pulled on some jeans and a crumpled T-shirt from the floor, and left the room. Mickey was sound asleep on the sofa.

Navigating the darkness, Viviano tried to forge the familiar path to the front door, but a stray shoe thwarted his plans and sent him crashing into the coat rack.

'Merda, merda!' he cursed under his breath, waiting to see if anyone had stirred, but the house was silent.

No longer able to restrain his legs, Viviano eased the door open, flung his body down the stairs and out into the night. His fingers typed instinctively:

> Where are you?

The reply came quickly.

> Nearly at Stan's. Are you coming?

> 10 minutes

The only sound was his breath as Viviano jogged down the maze of backstreets towards the river, with nothing but the odd street lamp and scavenging rat for company. At the bridge, voices echoed from underneath the arches and Viviano descended to the footpath.

'Viv! *Ciao!* Over here.' Camilla's beaming face came into view as she stepped out from the shadows by the murky water. 'I didn't think we'd see you tonight.'

With a nod, Viviano's eyes flickered over the familiar faces and then down towards Stan, who despite the humid air, was huddled in a blanket on the floor.

'*Come sta, signore?* How are you?' Viviano asked.

'*Come un pappagallo testardo,* like a stubborn parrot,' Stan replied.

'Who doesn't love a parrot?' said Viviano. 'Beautiful creatures.'

Without baring his gappy teeth, the ageing man mustered something like a smile, but continued to stare into a different universe.

'We've bought you some minestrone,' said Camilla, kneeling next to his spindly legs and tending a flask which he received with blackened fingernails.

'We've got you a fresh blanket, too, if you want it,' said Nico, another volunteer, whose beanpole silhouette resembled that of a lamppost.

'I like this one,' said Stan, pulling the squalid rag tighter around him.

'I know.'

'Did you perform today, Viv?' he asked.

'Leonardo the cat was indeed out and about. I came to say hi, but you weren't here.'

'Maybe I was walking.'

'That's what I thought.'

'Will you come to the centre soon, Stan?' Camilla asked, lightly stroking his forehead with her thumb. 'Let us give you a haircut and clean you up a bit? Of course, you're beautiful anyway, but you could do with some TLC.'

'Every time you make me look nice, I want to show my wife,' replied Stan. 'I'd rather stay here.'

Camilla nodded.

'*Sono così stanco,* I'm so tired,' he said.

'We'll leave you to rest, *caro,* but we'll come again tomorrow.'

'My boy would have loved your costumes,' Stan said, his limp fingers briefly holding Viviano's wrist, before he turned and pulled the blanket over his head. 'Thank you all for coming,' he murmured.

As they trudged back up the stone steps, Viviano greeted Camilla, Nico and Serena with a hug.

'Where to next?' Camilla asked, her voice cracking slightly. She tried to hide it with a cough as she glanced back at Stan's sad figure.

'Let's go and see Lady Red. Make sure she is keeping out of trouble,' said Nico. 'Maybe we can convince her to come in tonight.'

Camilla nodded. 'You two take the motorino, Viv and I will follow in the van. I need to stop and pick up supplies on the way.'

Viviano slid his door closed while Camilla hopped in the driver's seat and started the engine. At this time of night, they relished the lack of traffic in streets that normally heaved like clogged arteries.

'I'm happy to see you,' Camilla said, taking her grey eyes off the road for a second and smiling at Viviano. 'It's always more fun when you come along.'

'It's nice to join you guys,' said Viviano. 'Are you alright, Cams?'

'Yeah, thanks,' said Camilla with a nod. 'Stan always gets me, you know … I think because I knew him and his family before the accident. They were so happy and, he was so … normal. Some people get a terrible lot in life.' She stared out at the open road. 'I hope one day he'll find some kind of peace.'

Viviano squeezed her shoulder. Camilla felt everyone's pain as if it were her own. It was both a blessing and a curse.

'You know, before you abandoned me at law school …' she began to say.

Viviano rolled his eyes and Camilla laughed. She always started every other sentence like that.

'No eye rolls! Before you abandoned me at school, I always thought we'd have our own practice together.'

'Really?'

'Yes, me the brilliant legal assassin and you, the goofy clown that cheers clients up when cases aren't going well.'

'I believe I could do that now, without a law degree,' Viviano said.

Camilla shoved his arm and the van veered slightly. 'You were a better lawyer than me,' she said.

'Come again?'

'Well, you weren't. You never applied yourself and you didn't come to the exams. But, if you *had* stuck with it, you would've been brilliant.'

'We'll never know,' Viviano said.

Camilla shrugged.

Suddenly, without warning, she swerved up the pavement and slammed on the brakes by the charity headquarters, parking the van at a violent slant between a lamppost and a bicycle.

Viviano looked over at her. 'You can't be serious.'

'What? What you just saw takes a lot of skill.'

'I actually think the van might tip over.'

'Well you better get out then. It's just a quick pick up anyway,' she said, hopping down. 'We got a late delivery from the deli around the corner. A couple of trays … Here they are.'

Two large, rectangular boxes were stacked on the doorstep. They contained rows of sandwiches filled with cured hams and cheeses. Together, Viviano and Camilla carried them to the van and jumped back in.

As Camilla pulled off, there was a crunching noise as the lone bicycle was swept under her wheels. Viviano didn't think she had even noticed.

In silence, they navigated a few empty streets.

'It's not working out with Diego,' Camilla said after a while, lifting her hands from the steering wheel to tie her hair and prompting Viviano to steer in her place – something he had found himself doing since their days at university together.

'*Mi dispiace*, I'm sorry,' he said. 'How come?'

'Work is too chaotic,' Camilla replied. 'If I'm honest, I know I could make more time for him, but I'm not … Look at tonight. It's my first evening off in ages and I'm here.'

Viviano nodded. 'How do you feel when you think about him?'

'Like I'm happy he's there, but if he wasn't, I wouldn't mind.'

'What every man dreams of hearing,' said Viviano. 'I'm sorry, Cams.'

Camilla gave a little sigh. 'And how about you? How is the most happening bed in Rome?' she asked, poking his ribs and emitting a derisive snort.

'*Niente da dire,* nothing to report,' they said at the same time, with Camilla mimicking Viviano's casual manner.

'As always. Nothing. Really? Viv, I've never seen you with anyone since I've known you!'

'Nothing,' Viviano shrugged.

'OK,' said Camilla, 'but you have *seen* you, right? Every time you meet my friends, they harass me for your number.'

'And yet you never pass on the message.'

'Do you want me to set you up?'

'No, you know, I do fine. I'm seeing different people.'

'I take it back,' said Camilla. 'You would have been a terrible lawyer, you can't lie for shit. We're here.'

Lady Red was hiding under some bushes near a lamppost. Nico and Serena were opposite, trying to coax her out.

'Do you have a message for me?' she enquired, as she always did, in her hoarse voice. The elegant, floor-length red dress which clung to her body was filthy from years spent on the streets.

Gaia had been one of their first case studies back in law school, during a module on the consequences of legal blunders. At the time, she was a young mum with a heroin addiction. Her partner, known to deal and shoot up himself, had run away with their baby girl. While fighting in the courts, Gaia had undergone treatment and weaned herself off the drugs – for her one-year-old Lila, everything was possible. But Lila's dad was from a wealthy family and they wanted Gaia out of the picture. In their eyes, she was the vermin that had corrupted their darling son.

During the trial, expensive Rottweilers had done their best to portray Gaia as an unfit parent with no hope. But the jury were unconvinced. They saw her will to change and the steady progress she was making. Things looked in her favour.

Just as Gaia could feel her daughter's warm body returning to her chest, the case unravelled. A drug test she failed to attend, due to a miscommunication with her lawyers.

'That's so unfortunate,' one Rottweiler said as the judge ruled against Gaia. 'You must have missed the message.'

Scrambling, her legal team immediately launched an appeal, but the heartbreak was too much for Gaia. Instead of a baby, her arms were greeted with needles, and she lapsed back into addiction. The charity had been supporting her for some time now, and if she could stay clean, Camilla promised she would help Gaia see her daughter again. Little by little, the tide was turning.

'How are you feeling today?' asked Viviano, handing her a sandwich and a bottle of water.

'*Come un coyote astuto,* like a wily coyote,' Gaia whispered, reaching out a bony arm. 'I … I went to my rehab earlier,' she said, timidly. 'The group is nice this time. We're helping each other.' She hesitated, then took a sip of cold water. 'Can I come in tonight?'

Camilla couldn't hide her beaming face. It was the first time Gaia had asked, without having to be persuaded.

'Of course, you can! I can take you back in the van. We always have a bed for you.'

Gaia nodded. 'I'll leave a note so that if anyone comes with an important message, they'll know where to find me.'

'I can drive,' Viviano offered while they helped gather her belongings. He didn't want Camilla to kill Gaia in a road accident just as things were starting to look up.

Back in the van, Camilla noticed that the petite woman next to her was shaking. '*Stai bene,* are you OK?' she asked, placing a hand on her shoulder.

Gaia let out a yelp. 'Maybe I shouldn't go after all. I feel nervous.'

In the mirror, Viviano caught the crestfallen look in Camilla's eyes.

'Let's play a game,' he said.

Gaia was silent.

'I spy with my little eye something beginning with … Um, that traffic light over there.'

'What?' Viviano heard Gaia's voice from the back. 'That's not how you play. You're not supposed to tell us what you spy.'

'Oh, *scusami,* you're right. What was I thinking? Let me go again. I spy with my little eye, something beginning with … my very own hands on the steering wheel,' said Viviano. 'Ha, that's a tough one for you guys.'

'*Ma sei pazzo?* Are you mad?' said Gaia. 'You just told us again. Here, let me show you how to play.'

'I spy with my little eye, something beginning with … D.'

'Driver.'

'Viv, not everything is about you.'

'Drone.'

'Do you see a drone?'

'Driveway?' asked Camilla.

A thousand guesses later, Viviano and Camilla gave up.

'It's George Clooney,' said Gaia, a coy smile on her face.

'That doesn't have a D anywhere in it, and he's also not here,' said Viviano.

'Yeah, but you didn't know how to play either,' said Gaia, letting out a cackle so boisterous it caused Camilla to erupt in fits of giggles. 'Is it my turn again?' Gaia enquired.

'Absolutely not,' said Viviano. 'Anyway, we're here.'

With wide eyes, Gaia contemplated the grey building. There were times, in the past, when it had loomed large like a shadowy lynx with amber eyes, threatening to devour her. But today, the yellow light pouring through the windows looked homely, inviting her to rest.

'I am looking forward to taking a shower,' she said.

Another volunteer came out, and with a gentle manner, she led Gaia to get settled for the night.

'I think that's me done,' said Camilla. 'Serena and Nico are going to take care of the rest, if you want to join them, but I've had a long day. I'm just going to drop the van back to them.'

'No, I'll head off too,' said Viviano.

'Where are you going to go?'

'Out and about.'

Camilla laughed and shook the heavy fringe from her face. 'Thanks for taking the time,' she said. 'It always feels a bit lighter when you come.' With her eyes closed, she pulled him into a tight hug and then lingered there, her soft breath warming his neck. 'You can kiss me, if you want, Viv,' she whispered. Feeling Viviano immediately freeze between her arms, Camilla pulled away and smiled with embarrassment. 'You don't want to,' she said. 'I knew it anyway. It wouldn't be a good idea.'

Viviano cocked his head to one side as his friend's grey eyes dodged his. '*Madonna mia,* my God, Cami,' he said with a gentle laugh, 'how tired are you?'

Cautiously, he brushed the strands of hair from her eyes, and then, like a hairdresser conceptualising a creation, began to ruffle her parting so that, within seconds, a bird's nest had formed on top of her head.

'I changed my mind,' Camilla said, eyebrows raised, unamused by her new look. '*So che siamo amici,* I know we are friends, my dear.'

Viviano shrugged. 'Suit yourself. I thought you might at least fight for me,' he said, jumping down from the van.

'*Idiota,*' Camilla retorted as she revved the engine and sped off into the night, the door still wide open.

'Close the fucking door, Cams,' Viviano shouted, shaking his head.

After one final glance at the shelter, Viviano left. He knew exactly where to go.

CHAPTER TWENTY-SIX

Killing me softly

Viviano's legs guided him through the streets and along the river, past eerie churches and ancient monuments, until he was standing in front of a newsagents. Even at 3 a.m., its neon white lights shone brightly, reassuring night wanderers that they weren't the only ones awake.

'*Signore,*' Abdul said as Viviano stepped inside among the rows of pantry essentials, chocolate bars and cleaning products. 'It's in full swing.'

'*Grazie,* sir,' said Viviano, slipping down the back stairs where the white wall paint was peeling and the steps sagged under his feet.

At the bottom, there was a heavy, metal door.

As he opened it, just a millimetre, a deafening wail escaped from within, and Viviano slipped in.

Inside, about thirty people were sardined together, some standing, others sitting on beanbags which were strewn across the floor like blotches on a Twister board. Sweat had crept over their skin, hair and clothes. Overhead, a dim light was trying to permeate the darkness, making everything look like a grainy old film.

Viviano fought through the wall of noise and slumped onto a beanbag in the corner. Through the various figures, he could make out a musician in the middle of the room. The thick earplugs wedged into her ears ensured the woman couldn't hear anything around her – that was the condition upon which she agreed to perform. Softly, she launched into a rendition of Norah Jones' *Sunrise*, plucking delicately at the strings of her acoustic guitar.

'*Sunrise, Sunrise, looks like morning in your eyes …*' screamed the audience in a collective, out-of-tune howling, which was enough to make demons from the underworld beg for mercy. Some people refrained from any lyrics at all, preferring a long groan like a foghorn or continuous high-pitched shrieks.

Viviano willingly joined in. For him, and everyone else there, this was therapy.

The smooth classics kept rolling – *Dream* by The Everly Brothers, Elvis' *Can't Help Falling in Love,* Al Green's *Let's Stay Together.*'

Like dogs, they barked the lyrics at the top of their lungs. Viviano closed his eyes and tried to let the pounding din drown out his thoughts.

When he opened them, he saw a woman wandering towards him.

Her rainbow hair was plaited, and she was covered in shiny piercings and tattoos. Aurora, his last one-night-stand. Sitting down beside him, she nodded in acknowledgement, her face tinged with blue glitter.

At the time, Viviano didn't think either of them had really enjoyed the night they spent together. A whirlwind of vodka shots had led them from the shouting room to Aurora's cramped flat where they had searched for some kind of complicity or escape from this world. But in the haze of morning, they both knew it wasn't meant to be.

As the performer launched into a new song, tenderly picking the strings of her guitar, Aurora rested her head on Viviano's shoulder and began to wail. Viviano stared around the room, seeing Munch's *The Scream* produced over and over again on faces that appeared to have nothing in common. Then he started yelling until his throat was on fire.

After a long while, Viviano rose, slid through the swamp of bodies and made his way out, past Abdul and the neat rows of toothpaste and dried pasta, onto the street.

He climbed the side of a building and climbed down again, passed a dive bar and downed whatever potion the barman handed him. On nights like these, nothing helped. Nothing helped. Nothing could soothe the restless sadness, the tunnelling shame and accusations, the tears that drowned his insides but never spilled out of his eyes.

Just beside him, a pack of runners jogged past, marathon training at the crack of dawn before the sun made any physical activity feel like a sin. Grouped together, they puffed and encouraged in equal measures, sweeping Viviano up with them.

Why not? he thought, embarking on a breathless tour of the city.

The circuit eventually spat him out by the river, and Viviano keeled over on the bridge. The pavement smelt of the Roman labourers who had built it and a thin layer of gravelly dust stuck to his face.

After a period of stillness, he struggled to his feet and leant over the side. Below, the dark waters rushed over jagged rocks lurking underneath. Across the ripples, her face began to appear. The impossibly dark eyes bore into his, her black curls wove into the waves and the tip of her nose peeked through the surface.

'I want to meet you,' he whispered.

The woman's eyes blinked rhythmically and Viviano felt his heart rate slow.

As he stared, lost among her watery features, a noose began to descend over the beautiful face. It settled around her neck and tightened. The water swirled and spluttered as the woman without a story thrashed against the cord.

Viviano shook his head violently and turned away.

'I can't meet you,' he said. 'I would just ruin everything.'

CHAPTER TWENTY-SEVEN

The two sides of the wall

Slowly, he moved in, his gaze fixed upon her like a lion circling its prey. Just millimetres away, he stopped, their bodies barely touching. Laure froze and the hairs on her neck and arms stood on end. Her heart thumped against her ribcage.

For a moment, they were both still, neither one daring to proceed. Then, with agonising caution, he lifted a hand and traced his fingertips lightly down her arm, sending a shiver of excitement through her body.

'I haven't been able to stop thinking about you,' Marco whispered as he leant in and kissed her, parting her soft lips and exploring the intricacies of her mouth.

A gentle moan escaped from Laure's throat as his tongue descended to her neck. Reaching out, she discovered the shape of his shoulders, the hairs on his chest, his firm torso, until her fingers collided with the seams of his dark jeans.

Like two excited animals, they began to pant and the kisses became clumsy and wet. Marco sunk his teeth into Laure's bottom lip, and with the force of his body, pushed her backwards against the desk. The tip of his tongue circled hers and Laure's legs slid open. Instinctively, his body slotted between them.

'Do you want me?' Marco asked, unbuttoning her shirt, licking and kissing the skin that revealed itself.

'*Oui,*' she whispered, her head rolling backwards.

Marco let out a low growl as Laure's fingers found the erection straining against his boxers. With strong hands, he pulled her legs around him and threw her onto the bed. Here, in the dim light, his dark eyes searched her half-naked body lying before him.

'I want you so badly,' he murmured, slipping off her knickers.

Laure felt Marco's lips brush over her breasts, her stomach, until he reached her thighs.

'I can't believe this is happening' she said breathlessly.

The door slammed and Laure awoke. Every part of her body was tingling and a light perspiration clung to her skin.

'What's going on?' she said hazily, trying to get her bearings.

Halfway between sleep and consciousness, she shut her eyes again, and searched for the fading dream. The feeling of Marco's touch was so vivid that Laure's hands wandered up her legs to her knickers, desperate to lapse back into fantasy.

'Hey, babe.' The vibrations of Marco's deep voice came floating through the wall, fluttering against her ear drum and entangling itself with her reverie.

This is surreal, Laure thought, swaying a little closer to reality. Eyes still closed, she tilted her head towards the wall, but there was silence. *Am I dreaming? Was he actually talking to me?* She shuffled up, searching hungrily for Marco.

'You still not speaking to me?' The voice resurfaced, smooth and inquisitive.

He's next door, talking to his girlfriend, Laure thought with a heavy sigh, *just like every other night.*

In her mind, Marco was back in her bedroom, back on top of her, his lips circling the top of her inner thigh, edging closer and closer.

'I'm not *not* talking to you, Marco. I just don't know what to say,' came Valeria's razor-sharp response from the other side of the wall.

...

Next door, Valeria was sitting on their grey sofa, her knees drawn in and arms gripped around her legs.

'You know what I've been thinking,' Marco said, nestling next to his girlfriend and rubbing his nose tentatively against her cheek. 'We've been putting too much pressure on ourselves. We've let things get so heavy. It's not healthy for us, for our relationship.' He kissed her cheek and stroked the outside of her leg. 'We should go out tonight together,' he continued. 'It's Friday. Let's go out, *amore,* and take it all back to the beginning.'

Valeria looked straight ahead, lips sewn shut.

'We can go to Mega Bar,' Marco pressed on, trying to snuggle his face into her neck. 'You remember, we used to go there all the time.' He laughed, desperate to build up some kind of momentum between them.

Valeria's face was expressionless.

Marco persevered. 'You know, I'd go back in a heartbeat, just for the DJ, right? Remember, *amore,* he was so talented!' With a stiff smile, Marco gazed hopefully at his partner, begging her to laugh or to detect even a hint of amusement somewhere in her solemnity.

The pleading overtures swirled through the wall to Laure.

Marco's thinking of me, Laure thought, her body quivering like a leaf in the breeze. *He wants her to laugh like I laughed this morning.*

Laure's fingertips slipped underneath the thin fabric of her knickers and she began to touch herself.

Next door, instead of begrudging goodwill, Marco was greeted with icy disdain. He pulled away from Valeria's side, hurt by her coldness.

'Just another night of this attitude then, I guess,' he muttered, standing up.

'My attitude?' Valeria said, an unequivocal quiver in her voice. 'Marco, I was so upset last night, I didn't sleep at all. Everything we said to each other was going around and around in my head.' She paused and shut her eyes. 'I have been here waiting for you, feeling so nervous, expecting to have a conversation about it. But you just came in and acted like none of it mattered, like you didn't say any of those things.' Her voice began to crumble. 'And on top of that, you have the ego to demand that I act as if everything is OK, too, because you've decided that it is.'

'I'm not demanding anything,' Marco said, angst flooding his face. 'I know we said some hurtful things, we were angry. But that's why I think we need to get out, blow off some steam and reset. Everything has become so intense.' He shook his head.

'Trust me,' said Valeria. 'I heard very clearly what *you* think.' She cocked her head to one side and adopted a cloying tone. 'Our relationship is too heavy, and you'd like for everything to be new again.' Thin streaks of dismay lined her face as she contemplated her boyfriend. 'I really don't know what's going on with you.'

On the other side of the wall, Laure grazed her teeth along Marco's ear. It drove him wild. Making wide circles, she ran her nails along his back, digging in ever so slightly. He caught her wrist and pinned it to the mattress, then slowly, he began to touch her, finding all the right places as she moaned into the night air.

In the flat next door, Valeria walked towards her partner.

'I don't want a new relationship,' she said, looking Marco dead in the eye. 'I want *our* relationship, the one that we've been building together for seven years. I just want to make it better, and I thought you did too …' Valeria trailed off, visibly at a loss to understand. 'You need to think about the way you're acting,' she said.

'Do I?' Marco replied, irritation itching his skin. 'Well, maybe I'm tired of constantly pandering to whatever you want.'

'Oh, what on earth are you talking about?' Valeria screamed, a fire roaring behind her eyes. 'It's called compromise, and it's what you do when you build a life with someone.'

'I can't believe we're doing this,' Marco whispered to Laure in her fantasy. The walls of her body shivered with sensitivity as he pushed inside her. Leaning down, he kissed her and then, steadily, began to thrust, sending ripples of pleasure cascading through her to the tips of her toes.

'I'm bored, OK,' Marco bellowed at Valeria as he erupted with rage next door. 'I'm bored of this monotonous shit. I'm bored of your whinging and this constant fighting.' He glared at his girlfriend. 'You know, there are other ways of being together, Valeria. There are couples who have fun together. A relationship doesn't have to be like this.'

'Oh *mon Dieu*, Marco,' Laure gasped, holding him close as a desperate urgency ignited inside her. Spurred on by the encouragement, Marco thrust deeper into her body, his fingers grasping the flesh of her buttocks.

On the other side of the wall, a layer of tears had formed over Valeria's hazel eyes.

'Well, guess what,' she said, trembling. 'I'm bored of you too. I'm bored of your selfishness.' She let out a feverish laugh. 'I don't know why I'm even bothering to try when you clearly don't give a shit.'

Gazing down at the floor, Marco said nothing.

Valeria shook her head. 'I can't be here anymore.'

'Marco, I'm going to come,' Laure moaned, feeling a tidal wave breaking inside her as, back in reality, her own fingers worked their magic. In her mind, Marco kept his pace, desperately staving off his own ejaculation.

Next door, Valeria shot one last-ditch glance at her boyfriend. 'I'm going to stay at my parents' tonight,' she announced.

No objection was lodged, and so she left, slamming the door with so much force that tiny fissures wormed through the plaster.

Laure's body began to convulse. Feeling her come was too much for Marco. He let out a violent cry and shuddered, his face contorted in anguish, before the weight of his sweaty body collapsed onto her. Tangled together, they lay there, panting.

In the dark room, as the last ebbs of her orgasm melted away, Laure opened her eyes. She was lying alone on the bed, and an eerie silence hung around her clammy body.

Through the wall, Marco was staring out at the empty flat. For a while, he was perfectly still, as if petrified in stone. Then, slowly, he drifted over to the dining table and picked up a crystal vase they had been given by friends for Christmas. Rolling it around and around, he watched its ornate grooves blur together. Then, with all his might, he hurled it against the wall, showering the floor with thousands of tiny icicles before slumping down on the sofa, head in his hands.

...

From the floor below, Valeria heard the racket. She had been waiting in the stairwell, leaning against the cool wall, for Marco to come after her.

He would come, she reassured herself. He loved her.

But as the minutes went by, a nagging panic began grow.

Something had changed, she thought. It was true that this was a particularly unhappy patch for them, but they had weathered worse storms and it had never been like this. He had never been like this.

Her cheek sunk into the white paint.

She hadn't meant it when she said they should end things. It was a bluff, an attempt to make him behave differently. *Could those words, spat in anger, really have cut him so deeply?* she wondered, running the events of the past week through her mind. Or was there something else?

As she gazed up the stairwell, thinking that at any moment his figure might appear, Valeria's eyes started to droop.

I'm so tired, she thought.

Shadows shifted across the walls and she lost track of time.

Eventually, she gave in. Marco wasn't coming. Feeling a warm, salty tear drop onto her lip, Valeria lifted her heavy head and trailed down the stairs into the night.

...

Back in the flat, Marco unclenched his fists like a fossil coming back to life.

It was good that Valeria had left, he thought, bringing his breathing under control.

I can't handle another night of arguing and I'm tired of sleeping on the sofa.

Several times, he rose to his feet and then sat again, like a tightly wound coil needing a release.

In his subconscious, Laure crept out of her hiding place, wild hair and dark eyes. She would be awake now, probably charming strangers with her unassuming smile. *Between us, nothing is complicated,* he thought.

Marco pulled the phone from his pocket and opened their conversation.

> Can we meet tomorrow?
> *Ti voglio vedere.*
> I want to see you.

For a moment, he lingered over the send button and then clicked.

Next door, Laure's phone emitted a lazy buzz and she caught the edge of it with her fingertips. The backlight startled her eyes as the message appeared. She replied, then rolled over and fell back into the clutches of sleep.

> I want to see you too

CHAPTER TWENTY-EIGHT

Pâtes au pistou – Pasta Pesto

Twelve hours later, Laure came back to life.

So deep was her sleep, it felt like she had awoken on a seabed, cut off from the chatter of reality which bubbled above. Gradually, every inch of her body yawned and she drifted towards the surface. On the way up, Marco and his girlfriend glided alongside, asking a thousand questions, but only bubbles came out of their mouths. 'I want to see you,' Marco finally spluttered as they broke through the surface into the hot summer air. His girlfriend evaporated with the sea foam.

Laure's eyes opened with Marco's late-night proposal simmering in her mind.

Had he been serious? she wondered. And, reconsidering the situation in the light of day, would she really want to go?

'I didn't expect to find myself here,' Laure murmured, pulling the bedsheet over her head. Hidden from the world, she thought about Marco, and how it felt when his sparkling eyes lingered on her. The heat of last night's dream still simmered in her bones. 'I do want to see him,' she admitted.

In one swift motion, Laure swept the sheet from her body and began to face reality. Initially, her phone revealed the standard weekend messages: A poem from Eva about erectile dysfunction, told from the perspective of the penis. Laure read the first line, gagged and deleted it.

Then, there was a missed call and a voicemail.

'Ciao, Laure, it's me, Marco. I guess on a Saturday you are in recovery.' He laughed, but his voice sounded tired. *'I'm sorry I texted you again so late. But listen, I meant what I said, I really would like to see you ... Today, if you are free. I was thinking we could go to Da Antonio, since it's near for both of us. At around three this afternoon? We could have a drink, get your evening off to a good start ...'* More insecure laughter. *'It would be nice to see your smile.'* The message clicked off.

There it was, she thought. The morning after and the offer still stood.

Clambering out of bed, Laure appreciated how different she felt after a proper night's sleep – it had been ages. Various items were strewn across the floor. She tip-toed around them and began to prepare a pot of coffee.

Over the week, the flat had become something of a pigsty.

'I haven't really been taking care of myself lately,' she acknowledged, as her stomach whined like a disgruntled cat.

With a stick lighter, Laure lit another hob, let a pan fill almost to the brim with water and located some pasta and a jar of pesto. It wasn't a typical breakfast but actually, she reasoned, it was nearly lunch time. The little Moka machine began to overflow with silky streams of coffee, and after filling up a cup, Laure perched on the small ledge by her window. Below, Trastevere was also just awakening. It wasn't a morning city, no, *la bella Roma* was a night owl: dinners were late, drinks were later, and lie-ins were sacred.

'*Svegliarsi presto? E perdersi la notte? Assurdo!* Wake up early? And miss the night? Ridiculous!' a true native would tell you.

Leaning back against the wall, Laure felt the sunshine on her face.

This is nice, she thought, breathing softly.

Tu sais, you could just stay here all day if you wanted? her brain said. *Eat your pasta pesto, put some music on, relax and forget about this sticky Marco situation.*

Laure smiled, the idea making her feel safe and secure.

It'll be great, her brain continued. *You can veg out, pretend you're having sex with someone. You know, the usual. And then, you can get stuck into some poetry about men who are struggling to get hard.*

'I deleted that,' Laure snapped, defensively. 'Anyway, I want to go,' she announced to the empty room. It was true. She was curious about Marco and tired of rejection being the only constant in her love life. 'I'll go for a bit. Maybe I'll say I have plans for later. I just want to see if there really is something between us.'

Laure, he doesn't know anything about you. He thinks you're a hot mess and that's why he's interested, her brain said.

'I am a hot mess,' Laure replied.

Oui, ça c'est clair, that's for sure. But you're not a fun, party-animal hot mess, who loves indulging in cigarettes and coke until the sun comes up. You've got some unaddressed mental health issues and have been spying on your neighbours through the wall. Is that what you think he's after? Her brain tailed off.

'Frankly, quite mean,' Laure said with a frown. 'I am going, but I'm going to be myself. I'll tell him some real things about me, and see if he still looks at me like I'm someone special.'

What about his girlfriend?

'You know,' said Laure, feeling increasingly annoyed. 'Sometimes, couples do break up and sometimes they aren't built to last. From what I've been hearing, these two are doing a pretty good job of tearing themselves down.' Her resolve strengthened. 'Anyway, do I really owe this woman anything? Are relationships first come first served? I want to see where Marco and I stand when it's just us.'

Very philosophical, said her brain.

'Oh, *tais-toi,* shut up,' Laure said, rising to her feet to toss some spaghetti into the bubbling pot of water.

She replied to Marco:

> *Ciao.* Three sounds good.
> I'll see you there

As she was about to engage in all-out warfare with her brain, Laure saw another message come through, and just reading the name made her smile. It was from Julie, one of her best friends back in Paris. No matter how busy their lives were, they tried to touch base at least once a week. When Laure first arrived in Italy, Julie had been her rock, calling daily to check she was OK.

> *Bonjour ma chérie*, I hope you're having a beautiful weekend. I was just watching the news and there's this story about a Roman diamond thief. They caught him on the run using a fake name, Stefano Uccello.
> Could it be the mysterious Davide?
> He tunnelled right underneath the bank, apparently. I remember you said Davide was into caving. Anyway, there was no photo.
> Love you!

Laure stared down at the message, perplexed. 'Why do all my friends think I was dating a criminal?'

It had now been suggested too many times to ignore, and her curiosity piqued, Laure typed *'Stefano Uccello, diamond thief'* into the search engine and clicked on the first link that appeared. Despite knowing it was nonsensical, she held her breath and read.

Marauding under the name Stefano Uccello, Massimiliano Venchio, 30, was apprehended by police in the mountainous region of Oulx near the French border, in his rucksack, the stolen diamond stash.

Underneath, there was a photo of a young man with dark hair and trickster eyes.

'I knew it wasn't him,' Laure said, placing the phone back down to tend to her lunch. 'Although, I have to say, I like the story.' She looked out of the window. 'And, maybe the real Davide might never resurface. Perhaps today is an opportunity to move on to something different, to feel different.'

The pasta was ready and Laure mixed in a jar of creamy pesto. On the small kitchen island, she laid the table neatly to have at least a semblance of order and control before heading into the unknown. The fork prongs twizzled with ease among the mass of silky spaghetti strands, and with the first comforting bite, she closed her eyes and breathed a sigh of relief. The plate was soon empty and Laure devoured seconds, polishing off everything and scraping her spoon around the pan.

There was still some time before meeting Marco, an opportunity she gratefully embraced to tidy the flat and take a long shower. After emerging from the steamy bathroom in a fluffy white towel, Laure felt more human than she could remember and the mirror revealed that the dark bags under her eyes were somewhat reduced.

She scoured her wardrobe, trying on several outfits before settling on a summery blue jumpsuit.

Something pretty, but not too out there, she thought, pulling her hair into a half up-half down style.

Touches of makeup made it look as if she'd had weeks of replenishing sleeps, and Laure reminded herself that Marco had certainly seen her looking worse.

Time was ticking. A glass of wine seemed like a good idea to calm the butterflies. As she poured a considerable over-measure, music began to drift through her window, and in a heartbeat, Laure was transported back to her childhood living room and her mum dancing around an ironing board, singing at the top of her lungs.

'Jean-Maxime La Croix Montagne,' she said aloud, pressing her ear against the wall, a position that was becoming far too familiar.

On the other side, Marco was singing away to '*Les Flammes de Notre Amour*' – *The Flames of Our Love* – and Laure stifled a laugh. Was this his 'French date' preparation? It was quite endearing, but she'd have to introduce him to some new artists. This was old school and personally, she'd never been a fan. Quickly tired of the romantic crooning, Laure drowned it out with some music of her own, the nerves swelling inside with every second.

To avoid crossing paths, she left the flat much earlier than needed, creeping like a mouse past Marco's door. It was a relief to hear that he was still having a ball with *Monsieur* La Croix Montagne.

The backstreets behind Da Antonio were her hiding place, and after toiling down the twisting alleys to kill time, Laure came out onto the main road by the bridge with a plan to stroll casually to the café from this direction.

Does none of this behaviour strike you as strange? her brain asked.

Laure ignored the comment. 'There are no obstacles now,' she said. 'No apartment walls, no girlfriend, no façade to hide behind.'

Her heart was racing and she focused only on placing one foot in front of the other, but the closer she got, the more it was like walking through cement.

Why am I doing this? she wondered, starting to feel sick.

'Just breathe, Laure,' she told herself. 'No pressure, it's just a drink. Imagine you don't live next door, and he's just a friend. You're just meeting a friend.'

With a few more laboured steps, Da Antonio came into view, and from a spot under the veranda, Marco waved.

CHAPTER TWENTY-NINE

I just want to get to know you

Laure's anxiety abated. At least if Marco's girlfriend walked by, she would never spot them on the terrace overflowing with customers.

'*Ciao,* Laure,' Marco said, rising hurriedly to greet her with a kiss on both cheeks. 'You look very nice.'

In his voice, there was the same nervousness as in the earlier voicemail, but his smile was genuine and Laure could see how pleased he was that she'd come.

They stood together, waiting for someone to break the ice.

'So …' said Marco, after shuffling on the spot and nervously patting his jean pockets a few times as if checking for his keys and wallet. 'That gas mask story was crazy!'

Laure laughed and silently thanked the Lord for Rob's mental breakdown.

'I know!' she said, her voice hitting a shrill octave as all the angsty energy inside came tumbling out with her words. Her eyebrows shot sky high as if to say, 'A gas mask, can you believe it?'

Laure might have felt embarrassed by her awkwardness, but apparently Marco had also entered the 'supersize my emotions' competition.

'So, what happened to him?' Marco asked, his own eyebrows rocketing north, squashing the skin on his forehead into a thousand tiny folds. One hand came to rest under his chin and his head tilted sideways, it appeared to be the most interesting story he'd ever heard.

'No idea!' Laure said, her shoulders shrugging up to her ears. 'I guess we'll see on Monday!'

'Crazy, just crazy,' they both muttered, shaking their heads.

Silence fell once again, and across the gulf of uncertainty, their eyes met.

'Let's get a drink,' Marco said, exchanging his stiff manner for a sheepish grin. 'I have to admit I already had a small glass of wine before I left.'

'Oh, good. So did I,' Laure said, her trembling hands steadying in her pockets.

'*Perfetto.* How about a Spritz?'

Lorenzo bustled over to take their order, and from behind the bar, Antonio noted their presence.

The pair sat down, nestled next to the window and hidden among the chic dressers and sunglass wearers who were loudly recounting their summer adventures. Within seconds, two large glasses of fizzing, orange cocktail were placed before them. Marco pulled out a packet of cigarettes and extended it to Laure, who contemplated the shiny white box.

You have got to be kidding me, her brain said, unable to stay quiet. *Just tell him you don't fancy one today, or admit that you don't actually smoke. That's why you're here, n'est-ce pas, isn't it?*

'Oh, my saviour, I'd love one,' Laure cooed after a moment's hesitation. With a sip of Spritz, she began to enjoy herself.

I see, said her brain.

Laure's willingness to ingest tar was rewarded with a pearly beam from Marco. Without visible trepidation, she inhaled and searched for that insatiable addiction that had hooked so many, as smoke billowed out between the gaps in her teeth.

Is this attractive? she wondered, her head filling with fumes.

Marco hadn't noticed, as he was too busy making love to his own cigarette.

'Knowing yourself is the beginning of all wisdom. I think that's Aristotle,' Marco said, leaning back in his seat. 'Tell me Laurrre …'

Laure's thoughts began to wander off along tentacles of smoke snaking through her mind. Marco's eyes seemed to melt like glossy chocolate before her. She liked the way he rolled the 'r' in her name. 'Laurrre.' It made her sound like a Cuban ballerina. Last night's dream swirled in her head and she felt flushed, noticing how the white T-shirt clung to his muscles. She imagined introducing him to friends. 'It was a complicated beginning with Laurrre,' he would say, holding her tightly, 'but it turned into something beautiful.' Then he would kiss her on the cheek.

'Laurrre?' Marco was looking at her, a smile pulling at his lips as she snapped out of the smoky trance.

'You are daydreaming,' he laughed. 'Obviously, my philosophical musings are not very engaging. Noted. I will not put myself down as the next Sartre. Tell me, what did you do last night?' he asked, stubbing out the cigarette, his eyes glittering in anticipation.

Channelling Sophia Loren, Laure took a puff of cigarette.

Come on, Laure. How are you ever going to know if you're compatible with Marco if you keep lying?

You're right, Laure thought.

'Actually, last night, I had an evening in. Sometimes I like to do that too,' she said, her whole body tense.

'On a Friday night?' Marco said, his jaw dropping. 'Laurrre, I don't believe you. You're having me on!' He nudged her arm, leaving a lingering tingle on her skin.

Marco's stunned reaction to the very un-shocking admission that sometimes she liked to stay at home, made Laure laugh. 'No, really,' she said. 'I mean, I know it's not like me to do that, but it's true.' She looked at Marco, willing him to accept her.

But it was a lost cause.

'*Dai,* Laurrre, come on,' he said, desperate to be allowed in on the joke. 'You have a poker face, but I know you are messing with me.'

His dark eyes scanned over her.

112

'Oh. OK, you got me,' she said, relenting. 'I can't fool you.'

From somewhere inside, Laure heard the familiar knell of relationship doom chiming solemn warnings. But Marco was beaming.

'It was just a house party,' Laure said, engaging with the story and drowning out the chimes with more alcohol. 'Some friends, some dancing, that sort of thing.'

Her eyes searched for his adoration.

You are so weak, her brain tutted. *Why don't you just ask for another cigarette?*

'Marco, can I have another?' Laure said, gesturing at the packet.

Her brain put out an alert for other jobs.

'Anyway, I knew it,' Marco said, lighting Laure's cigarette with boyish glee. 'I know you, Laurrre. You are like me.' His expression became serious and Laure could see the Spritz starting to take effect. 'You know,' he said, 'I was listening to some Jean-Maxime La Croix Montagne earlier.'

'Yes, I heard!' Laure said, feeling tipsy herself.

As soon as the words left her mouth, she froze.

Marco looked at her. 'What do you mean, you heard, Laurrre? Are you omniscient too?' he asked with a puzzled smile.

'Ha,' said Laure, trying to keep the panic out of her eyes, her skin suddenly burning in the summer heat. 'What did I say? "I heard"? Sorry, that's my Italian. I meant "I'm sure!" I know Jean-Maxime La Croix Montagne is famous all over the world and very popular in Italy,' she said, coughing at the end of the sentence to hide a wheeze.

Marco leant in closer. 'Do you like him?'

'Ha.' Laure's strained laugh rang out again, although this time it sounded distinctly more like a groan. 'Of course,' she said through gritted teeth. 'He's a national treasure.'

'I like him,' said Marco, staring into Laure's eyes. 'He's romantic. You know, like romance used to be – spontaneous and overpowering.'

'Sure,' Laure said, caught up in his gaze.

With a deep drag, she felt herself giving in to the persona of 'Laurrre', and Laurrre wanted to throw caution to the wind.

'Well, of course, it doesn't surprise me that you like him. He's French,' she said, blowing out a coquettish cloud, and feeling like she was getting the hang of smoking. 'Everyone knows that French culture is the most romantic. The music, the language, a certain *je ne sais quoi*. I mean there is no comparison really.'

'Eh, hang on. I mean, let's not get carried away,' said Marco.

'You said it yourself,' Laure said. 'The great Jean-Maxime La Croix Montagne, a true genius, far better than anything else ... from any other country ...' she trailed off.

'But Laurrre, of course, I didn't say that! Here in Italy, we have many of our own music legends.'

'I'm sure you do. It's just ... none come to mind.' Laure's eyes sparkled. 'And of course, our food is perfectly romantic too, accompanied by a rich glass of French red. Tell me,' she asked, 'is a bowl of spaghetti really as elegant?'

Laure grinned into her drink as Marco struggled with every fibre of his being to take her words lightly.

'Laurrre,' he finally said, his hands telling the story for the hard-of-hearing. 'I'm sorry to tell you, but what you're saying is nonsense! You might have decent dishes, a bit too much butter for my liking,' he added, tartly, 'but, none of you know how to cook! The golden years of *la cuisine française* are long gone! Listen to me, pasta is the sexiest food there is, without exception. Clearly, you don't know what home-made pasta dish can do for a relationship. It can make you fall in love, Laurrre. It's as simple as that.'

Laure scoffed and Marco moved in closer, brushing his leg against hers.

'I mean our ancient and powerful civilisation practically wrote the rules of love,' he whispered.

Laure's heart stopped as Marco leant in so close, she could smell the scent of his shaving cream. Timidly, her eyes flickered over his face, revealing within them the flecks of desire, anticipation and self-doubt. But, as she stayed, on the cusp of cardiac arrest, Laure noticed Marco's expression beginning to change. He had detected the success of his smooth act and couldn't hide the celebratory grin.

Immediately, Laure pulled away and eyed him with suspicion. 'Whatever. Big talk,' she said, swallowing hard.

Marco's smirk grew wider.

'I don't know what to tell you,' he said. *'Voilà,* the Italian charm.'

Laure laughed, but she felt anxious. For the first time with Marco, her guard had come down, and as their eyes met, she felt a delicate spiders web being woven between them.

On the table, a phone began to bleat, and realising it was his, Marco swiped it into his pocket, but not quite quickly enough. Laure had seen it was Valeria, and like a lead balloon she plummeted back to earth.

'Va bene, OK,' she said, feeling Laurrre fade into a ghost. 'Italian culture can per-haps be a competitor. I mean,' she said, gesturing to where the phone had been, 'you and your girlfriend are both Italian. I bet there is a lot of romance, right?'

At the mention of Valeria, beads of sweat appeared on Marco's upper lip. Clearly, he wasn't ready to engage with reality. After fidgeting in his seat and staring down at the shiny table, he reached for another cigarette.

'You know,' he said finally, staring off into the distance, 'me and my girlfriend have been together for so long, romance, in the end, it fades away.' He breathed out a smoke-laced sigh. 'For us anyway, things get so complicated.'

'I'm sorry,' Laure said.

'Do you believe in finding the one?' Marco asked.

Laure shrugged. 'I'm really not the person to ask,' she said truthfully. 'I don't know much about love and relationships.' She paused, and then thought out loud. 'But … shouldn't you know the answer to that question? I've always been told that when you meet the right person, you just know it.'

Marco's stare was so intense, Laure could almost see the washing machine of emo-tions churning inside him.

'Well now, that is very romantic,' he finally said. 'Cheers to that.' In one gulp, he downed the Spritz, and seemed to decide that reality could wait. Being on the run was much more pleasant. 'Let's get another one,' he said, gesturing towards the waiter. *'Monsieur, Monsieur.'*

'Why are you ordering in French?' Laure said, laughing.

'Just to be stupid,' Marco said. 'I like being an idiot with you.'

Laure leant back in her chair and contemplated the perfectly symmetrical man opposite. She could imagine all the places the evening might lead them, but a visceral instinct inside was telling her to leave.

'Actually, I have to go,' she said, pretending to glance at her watch. 'I'm sorry, some friends are coming over tonight and I haven't prepared at all.'

Marco's face dropped. 'Really? Are you sure you can't stay?'

'I'm so sorry, I can't. I can't keep them waiting.'

'The fun just doesn't stop for you, does it?' Marco said, his playful words unable to belie the disappointment.

Laure smiled and reached for her purse, but Marco waved her away.

'Don't worry,' he said, clipping fifteen euros under his glass. 'It would be my pleasure. I can't make overtures about Italian chivalry and then let you pay.' Before getting up, he reached out and took Laure's hand. 'This has been so nice,' he said.

'I've really enjoyed myself,' Laure replied, her cheeks turning pink.

'Should I walk you to your place?'

'Oh no, that's really OK. I can definitely manage,' Laure said quickly, trying to sound as decisive as possible and praying he wouldn't insist.

'OK, *cara. Buona serata,* then.'

Before they parted ways, Marco kissed her cheek, and just for a moment, Laure leant in, resting her body against his chest.

'Ciao,' she said, and disappeared among the crowds.

CHAPTER THIRTY

Excuse me, but I also want to get to know you

Once out of sight, Laure scuttled down a side road and flopped against the wall. She had been having fun with Marco and there was definitely chemistry, so why had she run away?'

Because you were acting. You weren't being yourself, said her brain.

'I think I just felt too conflicted.'

As she looked around the dingy alley, Laure heard a scratching noise in the far shadows and ventured further in. A few metres away, a squirrel was clawing furiously at the ground and Laure saw its foot was trapped in a rusty grate. The creature was lashing around, its beady eyes full of fear.

'Shhh, *mon chou,* it's OK,' said Laure.

Slowly drawing closer so as not to startle the frightened animal, she knelt down to assess the issue. Its tiny leg looked limp, caught at an awkward angle under the rigid iron bars.

'*Je vais t'aider,* I'm going to help you,' she whispered. 'Just try and stay calm.'

In Laure's head, she was pulling on a white doctor's coat, and with great care, she began to shuffle the squirrel's foot along, millimetre by millimetre. To her amazement, the furry creature stopped fighting and became still, the white fur on its belly quivering with nerves.

There was a distortion in the grate where the bars diverged, and Laure eased the little leg until it came free.

'*Voilà,*' she said. '*Bravo, mon petit,* well done, little guy.'

The animal stared up at her with wide eyes, but its foot wasn't in good shape, a sore cut lay across the side.

'Let's clean that up.'

Laure splashed some water over the wound and then, from her bag, retrieved antibacterial spray and a tissue. With steady hands, she fashioned a bandage of sorts until the squirrel looked like it was wearing a snow boot, with tiny claws poking out of the bottom. It seemed to do the job. The small being brushed up against Laure's leg and then scurried up the side of a building.

Laure slipped back out among the masses. While walking, a sense of satisfaction lightened her steps. It was different to what Marco had made her feel. It blossomed entirely from within, straightening her spine and no one could touch it.

It feels good be helpful, she thought.

And, what about Marco? her brain asked. *Will you see him again?*

Laure's mind wandered back to their date, the laughter, the subtle glances and the way her body lingered on his touches. But any excitement was quickly eaten up by a dull sense of guilt. These muddled feelings stole the energy from her legs and Laure came to a complete stop next to Da Antonio. She stared at the spot where, not long ago, they had been sitting together, and then her eyes turned to the twisting vines in front of her.

'I don't really know how I feel,' she said aloud.

'Not the best date?' the vines replied.

With a high-pitched scream, Laure leapt into the air.

'Scusami,' said the vines. 'I-I didn't know when to introduce myself. It got more and more awkward the longer you stood there.'

Laure placed a hand on her chest to calm her racing heart and stared into the vines again. She let out another yelp, as this time, she saw two emerald eyes peering back. The face painting was impeccable – the man was almost invisible.

'Mon Dieu,' she said, taking a step backwards. 'You gave me such a fright. I had no idea you were there.'

'Well, normally I'd be flattered,' said Viviano. 'If I hadn't scared the life out of you. Most people spot me a little earlier. It's the legs that give me away.'

Laure looked down to see a pair of knees protruding from the tangle of leaves. They were intricately painted in earthy brown tones to resemble gnarled tree stumps.

'I'm working on a way to hide them better.'

'Oh, good,' said Laure, still trying to get her breath back.

She was about to bid the tree man good evening and continue on home, when suddenly, he said: 'That guy's got a girlfriend, you know.' As he spoke, his voice wavered. 'I used to see them here all the time. She's nice. I mean, he's nice too. A little on the dull side, but whatever ...' He trailed off.

'I'm sorry,' Laure said, understanding nothing. 'Are you talking to me?'

'I hope so,' the tree replied, with a shy smile.

'But ... what are you talking about? Were you spying on us?'

'Well, this is kind of my spot,' Viviano said, gesturing at the place he was standing. 'And then, I found that I couldn't look away.' The vines fell silent for a moment before adding, 'I'm sorry, I didn't mean to pry. I just wanted to tell you that he has a partner, in case you didn't know, 'cause I didn't really think that was your thing.' Viviano took a deep breath. His heart was pounding.

'My thing?' asked Laure. 'But you don't know anything about me.'

'I know,' Viviano said, spikey twigs scraping his face as he shook his head. 'It doesn't make any sense. I know everything about everyone, without even trying.'

Laure smiled sympathetically, while planning how she was going to leave.

From the leafy nest, Viviano's eyes caught hers. 'But it's different with you. When I see you, my mind goes blank. Oh, actually, HA!,' he suddenly said, as if recalling the *funniest* joke.

This poor man is crazy, Laure thought.

'Sorry,' Viviano said, trying to regain composure, but unable to stop ripples of laughter cascading from his mouth. 'Yes! I do know one thing about you, of course. I know you don't smoke!'

'*Che?* What?' said Laure, feeling her cheeks burn.

The statue was shaking, abandoned to the Gods of mirth. He lifted a leafy hand and wiped away the tears which were smudging his face paint. 'But to be honest,' he spluttered through gulps of air, 'anyone who has seen you smoking knows that!'

With viney fingers, Viviano pretended to hold a cigarette and then contemplated his hand fearfully, like it might explode at any moment. His lips made a big round O and he slotted the invisible cigarette squarely into the centre. He then proceeded to inhale aggressively and blow out in all directions, like a rotating fan. 'Oh, *mi piace,* I love this!' he declared, with an expression on his face that suggested he might be sick.

'Stop it!' cried Laure, turning a deep shade of violet and putting her face in her hands. 'My God, this is so weird.'

'I mean, how he hasn't called you out on that is frankly shocking! And then!' Viviano continued, his amusement insuppressible, 'If he hasn't said anything because he actually believes you smoke!' His eyes widened in astonishment. 'Well, that is even worse. He'd go way down in my estimation, and he already didn't seem like the sharpest knife.'

Laure stared at the leafy man, her face stinging with incredulity. 'Well, I'm very sorry he doesn't match up to the expectations of a nearby vine,' she finally managed to spit out.

The statue grinned at her, his green eyes crinkling at the corners. 'Fair point,' he said.

It might have been wise to stop here, but Viviano found he couldn't close his mouth. 'And then there's the way you act around each other. It's so weird … quite forced,' he reflected. 'Anyway, there's something wrong with it.'

'Alright,' said Laure, sharply shutting down the life commentary before the tree could launch into another impression. 'I don't think I have to tell you how creepy this is, but I'm going to go,' she said, glaring at the hidden face and turning to leave.

'You just don't seem like yourself when you're with him,' Viviano said quietly.

It was the last straw. A lightning bolt shot down Laure's spine and she turned back with thunder in her eyes. 'Listen,' she said. 'I don't know who you are, but you're being completely inappropriate. You don't know anything about me,' she said, pronouncing each word clearly. 'So, please, mind your own business.'

Viviano's head began to spin. The adrenaline that had pushed him, finally, to speak to her was wearing off, just in time for him to realise how offensive he was being. Suddenly, the evening heat was suffocating and his throat closed up. In all the millions of times he had pictured their first conversation, never once had he acted so arrogantly, or found such hatred in her eyes. This wasn't how it was supposed to be.

'I'm so sorry,' he stammered. 'I've done this all wrong.'

Laure stared back, eyebrows raised.

'You're absolutely right, I don't know you.' He wanted to explain, but he didn't know how. It was too difficult. Furious at this feebleness, Viviano bowed his head, but then he saw Laure turning away. 'It's just that for me, you've always represented calm,' he said, 'like the sea.' His eyes dared to meet hers. He was trembling from head to foot. 'I love that I don't know anything about you,' he continued. 'I-I want to get to know you.'

'Well,' Laure said, arms crossed like iron locks. 'Maybe that there with Marco is who I want to be, did you ever consider that? Maybe I'm tired of being me and maybe I don't appreciate the opinions of an obnoxious tree.'

'I'm so sorry,' Viviano said again, stumbling over his words. 'I was being an idiot.' But he could hear how hollow the soupy words sounded. Suddenly, he was a child again, back at the foot of his mother's bed, trying to make things better, and nothing he could say was right.

I'm tired of failing, he thought. *I need to act.*

'Would you come out with me?' he blurted out.

Laure stared at him. 'What? What do you mean?'

'Would you let me take you out? Tonight,' he said with a little more confidence. 'I know the city like the back of my hand. I promise it won't be boring.'

'Me?' Laure asked.

'Please,' Viviano said. He tried to smile, but his gnarly legs were wobbling. 'Ditch Marco life crisis over there.'

At these words, Viviano detected the smallest flicker of amusement on Laure's face, and his racing heart calmed. 'And, I-I promise, I'll only make you smoke as part of a street comedy act, if we're short on cash,' he added, a laughter-tinged exhale escaping his lips.

'You think you're very funny, don't you,' said Laure, but the hint of her smile was still there.

'Unfortunately, I can't take credit for your smoking.'

Laure shook her head.

'So,' said Viviano. 'Will you come? At 9 p.m. tonight? Piazza di Santa Maria?'

Laure was silent. 'Will you be dressed as a tree?' she asked, finally.

'I will not.'

'OK,' Laure said, beginning to back away, 'I'll come. I'm going to go and lie down for a while now and see if this is all real when I wake up.'

With that, Laure turned and walked away, making no stops and looking only at her feet, lest anyone else should decide to approach. At her building, she helter-skeltered up the stairs, listening out for any sign of Marco and his girlfriend. The coast was clear.

'That might be the strangest thing that's ever happened to me,' she said, closing the door behind her and flopping straight into bed.

It was six o'clock. Three hours until the meet-up.

From where she lay, Laure looked up at the ceiling and traced her eyes along the slight cracks in the white paint, wondering why she had agreed to rendez-vous with a man dressed like a tree. Was she experiencing severe dehydration?

Bon bah, I think it's risky, said her brain.

'Maybe you're right,' said Laure. 'He's a complete stranger. But at least when I meet him, I don't have to pretend. God knows he isn't trying to keep up appearances.' *"For me you represent calm"*. The statue's words echoed in her head. 'How could I represent calm to anyone when I feel like such a disaster?'

Through the wall, the faint sound of crying reached her ears. Laure edged closer, but she already knew it was Marco's girlfriend.

She must've come home to an empty flat, she thought.

The sobbing was soft, a million miles from the exaggerated drama Laure had come to expect through the wall. Valeria sounded like she was evaporating into thin air. Laure's insides shrunk up. Meeting Marco for a drink felt very different from this perspective. She crossed her arms over her face, but was unable to block out the noise.

I'm implicated in this woman's misery, she thought, bathed in shame.

Hidden from the world, Laure stayed there until she eventually escaped into the forgiving hideouts of sleep.

CHAPTER THIRTY-ONE

If a tree dates in the jungle, does it make a sound?

Laure awoke an hour later in a sweaty panic – she hadn't meant to fall asleep. The sound of crying had ceased, and as she took a sip of water and rolled the glass across her forehead, Laure heard someone come in next door.

'Valeria?' Marco said. 'Are you over there? Why are you sitting in the dark?'

'It's been so hot all day,' Valeria's mouse-like voice came back. 'I just needed some coolness, some space to think. Where have you been? I tried to call you.'

'I was out.'

'I thought you'd be here when I got back,' she said. 'To be honest, I didn't think you'd let me leave yesterday.'

...

On the other side of the wall, Valeria's voice trailed off and her eyes searched Marco for any gesture of compassion, but she found none.

'We were too hot-headed yesterday,' Marco said. 'I think some space was good for us.'

'You've never wanted space before,' Valeria said, her fingernails leaving dents in her palms as she tried to maintain a fort-like exterior. 'I ... I thought you would want to apologise.'

'Why would I apologise?' Marco asked. 'I don't actually think I did anything wrong. Unless you think running away from old *Signora* Mancuso downstairs is wrong.' He snorted. ''Cause I definitely just did that, and it wasn't very subtle.'

'Have you been drinking?' asked Valeria, her eyes like deep voids.

'I might have had one or two,' said Marco. 'It's Saturday, after all!' He lifted his arms and did a little jig on the spot. 'Oh, I forgot, it's *impossible* to make you laugh nowadays, isn't it?'

Valeria looked as though she'd been hit with a stun gun. Slowly, she studied Marco's face, his dark hair, his elongated, espresso eyes, the permanent dimpled crease on his cheek that burst open when he smiled. But even though it was him, he was a stranger.

'Am I just the butt of your jokes now?' she asked, unable to stop tears sliding down her cheeks. 'To think that I've been waiting here for you all day, even after the way you've been acting, and you come back and treat me like I'm worthless.'

Suddenly, she stood up sharply and lunged at Marco, shoving him over and over again. 'What is the matter with you?' she screamed. 'I have no idea who you are.'

...

On the other side of the wall, Laure pulled her ear away, feeling sick. She didn't want to hear anymore. With light steps, she scuttled to her laptop and put on some music, turning the volume up until it drowned everything out. Then she went and hid in the bathroom.

At the sink, Laure drenched her face with icy water and scrunched it into a towel, breathing in and out until the worst of her anxiety subsided.

'It will be good for you to get away from this,' she told her reflection. 'Just calm down and focus on getting ready, OK.'

From a small pot on the shelf, Laure selected a dark eyeliner, and steadying her nerves, traced it under her eyes until they stood out like glistening black jewels.

'You could have stayed with Marco today, but you left,' she repeated over and over.

Laure never usually bothered with much makeup, but today it served as a kind of shield, in case the anonymous tree really could see right through her.

'I don't know how tonight will go, but I want to be open-minded,' she said, applying a deep rose lipstick and layering some mascara.

The tree might kill you tonight, her brain suggested.

'True. But he probably won't,' Laure replied firmly as she straightened her necklace. The delicate gold chain had come from a jeweller's in Marrakesh. Both she, her brother and sister had been given one on their eighteenth birthdays. Laure knew her grandparents had saved and saved to offer them the precious gifts.

What would lalla say if she saw me in this situation? Laure wondered, running her fingers along the shiny links. *She'd probably stroke my hair and remind me that growing up is a journey.*

...

Isabella's mouth dropped like a dead weight as she poked her head around the door and caught sight of her son. Viviano was wearing a light-grey shirt which was ironed and crisp. His jeans were smart, and the curls around his face had been coiffed and were free of their signature knotty tangles.

He never made an effort, and for the very first time, Isabella felt like she had a grown-up son. With a hurried hand, she swept away the tears that filled her eyes, not wanting to alarm him.

'Where are you going all dressed up, *tesoro?*' she said, trying to hide her amazement.

Startled by her voice, Viviano swung around and his cheeks turned pink.

His mother's eyes widened. 'Have you got a date?' she asked, stepping tentatively into the room. 'An actual date that you are making such an effort for?'

Viviano brushed off the comments. 'I wouldn't call this such an effort,' he laughed, but then he turned back to her with uncertain eyes. 'I mean ... would you?'

Isabella felt like dancing on the rooftops. 'You look so handsome, my boy,' she said, glowing with pride. 'So, who is she?'

Viviano rolled his eyes.

'Come on, *tesoro,'* she pleaded. 'I've never *seen* you like this before!'

'It's a female tree,' Viviano said. 'We fell in love today.'

His mother threw the dishcloth in her hands at him. 'I'm just going to hope that isn't true,' she said, making the sign of the cross before disappearing behind the door.

Viviano detected a skip in her step as she went.

She is going to ring Aunty Rosa, he thought.

As the smart reflection blinked back at him, Viviano fought hard to control the jumble of butterflies swirling in his stomach. She was coming to meet him. He had pinched his arm so many times, it had left a red patch.

Their meeting had got off to the worst start imaginable, but against all odds she had given him a chance. Now he needed to make it up to her. He was scared, though. For a year he had been watching this woman, waiting for her to appear at any and every moment. She had no idea.

It sounds so creepy, thought Viviano. *If she knew, she might feel afraid. She might think I've been stalking her, without any idea that every time she materialises, I'm too nervous to even take a step in her direction.*

How could he communicate the effect she had on him when he couldn't even explain it to himself? Maybe it was better not to mention it at all. Despite all the questions and the biting anxieties, one thing was clear to him. He was going to meet her and he couldn't disappoint.

'Yes, Rosa, I couldn't believe it either ... a shirt!' His mother's hushed tones rushed into Viviano's room. 'Oh no,' she giggled like a school kid, 'I couldn't take a photo ...'

This statement was followed by the sound of heavy tiptoeing and a small portion of his mother's head appeared around the door. But when her eyes fell upon her son again, the phone hit the floor with a clatter.

'Viviano, what are you doing?' she shrieked. 'Oh no, no, no.' She shook her head in despair. 'Why, why, *why* are you putting on makeup?'

Viviano turned from the mirror where he was accentuating his lashes with black mascara.

'It's all about equality these days, Ma,' he said with a little shrug. 'I don't want her to think she made more of an effort than me. That's not fair ... Actually, since you're here, do you have any waxing strips I can use for my brows?' He winked at his mother.

Isabella looked like all her dreams had been shattered. Eyeballing her son, she retrieved her phone from the floor.

'Forget it, Rosa,' she spat into the speaker, turning on her heel and leaving the room. 'This boy is a lost cause.'

Viviano admired his efforts. Some blush might give him a wholesome glow.

…

Laure slipped on a dark-green maxi dress. As she pulled the stretchy material over her head, the electro music pulsing from the speakers drew her attention. Laure could remember the exact moment she had first heard the song at a festival just outside Paris a little over a year ago. In the dazzling sunlight, she and her friends had danced with total abandon together, like other-worldly creatures, unaware of life around them.

That was the night she had decided to leave France. Something about the intense high of the day brought out a shadowy low looming within her. As the sun set, surrounded by her friends and after one too many beers, Laure had begun to cry.

It was her second week of sick leave from work.

Immediately, everyone had piled in around her, and squashed between their hugs, Laure realised she felt completely lost. The career that she had fought so hard for was leaving her in tatters, and what about a love life? While everyone else seemed to be settling down, Laure had forgotten what being in love even felt like.

'*Je me sens vide*, I feel empty,' she whispered, her face smushed into the soft cotton of her friend's cardigan.

Two weeks later, her bags were packed for Italy. 'I'll find my way when I'm there,' she had told herself. 'I just can't be here anymore.'

Now, as her dress fell down over her body, stopping an inch from the floor, Laure shut her eyes and let the music wash over her. The green material reminded Laure of the dense foliage that covered Rome's walls and which had cloaked the statue in nature that afternoon. To Laure he seemed free, unaffected by society's norms and expectations.

Swaying to the melodic beat, Laure found a brown eyeliner and began to trace a root-like line from the tip of her middle finger downwards. The edges of her mouth curled into a smile at the effect. She drew another, this time starting on her index. When it reached her wrist, she thickened it, adding curves so that it coiled like the gnarled detail of a branch. With every stroke, she edged the pencil further. The next one skirted around the spiral pattern and snaked its way up to her elbow where it finished in an intricate knot of lines. Still Laure continued, finding a soothing rhythm in the movements.

I'd like to let go too, she thought.

By the time she put the eyeliner down, Laure's hands and arms were covered in twisting vines, and brown swirls spun around her ankles and disappeared under her dress.

Glancing in the mirror, she felt a mix of pride and embarrassment.

'It's definitely a look,' she said, gliding over to the kitchen to pour some wine.

8.45. It was time to go.

...

Across the wall, things were not so meditative.

'Don't you love me anymore?' Valeria asked, finally voicing the fear that was shredding her insides.

The tormentuous confusion in Marco's head was painted on his face. 'Of course, of course I still love you, but ...'

'But what? What is it, Marco?' Valeria asked, her own face as white as chalk. 'Do ... do you want this to be over?'

A floundering wail fell from Marco's mouth. 'Argh!' he yelled, 'I can't think straight with this shit music next door thumping away in my ears!' Like a prisoner begging for relief, he pounded his fist against the wall.

Laure heard the banging, and as if answering Marco's prayers, shut her laptop, leaving the room in silence.

As she left, the tortured love story echoed down the stairwell, but Laure had already escaped out onto the streets below.

CHAPTER THIRTY-TWO

I'd like you to meet my friends

Piazza di Santa Maria in Trastevere had come to life under the orangey glow of the setting sun. A patchwork of people were sitting around the central fountain, sipping beers and sharing out pizza slices from big takeaway boxes.

Laure looked around nervously for any sign of him, her hands scrunching and unscrunching by her sides.

In one corner of the square, the faithful were still filing into the Basilica di Santa Maria, one of the oldest churches in the city. It wasn't an imposing building, but it had a faded splendour. Colourful hand-painted palm trees adorned the golden façade which shimmered in the light, and the ornate brick clock tower always made Laure feel as though she had been transported to a tiny Italian village.

As her eyes searched, it dawned on her that she didn't know who she was actually looking for.

All around, street sellers were working hard, touting their merchandise. They sent fluorescent spinners soaring high into the sky like cheaply-manufactured shooting stars, delighting the children below who were still tearing around, way past their bedtimes. As the spinners floated back to earth, the kids sprinted towards them, arms outstretched, hoping to catch one before it slipped back into the hands of its master. But they were never successful, and weary parents had to fork out the cash for a shooting star of their own.

Laure looked past them and her heart sank. Waiting nearby was a man in a full Santa Claus outfit.

'*C'est lui,* it's this guy,' she whispered, taking a few steps forward as Father Christmas stroked his beard. '*Merde.*'

'That's not me!' a voice announced behind her.

Laure spun around to find a man contemplating her with incredulity.

It was him, and Laure's eyes widened in disbelief. The tree was handsome, and he wasn't dressed like a tree at all but like a human person on a date.

'Oh, thank God!' she blurted out, staring at his dark, unruly curls and bright-green eyes.

The statue's smile grew. 'Come on,' he said. 'I wouldn't come to meet you dressed as Santa Claus. That's Rick. *Ciao,* Rick,' he shouted, waving over to the rotund man.

'Ho, ho, ho,' Rick bellowed back, jiggling his stuffed belly.

'Don't be fooled by the outfit,' the statue whispered to Laure. 'Rick may look normal, but he's an odd man.'

'Normal, right,' Laure repeated, still light-headed with relief that she wouldn't be riding around Rome on a sleigh.

'You've come as a tree!' Viviano said, staring at the branches on Laure's arms.

'Oh' said Laure, suddenly self-conscious. 'Um, *oui*, well, it wasn't really planned but … I got carried away.'

She looked at him. 'You're wearing makeup.'

'Just some mascara and a little blush,' he said. 'I didn't want you to think I wasn't making an effort and … I thought it might look cool.'

'I like it,' said Laure.

They smiled at each other, embarrassed.

'You look beautiful,' Viviano said.

Laure felt her cheeks burn. 'So do you,' she replied.

'What's your name?' Viviano asked, and the words caught in his throat as he prepared to discover the very first thing about this mystery woman.

'Laure.'

Viviano smiled and then fell silent.

'Um … and, what is your name?' Laure prompted after a few seconds had passed.

'Oh,' he said. 'Yes, sorry. I'm Viv … Viviano really, but everyone calls me Viv.'

'*Piacere*, Viv, nice to meet you,' Laure said, noticing the light freckles that clustered around his eyes under the tips of his black eyelashes.

'I still can't believe that if I hadn't intervened, you were about to go on a date with Rick,' Viviano said as they began to wander through the square.

'That's not true!' Laure said.

'You're right, absolutely not,' said Viviano. 'Who even suggested that?'

Laure rolled her eyes and Viviano laughed. 'Are you hungry?' he asked.

'Starving!'

'I know a good place. It's nearby.'

They zigzagged through the evening wanderers and were about to leave the piazza when a swirl of starlings scattered through the air, decorating the sky with patterns.

Laure and Viviano gazed up at the show, but Viviano's eyes kept wandering back to the woman by his side.

'I've always loved them too,' he said. 'Ever since I was little.'

'I don't know what it is about them,' said Laure, 'but I can never tear my eyes away.'

'I remember being about six,' Viviano said, looking back at the sky, 'and my dad carrying me up the Gianicolo Hill on his shoulders to see them flying over the city. There was a bright pink sunset and I thought the birds must be magic. We watched for hours. Well, it felt like that, and at some point, I was sure …'

'That they were going to crash into each other,' said Laure.

'Yes!' said Viviano. 'I had my fingers over my eyes and I was peeping out, just waiting for it to happen. You know, to this day, every time I see them, I can't help but feel a little anxious. It must be left over from that moment ...' Viviano felt suddenly dizzy and his words evaporated into silence. 'That's weird,' he said when he finally spoke again, 'I'd completely forgotten about that.'

'You know, I always wonder about that too,' said Laure, her eyes still fixed on the starlings. 'Sometimes I imagine how it would look. And then I think about all the journalists rushing out to cover the story,' she laughed.

As the birds' opening act drew to an end, the pair left the square via a tiny alley that Laure had never noticed before. Viviano led the way, criss-crossing the labyrinth of streets as if it they were tattooed on his eyelids. All of a sudden, he came to a halt outside a large open hatch from which a fountain of white smoke was billowing. The smell of meat and fragrant spices filled the air, and inside, Laure could hear voices chatting away in a language she couldn't recognise.

Viviano poked his head through the dense vapour clouds and suddenly disappeared from the waist upwards as strong arms from the other side pulled him into a tight embrace, leaving his legs dangling off the ground.

'Viv?' Laure said, addressing his floating feet while glancing around for clues about this place. Just around the corner, she found the real entrance and a sandwich board with the words 'Sunshine Café' written in fluorescent-yellow bubble letters.

The door swung open and a tall man with a warm smile stepped out. He shook Laure's hand and introduced himself as 'Jojo' just as Viviano rejoined them.

'Please, come in, my friends,' Jojo said, gesturing towards the café.

Inside, was a smallish white room, decorated with long, patterned tapestries that hung from the walls. The place was packed with people crammed around wooden tables and tucking into a rainbow of dishes.

'So, *amici*, what can I get you today?' said Jojo at the food counter. In the kitchen just behind, a stocky man and a slender woman were at work, one deep-frying plantain, the other chopping meat.

Laure studied the various silver trays filled with stews and curries – they looked like a paint palette.

'Viv,' said the stocky chef, glancing up from his work, 'the groundnut curry is particularly exquisite today.'

'Everything is delicious, as always,' Jojo said with a wink, 'but Maya has been perfecting her recipe and it tastes ...' He went weak at the knees and pretended to faint.

In the corner, Maya blushed fiercely while continuing to chop.

After exploring the different options, they decided on the groundnut curry and a spinach curry, jollof rice, extra plantain and a few beers. Jojo wrapped it for them.

'Come back and see us again soon,' he said, patting Viv on the back as he accompanied them to the door. 'And of course, that means you, too, my dear. It's nice to see Viv with a radiant lady on his arm.'

Now it was Laure's turn to blush.

'How do you know about that place?' she asked as they wandered back through the maze. 'I'd never have been able to find it.'

'Believe it or not, you find a lot of hidden gems when you spend your life roaming the city.'

Laure smiled at the unassuming response, trying to figure out what this man with an ethereal vibe was all about.

After a few more corners, they were back in the piazza, but in their absence, it had transformed. Dozens of street artists had swept in, turning the square into their personal theatre. In the greyish-blue light of dusk, Laure could see flame throwers, acrobats, impersonators and musicians prancing under the glow of street lamps which shone like fiery mini suns.

Naturally, all the artists were acquaintances of the tree man by her side.

Together, Laure and Viviano strolled by a swing band dressed in crisp suits, shiny shoes and with hair so immaculately slicked back, neat comb lines ran along their scalps. In perfect harmony, they twirled their instruments, swung their hips and crooned to the people that had gathered, living out their boyhood dreams of stardom.

'These guys have been here for years,' Viviano said, as the frontman slapped his double bass and let out a loud whoop. 'They came from Bulgaria. If you speak to them, they'll tell you it's getting harder and harder to make a living. Every year there are more restrictions and more performers to compete with.'

'So, will they have to stop?' asked Laure, watching the trumpeter weave through the crowds during a jazzy solo.

'Nah,' said Viviano. 'They say they'll do it right till the end, because they just love it. Oh! And do you see the astronaut over there?'

Viviano pointed to a statue in a golden spacesuit, standing impeccably still. A little girl approached, her eyes sparkling at the figure who seemed to have floated straight out of her bedtime stories. With a shy wave, she dropped a few coins into his briefcase and watched the spaceman come to life, his arms and legs billowing out around him as if on an exploratory spacewalk.

'That's Melly,' Viviano said. 'He's amazing. He used to perform in Venice, but then they banned artists from the streets so he ended up here.'

'I wouldn't even know he's human,' said Laure as the statue froze once again.

'I know,' said Viviano. 'But you might not see him for much longer. He's learning to paint landscapes with stencils and aerosols. That's all the rage at the moment and there's far more money in it. His wife and toddler are back in Pakistan. Whatever he makes, he sends back home.'

'Wow,' said Laure. 'It must be so hard to be away from them.'

Laure spun her head around to take a last look at the astronaut, and was surprised to see him feigning a loss of oxygen situation to a bemused couple.

'Sometimes he goes off script,' Viviano said with a grin.

Walking on, the pair found themselves at the edge of a packed crowd and Laure stood on tiptoes to peer over.

'Oh, I know who this is!' she said, spotting the tip of a party hat. 'Enrico the clown. I heard he's been performing here since long before we were born.'

At that moment, Enrico shot into view, balancing on a unicycle as tall as a house. He wore startling white face paint and a flashing red nose, and every time he wobbled, the crowd gasped. High in the sky, he waved his arms like an octopus as he tried to get steady, then out of thin air, he produced a gigantic bouquet of roses. Howling with delight, Enrico flung them up and watched as they scattered all around. As the crowd scrambled to retrieve a delicate flower, they vanished on the floor before their eyes.

Laure laughed. 'I still don't know how he does that.'

'No one does,' said Viviano. 'Enrico never reveals his secrets.'

By now, they had come almost full circle in the piazza.

'Some of the performers don't show their faces,' Viviano said. 'They arrive and leave in their costumes. I'm not sure if they're scared of getting caught, or just adding to the mystery. Running from the law maybe. I often think of stories ...' He trailed off. 'There are a few I've seen for years, but I have no idea what they look like.'

Laure looked around the square she had walked through a thousand times and felt as though she was seeing it all with different eyes. Then, without warning, Viviano pulled her sideways as a luminous spinner spiralled down from the sky right above their heads.

'Sneaky, Reggie,' he yelled towards a sniggering street seller who darted in to retrieve his toy at the very last second.

'You know everyone here!' said Laure.

'I love meeting the people here,' said Viviano. 'Everyone walks past these guys every day, but no one remembers them. And if you take the time to talk, they all have the most fascinating stories about what led them to this way of life.'

Laure nodded 'And, how about you? Why do you do it?'

Viviano considered the question, then shrugged. 'I don't know,' he said.

At the fountain, they claimed a spot on the stone steps and nestled among the various groups. Viviano began to lay out the food.

'Wow, look at all this!' Laure said, filling a cardboard bowl with rice, curry and plantain. With the first bite, she shut her eyes. 'Oh *mon Dieu*, it's delicious!'

'Isn't it?' Viviano said, beaming as he devoured a piece of chicken covered in a rich, peanutty sauce. 'I know that a time will come when I'll go there and find a queue halfway down the road, but here in Italy, we are so obsessed with our own cuisine that I can probably count on it being my little secret for longer than it should be.'

With a pop, Viviano opened a beer and handed it to Laure. 'Why did you do the branches?' he asked.

'I'm not really sure,' Laure said, savouring a mouthful of curry. 'My dress made me think of your costume, and then I just started drawing. At first, I think I just wanted to try it out, but then I found it calming, so I carried on.'

'Can I tell you something?' Viviano asked in a tone that suggested he was not entirely sure he actually wanted to.

Laure nodded, and felt a light fluster of nerves in her stomach.

'I was worried that, when I saw you tonight, I wouldn't be able to say anything at all,' he said, staring at the floor. 'I kept imagining myself completely silent, and you trying to make awkward conversation, until, in the end, you just left.' His heart thudded. 'You have this very strange effect on me.'

Laure listened, unsure how to respond. 'I don't really understand,' she said. 'Why wouldn't you be able to speak to me?'

'I can't explain it. Which, believe me, drives me mad. It's as if I've always had this sandstorm in my head, a kind of agent of chaos. Sometimes I call it that because it's just the enemy of calm. It stirs up and takes me to some strange places.'

Laure frowned, and for the first time noticed a quiet anxiety behind Viviano's eyes and a clench in his jaw that he was good at dissimulating.

'But when I see you, it pacifies,' Viviano said, looking at her. 'I get this feeling of tranquillity that I have never experienced.' Suddenly aware of his ashen cheeks, Viviano paused and took a breath. 'Usually it makes me completely freeze up. I didn't think I'd ever be able to speak to you.'

'Really?' said Laure, baffled by what she was hearing. She pictured herself, barely awake, hobbling towards Da Antonio in the mornings. It was hard to imagine she could be having a positive effect on anyone.

'It's true,' Viviano nodded. 'Then, today, all of a sudden, you were right there, looking at me, and I think something inside just said: "It's now or never". I knew I wouldn't have another chance.'

At this admission, Laure burst out laughing. 'O Dio! And, at the time, I was wishing you hadn't said anything at all!' she said. 'That silent thing you mentioned would have been ideal.'

'I'm so sorry about that.' Viviano groaned, embarrassment flooding his face which he hid in his hands. 'That was awful. I think I had been wanting to talk to you for so long and then, suddenly, I couldn't stop.'

'It's OK,' said Laure. 'Especially now I'm aware of this *amazing* power I have over you. Apparently, I can shut you up whenever I want.'

Shifting the food cartons, Laure shuffled around until only the spiral of a curl separated their faces.

'Is it working now?' she asked, looking deep into his eyes.

The probing gaze caught him off guard, and for a second, Viviano froze. From this close, he could smell the rose perfume on her skin and noticed the soft wave of her upper lip.

As she stared, fully committed to her joke, Laure saw Viviano's eyes begin to glaze over and lose their focus, and the muscles in his face slackened. This caused Laure's own expression to change from feigned seriousness to genuine concern. She stared as Viviano's green irises steadily shifted until they were looking in entirely opposite directions. There he stayed, motionless. It was only when his tongue began to loll haplessly from his mouth like a gaping animal, that Laure realised he was having her on.

'What on earth are you doing?' she said with a splutter of laughter as Viviano finally pulled out of his trance.

'Mamma mia! How long did it take you to realise I was joking?' said Viviano. 'Either I'm coming across so weird, or I am an excellent actor. Hopefully the latter.' A mischievous smile rippled across his face.

'Hmm … no comment.'

Viviano let out a laugh like a bark and took a sip of beer. 'Are you from France?' he asked.

'*Oui.*'

'How did you end up here?'

From their spot by the cascading fountain, Laure looked out at the blur of faces, the lives and conversations around them, and thought about what to say. 'I was having a hard time in France, for a couple of reasons. I wanted a change. Needed a change, actually.'

'I'm sorry,' said Viviano.

'Italy seemed like a good place to come.'

'Why Italy?' asked Viviano. 'Easier to hide from the law?'

'No,' Laure laughed. 'My friend told me about a job here. But actually, I've always loved Italy. I think it's because my dad is mad about Italian films, the comedies especially – Massimo Troisi, Roberto Benigni. When we were little, we would watch them together, me, my parents and my brother and sister. I must have seen some of them a thousand times. I know the words by heart. So, I guess for me, Italy was always laughter and security, even though I obviously moved away from my family to come here.'

'That's really sweet,' said Viviano. 'And what do you think of it, now you're here?'

Laure nodded. 'I'm settling in,' she said. 'I don't know if it's forever, but I do like it.'

CHAPTER THIRTY-THREE
Alla festa si va

Their conversation was interrupted when a small blonde woman, in a black bandit disguise, began marking off a patch of the square just in front, warning everyone to stay back. On tiptoes, she floated around the invisible perimeter, a container in her hands from which a stream of clear liquid spilled out onto the cobblestones. By now, a curious crowd was staring to form.

Standing centre stage, the bandit unfurled a heavy rope and draped it, like a python, over her shoulders. One at a time, she plunged each knotted rope end into a bucket of the same unidentified liquid, which sloshed over the sides and across the floor with each dip. From between her lips, the bandit produced a matchstick which she struck against the rope, sending a satisfying crackle through the air. Bright-blue and yellow flames erupted, casting a fiery glow across the faces in the crowd. Inch by inch, the fire licked up the cord towards the young woman in black. She stared out, as if completely alone in the world, and raised the burning serpent above her head.

It was time to perform.

Slowly, the bandit began to rotate the rope, as if acquainting herself with the flames, making friends. They danced together as she weaved her arms around, creating fierce orange shapes in the air which seared an imprint of their existence on the eyes of those watching, just for a moment, before disappearing forever. From somewhere in the darkness, violins began to play, accompanying the artist. Every so often, her rope grazed the glistening ground, igniting fires all around.

A battle for survival ensued where the bandit was always one step ahead. She leapt, cartwheeled and even somersaulted until she was nothing but a blur, lost in the blaze. Watching the show, Laure was leaning so far forward, another millimetre and the heat would have singed her eyebrows.

Suddenly, the bandit was gone. One wrong move, perhaps a misplaced foot or mistaken calculation and the flames had triumphed, abducting her into their fortress. The crowd gasped and exchanged alarmed looks. Some called out for the bandit, others tried to approach, searching for a sign of life.

Then, as if a giant had blown out the candles on a cake, the flames were reduced to embers, and she was there, appearing impossibly tall.

The applause was ferocious.

She threw her arms up, the music stopped and a pitch darkness fell across the piazza. The bandit looked out – *she* could see everyone. As if responding to a vendetta in her heart, she expelled a dragon's roar from her mouth. It was laced with fire which sent an eruption of yellow and orange into the night sky.

The audience was on their feet, shrieking and applauding as the bandit took a bow and collapsed onto the ground. She seemed to have given everything to the performance. Fans surged towards her, showering congratulatory words and brandishing coins for her case.

'Wow,' whispered Laure, watching the bandit coil into a restorative cocoon. 'Who is she?'

'She used to be in a circus,' said Viviano. 'A famous one, apparently. But that's all I know about her. She never speaks to anyone – just turns up, combusts and then leaves.'

'I'm not sure I'll ever forget that performance,' said Laure. 'There was something completely gut-wrenching about it.'

Viviano nodded. 'I've thought about it before,' he said, handing Laure a beer. 'I think she could actually die doing it. I don't think there's any tricks.'

'Really?'

'Yeah ... I'm just not sure she minds,' he said.

Laure swallowed hard before looking away from the bandit who was breathing softly on the cobblestones, her face still hidden away.

Everywhere else, the square was pulsating with energy. In one corner, a Michael Jackson impersonator was moonwalking, flicking off his sunglasses and screeching 'hee hee' to Billy Jean. Nearby, a woman who looked like she might be his mother was clapping. Elsewhere, a comedian was sidling up behind passers-by and imitating their movements with outlandish impressions. He teased the couple on a first date, mimicked the intrepid tourist and tried to distract a selfie-snapper.

Amid the medley of activity and performances, Laure realised she felt relaxed for the first time since she could remember.

A stout man, with slicked-back grey hair, approached and tapped Viviano on the shoulder. Laure recognised him as the swing band's trumpeter. Leaning down, he whispered something, the pointed tip of his moustache tickling Viviano's ear. Viviano listened with a very serious expression that Laure thought was almost certainly exaggerated to increase intrigue. The hushed discourse wrapped up almost as soon as it had started, and the man left.

Viviano pulled Laure to her feet.

'We have to follow the band,' he said.

'What?' Laure asked. 'Where?'

'Not sure,' said Viviano. 'But don't worry, I've done this before.'

'Very reassuring.'

'*Sbrigati!* Quick! We don't want to lose them.'

He took Laure's arm and began charging across the square.

'Viv, they're carrying huge instruments!' said Laure, trying to keep up. 'I don't think they're going anywhere fast!'

But as her eyes scanned around for the five-piece ensemble, she noticed they had all but disappeared. Only the scroll of a double bass could be seen before it whipped around a corner. Viviano and Laure ran in pursuit, rounding the bend just in time to see a metal door swinging shut. With a lunge, Viviano hooked his fingertips around the edge and kept it open, just.

Laure watched, understanding nothing at all.

Inside, a concrete stairwell greeted them, and above, there was a clattering of footsteps. Exchanging glances, they began to climb.

Every floor was identical to the last – a dusty, disaffected landing with one solitary door. Most were closed, guarding secrets, but a few had been left ajar. Laure peeped inside to find a stripped-out building site. Moonlight was streaming through square holes in the far wall, destined one day to be windows, and stray scaffolding poles and materials were strewn across the floor.

They continued upwards, Laure now taking full advantage of the handrail, her legs burning with every step. Every so often her eyes flickered over to Viviano. He pretended not to notice, not wanting to spoil the surprise. After what felt like hours, they reached the summit of the concrete mountain and Laure pushed open a heavy fire door, unable to bear the anticipation any longer.

A warm gust of wind swirled through the air, blowing her hair into her eyes and obscuring the view. Hurriedly, Laure brushed it away and then let out a gasp. Thousands of fairy lights were draped over the rooftop which had been transformed into a moonlit bar. Some spiralled up into the air, creating huge spiderwebs of tiny lights which hung over their heads like a forest canopy.

A waiter with pink, spikey hair offered them a champagne flute filled with a deep-purple liquid. Laure took a sip. It tasted of Morello cherries and vodka.

In the centre, the swing band were already serenading guests. Acrobats, painted statues, street sellers and performers were twirling and jiving to the jazzy notes in a vacuum of rhythmic chaos. Somewhere in the crowd, a young man with flowing blond locks, was blowing gigantic soap bubbles which sailed over their heads and off into the night. Viviano glanced nervously at Laure, wondering if this adventure might be a step too far, perhaps, but her eyes were glittering.

'I want to get into this,' she said, sinking the last of her cocktail and bounding into the crowd.

'Oh ... OK then ... cool,' Viviano stuttered, a smile plastered on his face as he followed suit. Together, they let the music inspire experimental dance moves, met everyone around them and explored the space. As Laure made wide hula-hoops with her hips, a woman dressed as a princess swooped in and lifted her onto her shoulders. Around and around she began to spin until the skyline of Rome was a rotating blur. When Laure was finally returned to earth, she collapsed on the floor, the twinkling fairy lights spinning furiously above her. With vacant eyes, she grinned up at Viviano who held out his hand and guided her to a bench.

'I love this,' said Laure as she sat down, placing a hand on Viviano's knee to steady herself. 'I feel like I've gone to a different universe.'

'I'm so glad,' Viviano said, trying to stop his leg from trembling. 'I didn't know if you liked dancing,'

'I really do, but I hardly ever do it.'

For a while, the pair sat, people-watching, statue-watching, watching the un-known. At one point, their attention was drawn by a mechanical dance-off between rival robot statues.

'My moves are natural, you're all AI,' one robot quipped to his frenemy.

'Sounds like jealousy from your cold metal lips,' the other said, blowing a robotic kiss.

When Laure and Viviano turned back from the scene, they found two serious-looking men standing before them. Without so much as a word, they took a palette from a briefcase and the next thing she knew, Laure saw a paintbrush being twirled towards her cheek.

'This doesn't normally happen,' Viviano muttered, keeping his expression still as velvety brushes caressed his face.

Once satisfied with their work, the men did a little bow and took their leave.

Laure and Viviano examined each other.

'What am I?' Laure asked.

'You're a lion,' said Viviano. 'How about me?'

'I think you're a mermaid.'

'Is it nice?'

'It is. You look like a *beautiful* woman,' said Laure, putting on a voice like a sur-geon revealing someone's new face.

'Ah, a dream come true,' said Viviano, and Laure giggled.

'What on earth is this place?' she asked, staring around.

'It only happens sometimes. They organise it in secret and then word spreads on the night. It's always somewhere different.'

'Who's they?' Laure asked.

'No idea, actually,' said Viviano. 'Gustav always tells me it's happening.' He gestured over to the moustached musician who was now perched on the fire escape, blowing his trumpet towards the sky as if in deep discussion with the moon.

Laure and Viviano rose and wandered over to the building's edge, collecting more drinks on the way – bright orange this time and tasting of tart clementines which made Laure's tongue quiver.

'What type of music do you like?' Viviano asked, looking out at the skyline as a light breeze rolled in from the distant coast.

'Everything, really,' said Laure, feeling definitely a little drunk. 'Depends on my mood. When I'm at home I like something chilled, but if I'm out, then something more intense that I can lose myself in. But, in general, I like everything.' Rome's buildings shimmered in her tipsy gaze. Then, without warning, she leant over the ledge and bellowed, 'Just not Jean-Maxime La Croix Montagne! For the love of God!'

'Woo, Jean-Maxime, yeah!' a passer-by shouted from the streets below, gazing up to try and spot a fellow superfan. Seeing no one, he sent a thumbs-up towards his other-worldly concert buddy, and yelled, 'Jean-Maxime La Croix Montagne! The best, the best!'

'Oh, for fuck's sake,' Laure said.

'Not a Jean-Maxime fan, I take it?' said Viviano, amused.

'Oh, um, it's a private joke,' said Laure, hurriedly trying to brush over her outburst.

'It's really funny. You should write it down.'

Laure gave his shoulder a little shove.

'Laure,' Viviano said, speaking with sudden clarity. 'There is somewhere else I wanted to take you tonight. I think you'll like it. The only thing is, we have to be there by midnight on the dot. What do you think?'

Laure looked at her watch. 'One more dance?'

'*Eh certo,* of course.'

The crowd welcomed them back for a slow rotating can-can where all the beautiful creatures linked arms and kicked their legs high into the air. As the song came to an end, Viviano kissed Laure on the cheek.

'Come on, lion,' he said.

CHAPTER THIRTY-FOUR

Do I really need to elaborate on my mental health?

The concrete descent beckoned, and Viviano urged caution as they began stumbling down. After a few flights, however, it became clear that Laure was racing, trying to slip ahead at every opportunity. With fancy footwork, Viviano sped up and over-took, and a ruthless sprint to the bottom ensued. Ten flights later, they burst onto the streets neck and neck. Midnight was approaching, and after claiming a false and elaborate victory which involved high-fiving strangers and a short, condescending speech to an eye-rolling Laure, Viviano hurried her across the piazza.

'Where are we going?' Laure asked as they sped past diners polishing off panna-cotta and tiramisu, and waiters cracking jokes on cigarette breaks. On every corner, music was spilling out of bars, but Viviano was leading them away from the city centre.

By the time the bridge came into view, Laure was panting. 'Viv, lets slow down for a bit,' she said pleadingly, trying to catch her breath.

Viviano slowed his pace.

'You move at about a million miles a minute!' Laure exclaimed.

'The faster you move, the more exciting everything is!' said Viviano, convinced in his conviction.

Laure laughed. 'But this night is already exciting! It's the most fun I've had for ages. But is it necessary to sweat all the way through it? Let's walk a bit.' She looked at her watch. 'It's 11.45. Will we make it to this place on time if we slow down just a little?'

'*Sì,*' nodded Viviano with a sheepish smile.

Away from the Trastevere buzz, everything was quiet. Leafy trees darkened their path along the riverside and only the sound of rushing water could be heard.

'Sorry,' said Viviano as they began to cross the bridge. 'Sometimes I get caught up in a rhythm of my own.'

Laure brushed his shoulder. 'That's OK, I find it funny. I've got no idea what you're ever going to do or say.'

'Likewise,' said Viviano, 'but it's nice getting to know you.'

'Really?' said Laure.

'You don't think it's nice getting to know you?' he responded with a smile and hint of irony in his voice.

Laure shrugged. 'I don't know, to be honest. For a while now, I feel like I've completely lost track of what I'm like.'

'Why do you say that?'

Laure paused and tried to articulate her thoughts. 'In reality, I think I only ever knew who I thought I should be, and that's just worn off over time.'

'Right,' said Viviano, 'and who was that person?'

'I wanted to be accomplished and passionate,' said Laure. 'A strong woman who seizes opportunities, the one my parents always said I'm capable of being.' Suddenly lost, she looked around, trying to find the words. 'But it's more than that,' she whispered. 'I've got no spine.'

'No spine,' said Viviano. 'I assume you mean figuratively.'

'I just let everything happen,' Laure continued. 'I've got no strength of character and I always tread lightly on this earth. I never make an impact. I'm too scared.'

'Scared of what?'

'I don't know,' said Laure. 'Scared of life.' She looked out at the cascades of dark water gushing below. 'You know, I think that's what happened with Marco,' she said, following her thoughts. 'For a little while, I just wanted to be someone else, someone confident, to break up this feeling of melting into nothingness.'

Viviano nodded, reached out his hand and lightly brushed Laure's fingertips.

'It sounds to me like you're being pretty hard on yourself,' he said. 'When things weren't working out in France, you moved to a new country, all by yourself. That's brave,' he said. 'Maybe you don't have strong convictions because life is nuanced and you see different points of view. And maybe you'll fight for something when you actually think it's worth it.'

Laure's eyes stared shyly up at him.

'You don't need to be a certain way, but you do need to value the qualities that you have ... otherwise you'll fight yourself constantly.'

'Sometimes the self-doubt is hard to cope with,' said Laure.

'I know,' said Viviano. 'Believe me, I think life is terrifying. I guess you have to try and carve out a bit of happiness within it, just for you, not anyone else, whatever that might look like. What do *you* want Laure?'

'I don't know,' Laure said, shaking her head.

'That's OK,' said Viviano. 'Start trusting yourself, and you'll work it out.'

Laure nodded and gratefully squeezed his hand.

'And, you know,' he said with a smile, 'if, after some soul searching, you decide what you truly do want is Marco from the café, even though he's as dull as ditchwater, so be it.'

Laure's expression twisted from quiet reflection into an incredulous snort, and she gave Viviano a scathing look.

'Ha!' she said. 'And here was me thinking you were my spiritual counsellor, above pettiness of any kind.'

'I'm sorry,' said Viviano. 'It may be useful to bear in mind that I spend most of my time dressed as a tree when assessing my advice.'

'*Oui,*' said Laure. 'That's true. Why didn't you lead with that? I feel better about myself now.'

'Hey!' said Viviano. 'Bad patient.'

'I'm joking! But how did the tree thing come about?'

'I don't know, really,' said Viviano, suddenly pretending he was being interviewed for a job. 'I've always loved nature, so I looked for a role in the field.' He lowered a pair of fictitious glasses.

Laure laughed. 'Stop it,' she said. 'I actually want to know!'

'Sorry,' said Viviano, looking rather uncomfortable at the prospect of peeling away this jokey demeanour. 'I'll try and answer properly. Parts of it are great. I love that I can be creative ... and you meet the most interesting people. But sometimes being a street artist is monotonous and, financially, it's not viable.'

'So how do you get by?' asked Laure.

'I still live with my mum,' Viviano mumbled, just loud enough for Laure to hear. 'Which, believe me, is not that uncommon for an Italian my age. But I would like to move out and be more independent.'

'So, do you have a plan?' asked Laure. 'Or is this what your patch of happiness looks like?'

'Um, not really,' said Viviano, beginning to fidget. 'It's just that every time I try to have a plan, things just get a bit serious ...' He tailed off.

Laure looked at him. 'A bit serious,' she repeated.

'I know, it might sound strange,' said Viviano, 'but I try to avoid stress and responsibility. I don't really want life to be serious.'

'Right,' said Laure. 'But is that a choice you get to make? Life might seem easier when you ignore uncomfortable feelings, but is it as fulfilling?'

'I can't really tell you,' said Viviano. 'As you get older, you get to know yourself, and I've realised it's just part of me.'

'I don't really understand,' said Laure. 'What is a part of you?'

For a while, Viviano was silent as he looked at Laure, out across the water and then down at the floor.

'You know, when I was a kid my dad left us,' he finally said, stumbling over the words and then clearing his throat. 'One day, he walked out and we never saw him again ... Those years of my life were so serious,' he murmured.

Laure watched as the man before her seemed to crumple. She wanted to intervene, but her instinct let him go on.

'My mum had a breakdown,' Viviano said. 'Lost her mind, actually. For a few years, I barely saw her – she wouldn't get out of bed. For me, she became a shadow in the house. All she did was cry.' Viviano shut his eyes. 'I remember, one day, she appeared in the living room in a beautiful summer dress. Even her hair was done. We couldn't believe it, my aunt and I. She rushed over and gave me the biggest hug,' he said, the words tumbling out. 'Her smile was so big, I remember thinking she was glowing like an angel. She whispered that we were going to watch a film together, just the two of us.'

He looked up at Laure, and for the first time, she saw not his eyes, but two wells of sadness.

'About ten minutes into the film, she leant over onto my chest and began to sob, and then she didn't move again, didn't look at me again. All night, we stayed there and she just shook uncontrollably. When my aunt came back the next morning, she helped my mother back into bed and tried to pat my shirt dry with a hanky, but it was soaked through.'

Viviano let out a sigh and offered Laure an uncomfortable smile. His whole body was like glass. 'I've never told anyone that before,' he said. 'Just after my dad left, I heard my aunt say he'd changed after I was born. Maybe it's true, because he never said goodbye to me.'

Laure moved closer and placed a hand on his trembling shoulder.

'You feel guilty for it all,' she said, tears pricking the back of her eyes. 'Like you caused all the sadness, the death of their relationship. Maybe, to you, it felt like a real death. It's not your fault, you know?'

Viviano shrugged and turned his head away from Laure.

'I think I only survived those years because of our neighbour, *Signora* Solari. She came and cared for me every day, took me to school, helped with homework and with life, when I had no motivation.' Viviano's voice went quiet, as if hanging from a thread. 'She just passed away, actually, after a long illness. The funeral is next week. I should go, but I can't face it.'

Suddenly, as if the air had been punched out of him, Viviano doubled over and began to gasp. He stared at the ground as tears spilled from his eyes onto the pavement. When he finally straightened up, it was like he'd seen a ghost.

Laure put her arms around him. 'I'm sorry,' she whispered. 'That must have been very hard to deal with when you were so young.' Taking a small step backwards, she found his eyes. 'You know, you don't have to feel apprehensive about sharing that with me, or with anyone,' she said. 'Actually, it's really important to address those feelings. That guilt won't go away unless you face it, it will just fester and re-emerge in some pretty horrible ways. Maybe it already is.'

Viviano stared at her. 'How-how do you know about that?' he asked.

'Back in Paris, one of my best friends was experiencing something that sounds similar. Once she got over the shame of her thoughts, we used to talk about what she was going through. She shared a lot with me. Therapy helped her to see it differently.'

Laure smiled at Viviano, trying to put him at ease. 'You know, kicking the shit out of yourself is more common than you might think, but given everything you went through, I think you could benefit from some professional help.'

Upon hearing these last words, Viviano flinched and shook his head like a cartoon character.

'Jesus,' he whispered, starting to laugh.

'What?' asked Laure, a sting of hurt in her voice.

'I'm so sorry,' he said. 'You're absolutely right. It's just, I don't think the words, "I think you could benefit from some professional help", have ever been said on a successful first date.' All of a sudden, he was bright red. 'I'm so sorry I told you that stuff. I don't know what came over me.'

'My gosh, it's fine!' said Laure, but she could see the window into his heart was closing.

'Laure,' Viviano said in a serious voice, his eyes dancing as if willing her to see him as she had before the admissions. 'I have a very important question for you.'

Laure was silent.

'Can I please still take you somewhere cool?'

He caught her hand in mid-air, twirled her round and dipped her to the floor.

Laure couldn't help but laugh. '*Oui,* you can,' she said, staring at upside-down Rome.

'Amazing,' said Viviano. He propped her up again and began to sprint.

Laure shook her head. 'Do you mind waiting for me, then?' she yelled, before chasing Viviano across the bridge and into the neighbourhood of Testaccio.

CHAPTER THIRTY-FIVE

The politicians, past and present, who party

Testaccio was an up-and-coming area that was still far more shabby than chic. Not a soul was in sight as they ran past blocks of flats, the neighbourhood's famed market place and rows of industrial buildings whose facades were covered with graffitied murals. The only noise was their own footsteps hitting the concrete and the occasional shout or a dog barking somewhere in the distance.

'Up here,' Viviano said.

'You're not serious,' said Laure, eyeing the rusty ladder which was barely clinging to the wall. 'Viv, this looks like it pre-dates the Roman era.'

But while Laure protested, Viviano was climbing, the corroded rungs screeching under his weight.

With a silent prayer, Laure placed a foot on the first step. In order to survive, she tried to imagine there would be another spectacular party waiting for them. But when her shaky hands finally found the top and she pulled herself up, there was only a filthy rooftop covered in pigeon excrement.

'So?' said Viviano, gesturing around. 'Whaddya think?'

Laure frowned at him. 'I think you're very special.'

He ushered her over to the edge.

Hmm, said her brain. *Is this where it all ends for us?*

'We have thirty seconds,' Viviano said, pointing towards a patch of pavement which was illuminated by a pale-yellow street lamp. 'Just keep looking over there.'

Together, they stared.

At the stroke of midnight, a rallying cry soared out of the building below, piercing the night's silence and echoing around the streets.

Laure glanced over to Viviano, but he nodded back to the spot.

From the darkness, a woman with cropped blonde hair and a tailored suit strode into the spotlight. Even from a distance, she oozed power and confidence.

Laure looked closer. 'Is that …?' Her voice trailed off as she watched. 'That looks like …' Laure squinted. It was uncanny. 'That looks exactly like Hillary Clinton!' she finally said, unable to dissuade herself. She whipped her head around to Viviano and then turned back to the former presidential candidate. '*Madame* Clinton, what are you doing here, in Testaccio, in the middle of the night?' she murmured.

A man in a buttoned-up jacket, with a mass of bushy black hair and a strong moustache also strolled into the circle. He didn't acknowledge Hillary, seemingly too engrossed in a book. The light bounced off his small oval glasses and Laure's eyes bulged.

'Is that Trotsky?!' she exclaimed.

As Laure stared, the man threw his political manifesto to the ground and scooped Mrs Clinton up into his arms. Together, they engaged in a jaunty foxtrot, hooting and yelping in delight.

Another Trotsky joined them, identical to the first. Intent on cutting in, he tried to take Hillary's hand, only to be rebuffed and unceremoniously pushed from the circle by Trotsky number one.

All at once, a carnival of people burst from the building below and scattered across the street. Laure spotted three or four more Trotskys and a Lenin. From the shadows, Germany's 'Mutti' Angela Merkel came hopscotching along the pavement, followed by Barack Obama giving Michelle a piggyback.

Everyone cheered as Christine Lagarde, the European Central Bank chief, emerged from around the corner, announcing she had lowered interest rates and bought 'great value' cigarettes for everyone. Somewhere in the chaos, a powerful beat erupted which shook the building to its core. Laure leant forward and saw a group, in traditional Indian dress, playing dhol drums. The politicians danced around them. Charles de Gaulle was breakdancing and Mandela was doing a jive.

Little by little, the bombastic crowd partied down the street. A man in a fluffy dog suit padded along after them.

'What on earth is going on?' Laure asked, her mouth hanging open.

Viviano laughed. 'It's mad, isn't it? I bet you didn't know Charles de Gaulle had moves like that, or that he was alive, actually.'

'But ... howww?' Laure asked.

'It's a drama school,' Viviano said. 'A really good one. We're sitting on top of their theatre. Every Saturday they rehearse until midnight, and then race off into the night together. Years ago, I used to take classes here, but now *this* is my favourite bit – watching them all appear. You never know who or what is going to come through the doors.'

'They look so authentic.'

'You should've seen your face when Trotsky arrived.'

'He was my favourite,' Laure said.

'So, do you fancy joining them?' Viviano asked. 'Usually, they head to this club around the corner.'

Assolutamente sì,' said Laure.

'I'm just warning you, they're completely mad! Some of them never come out of character.'

'I'm ready,' said Laure, turning back towards the death-trap descent. 'Come on. Let's go.'

But Viviano gestured towards the front of the building.

'You'd prefer us to step off?' Laure asked.

'I don't recommend it,' said Viviano, 'but there is a safe route down this way.'

Laure peered over and saw that he was right. Several golden balconies cascaded down the theatre's façade, connected by metal stairs to the pavement.

'I can't believe you made me go up that bloody ladder!'

Viviano shrugged. 'It would have ruined the surprise.'

After trialling her darkest look, Laure descended and once safely back on the ground, she sprinted into the spotlight where the show had unfolded.

'I am Queen Elizabeth II of England,' Laure announced in her best British accent, performing the royal wave to an invisible crowd and curtseying before Viviano.

'*Madonna mia,* you are weird,' said Viviano, attempting to walk straight past as if he didn't know this strange woman.

'Aha!' Laure yelped, her face flushing red.

'I'm kidding, I'm kidding!' said Viviano. He stared down at the floor, searching for his character. 'And I am ...' he announced, his head snapping up.

'Perhaps a king?' Laure said

'Jackie Chan!' Viviano bellowed into the night.

'Right,' said Laure.

'Come here, your highness!' he said, cutting the air with a series of karate chops and a flying kick.

In a swift movement, he scooped Laure over his shoulders into a fireman's lift, and tore off along the street.

CHAPTER THIRTY-SIX

Drugs? Have a strawberry instead

Hanging upside down, and with a view only of Viviano's back, Laure felt her surroundings before she saw them. The bass was sending tremors through the trees and making her ribcage hum.

As he put her down, the dilapidated house before them came into view. The windows were flashing different colours and a rolling wave of purple smoke billowed across the terrace. Everywhere Laure looked there were people: spilling out of the door, hanging out on the stairs or gathered in the street.

Just in front, a group of lads were sitting on the garden wall. Their oversized tracksuits hid intensively tattooed skin, and golden chains weighed on their muscular physiques. As if casting for the latest reggaetón video, they posed and pouted for passers-by. As Laure's eyes wandered past, her brain told her something was off and she looked back.

Instead of the surgically enhanced, scantily clad women you might expect to see draped over the wannabe bad boys, these men were in fact vying for the attention of several elderly ladies. Perched on their laps, the women fussed over the lads' hair and, from time to time, wiped their mouths clean with lacy hankies. The men looked around smugly, flaunting their conquests.

'I remember when …' Laure heard one grandma say, launching into a story about the unification of Italy.

Her toyboy listened, eyes full of desire. 'That's so hawt baby,' he said, before licking her face as the tale drew to a close.

Very unusual, Laure thought.

Through the groups of strangers, Laure and Viviano approached the entrance where two stony-faced bouncers looked them up and down before ushering them in.

Does anyone actually get turned away from this place? Laure wondered.

As soon as they crossed the threshold, a techno beat pounced on their eardrums. It possessed the air, forcing even the most disbelieving to pray before its unrelenting rhythm. Laure watched the disco lights dance over a sea of vibrating bodies. Every flash picked up a detail in the crowd, the colour of an eye, the shape of a nose, just for a fleeting moment, before leaving the dancer to their anonymity once again.

Hillary Clinton was up on the decks. Her neater-than-neat hair flew out in all directions as her head spun around and around. The tailored purple jacket had been cast aside, revealing a leather bikini with the US flag sewn onto the cups. The Obamas were making out in a darkened corner.

'Drinks?' Viviano yelled, signalling with his hand.

'Tequila!' shouted Laure, respecting what the setting demanded.

Viviano nodded and disappeared only to rematerialise moments later with a tray of shots.

'That was quick!' yelled Laure.

'*Conosco il tipo,* I know the guy,' Viviano mouthed.

'Of course you do!'

The poison of choice scorched her throat and Laure was about to shudder, when a piercing alarm like a final scream, knifed through the music, making her forget all about it. Panic assaulted her body, but as she swung frantically around, Laure noticed everyone else was cheering, their arms raised to the sky.

'Shut your eyes!' Viviano yelled.

Unable to think, Laure obeyed and waited, her heart thumping.

Something wet hit her wrist and shoulder, the top of her head, then suddenly, her whole body was being pelted as if the roof had lifted, letting in a heavy downpour.

When it finally ceased, Laure opened her eyes. A deluge of paint had come tumbling from the ceiling, showering everyone in an aurora of luminescent colours. Laure's whole body looked like a Jackson Pollock, her skin barely discernible through the bright splodges.

'Let's find our spot,' Viviano yelled, beaming at her with a paint-palette face. 'There's always somewhere that feels best.'

As they toured the club, Laure wished she had 360-degree vision to take it all in.

One corner was skulking with masked creatures, resembling anything from mythical animals, Venetian carnival goers or gothic demons. They sipped drinks through fissures in their disguises or moshed to the music as if it were heavy metal. A few were locked in tight embraces, unaware of their lover's identity under the mask. Laure and Viviano passed by.

Next, they mingled with an androgynous group of Freddie Mercurys, in an array of sparkling onesies, tank tops and yellow leather jackets. It was only after they left that Viviano and Laure realised their own hair had also been slicked back, and a neat moustache placed delicately above their lips.

'*Mi piace qua,* I like it here!' Laure announced, stopping in the middle of the dance floor.

'The Merkels sold it to you, did they?' said Viviano as a congregation of Angelas weaved sensuously around them.

'No, I like it cause it's under the fan!' yelled Laure, pointing up at the whirring silver blades on the ceiling. 'Although, the Angelas don't hurt, obviously!'

'*Das ist richtig,*' said one Merkel, leaning over and offering Laure a professional handshake and pat on the back.

'Yes, this is my spot!' Laure said with a grin.

Finally able to surrender to the music, Laure let her mind and body fall in sync with the beat, inaugurated into the cult of the club.

Time passed. It could have been minutes, or several hours, but when Laure opened her eyes, she saw Viviano next to her, also abandoned to the music, his glow of happiness reflecting golden light onto her. Laure noted that she had never seen anyone dance quite so badly as him – completely unaware of the rhythm.

'COMING THROUGH! COMING THROUGH! *MUOVETEVI!* OUT OF THE WAY!'

Ravers were knocked down like playing cards as a squad of muscular men forced their way through the club. Bulletproof jackets were hidden under their dark suits, and they carried something precious, which their stocky bodies, huddled in a tight circle, blocked from view.

At the moment they passed, one of the henchmen slipped, allowing a tiny chink to appear in their impenetrable wall. Laure's eyes widened as she caught a glimpse of a wooden barrel, filled to the brim with large ripe strawberries.

Unable to stop herself, she tapped one of the men in black on the shoulder. '*Scusami,* but what is so special about—'

He cut her off.

'*Signorina,* these are the finest strawberries you will find in the country. Nay, on the whole Goddamn continent,' he spat, clearly irked by the silly question. 'You think we get our award-winning cocktail here by chance? No, no, no, these heavenly fruits must be protected and patented!'

With that, he whipped around and continued to barge through the crowd, in perfect unison with his crew.

'Oh, right,' said Laure, raising her eyebrows. 'Maybe we should have ordered the Strawberry Daquiri.'

For a second, Viviano looked at her, scratched his head and tried not to laugh. 'There's definitely drugs under those strawberries, Laure.'

'Ah, *oui?*' said Laure, wishing the ground would swallow her up. Just as she searched for some words to restore credibility, a man with an impressive afro leapt into the air and landed on Viviano's back.

Apparently unfazed, Viviano held onto the man's legs and spun around.

It was Mickey.

'*Sei qui,* you're here!' Viviano said, dropping Mickey down and giving him a hug. 'This is Laure.'

Mickey's mouth dropped open. 'Are you an apparition from one of Viv's fantasy lands?' he asked. 'Or did someone slip something in my drink?'

Pleadingly, Viviano looked at Mickey, imploring him to not.

'Oh, right, yes, sorry. I mean, *piacere di conoscerti,* Laure, nice to meet you,' he said, giving her a kiss on each cheek. 'I don't know why I'm surprised, actually,' he continued. 'Viv has lots of dates, you know. *Tons* of girlfriends.' He offered his friend an exaggerated wink.

'Much better,' Viviano said. '*Grazie.*'

Laure laughed.

'Well, it really is an absolute pleasure,' Mickey said again, still looking at Laure as

148

if for tell-tale traces of a hologram. 'Lord, I never thought I'd see the day …' he muttered. Then, out of nowhere, he gave Laure a hug.

'Laure, Mickey is, unfortunately, one of my best friends,' Viviano said.

'Friends, yes!' Mickey said, his face bright and earnest. 'Now friends I really can say this man has a lot of. Very good friend of mine. He'd be an excellent boyfriend, I'm sure!'

Viviano placed his head in his hands.

'It's just … I've just never seeeen it.' With an unapologetic grin at Viviano, Mickey spun around and danced into the distance.

'So, that's Mickey.' Viviano said, visibly mortified.

With a soft smile, Laure leant in and kissed Viviano lightly on the cheek, just off his lips, causing him to blush fiercely.

As she leant away, their eyes met.

'I love this song,' Laure said.

Viviano nodded.

Face to face, they started to dance. The beat was fast, but they ignored it, their eyes closed but every so often, catching a glimpse of each other. Viviano wanted to kiss her, but he didn't dare.

There they stayed. Steve Jobs upgraded the decks, making the bass so fierce it almost brought down the roof, and a vicious fight broke out over the sumptuous strawberries, but they didn't notice.

At some point, the music stopped and the eccentric characters of the night began to trickle out of the club and onto the Roman streets.

Laure and Viviano opened their eyes, reluctant for anything to change.

The outside world felt like a different planet, and a blinding sunlight shone in Laure's face as she reemerged.

What time is it? she wondered, shielding her eyes.

As she reached for her phone, Viviano detached his hand from hers, brushed her shoulder and signalled that he would be back in a moment. He had spotted Mickey and wanted to say goodnight.

Six a.m.

Across the phone screen, a message from Marco appeared, and Laure noticed how that whole strange situation now seemed like a distant memory. With indifference, she clicked on it.

> *Cara* Laure. It's over between me and my girlfriend. I feel numb, but I can't stop thinking about you. I think you are the one I am supposed to be with

Laure stared at the message without comprehending a word. Again and again, she read it, but it wasn't registering. She gazed at Viviano who was roaring with laughter

149

next to Mickey, and then looked back at the phone.

Suddenly, a murderous hand grasped her stomach and Laure's head began to spin. Anxiety spread up her chest, squeezing her lungs until her breath came up short and fast. She had to leave right now. With desperate hands, Laure tried to wave at Viviano to signal that she was going, but he couldn't see her. Another moment there and she would faint.

Through her wheezes, she staggered in the direction of home, but after a few streets, her legs buckled and she slumped to the pavement.

'Deep breaths,' Laure said, letting her head fall between her legs.

The words of Marco's message sprung up before her eyes, like the pulsing lyrics to a karaoke song.

'How did I let this happen?'

Go home, Laure. This can all be sorted out. But you need to get home and sleep a bit, her brain said. *When you wake up, everything will be clearer. Rentre chez toi, just go home.*

As she tried to calm down, while the city around her was awakening, unusual thoughts began to creep through Laure's mind: Marco on a pony galloping off a bridge, Viviano in a poncho feeding her soup, Eva on a merry-go-round.

GO HOME, LAURE, her brain yelled, jolting her sharply from her drunken slumber.

Like a baby deer on fragile legs, Laure clambered up and began to wander.

It was early, but a handful of Romans were already up. She ignored the concerned glances from an elderly couple walking their dog, and kept her head down while shuffling past the merchants setting up their market stalls.

'*Mannaggia,* damn, I wish I was still young enough to live it up,' one said as Laure passed, but she barely heard.

Around the corner, a shiny shop window laid her reflection bare, and despite her pitiful state, a fountain of maniacal laughter burst from Laure's mouth, propelling her forward with such force that she had to grab her knees for support.

'Oh *mon Dieu,*' Laure whispered, wiping tears from her streaming eyes.

The lion-face art, which felt like it had been painted in another lifetime, had mostly sweated off, leaving dirty splodges across her pallid face. A superglued quiff of hair sat on top of her head, before exploding out into a bird's nest of tangles behind. And she was splattered from head to toe in fluorescent paint.

Quand même, it's astounding to me that someone wants to leave their girlfriend for you, said her brain.

Laure agreed.

What should have been a twenty-minute walk, took one hour, as Laure zigzagged through the streets, stopping twice to throw up. By the time her door appeared, she was done with life. Inside, she immediately removed her clothes and fell into bed.

I wish I could have told Viv, Laure thought as her mind shut down, *that I'm so sorry I had to leave like that … Marco!* The name suddenly leapt into her mind. *I never replied!*

Through squinting eyes, Laure managed to click on his message. In her dream, she was crafting a perfect response, sensitive but truthful.

> I'm so sorry, Marco.
> It's all a misunderstanding. We aren't
> meant to be. I wish you and your
> girlfriend all the best and really hope
> you can patch things up.

Back in reality, what she actually typed was:

> Doughnuts, thanks

Then she dropped the phone onto the floor and fell asleep.

. . .

In Testaccio, Viviano and Mickey had searched high and low for the mysteriously missing Laure. Their only clue was from a DJ who had seen a woman of her description walking towards the bridge.

'She definitely went home,' Mickey said, trying to reassure his friend after their two-hour search had turned up nothing. 'The guy said she was heading for Trastevere. That's her neighbourhood, isn't it?'

'You're right,' said Viviano, lost in a grey cloud. 'I just hope she's OK. I wish I could contact her. Why do you think she left like that?'

Mickey shrugged. 'Welcome to the world of women, Viv. They are hard to understand.'

Viviano frowned, and Mickey placed an arm around him. 'Let's go home for now,' he said. 'She'll turn up, *amico*, I'm sure.'

They began to walk.

'Does it worry you that I'm the only one you ever bring home from parties, *amore?*' Mickey asked.

'Yes, a little,' said Viviano, his eyes still scanning around for Laure.

CHAPTER THIRTY-SEVEN

The rude awakening

Laure awoke inside her oven-like room with little will to live.

Languishing on her back, she pawed out for the fan and, as the blades began to whir and waft cooler air around the room, she evaluated the state of affairs:

- *Un:* Her head was pounding, but throwing up had helped. She commended herself.
- *Deux:* She needed to burn her sheets. They looked like a rainbow had died on them.
- *Trois:* It was unclear what time, or even what day it was.
- *Quatre:* She had run away without telling Viv where she was going. She de-commended herself.

Despite the various ailments and misfortunes, Laure felt a glimmer of relief. At least she had dealt with Marco.

I wonder if he replied, and how he took it all, she thought, not yet ready to look. *I just hope he understands.*

As her heavy eyelids closed again, last night's date played out in her head like an old-fashioned film: the food, the fire bandit, the rooftop dancing, Hillary ripping off her presidential blouse, all the scenes and stories. It had been surreal from start to finish, exactly what Viv had promised. She thought about the kiss that had grazed the edge of his lips.

'I hope he's in his spot. I have to find him and explain.'

Laure pushed herself up and felt her arms wither in pain. 'Ow!' she groaned, remembering her death grip on the decrepit ladder in Testaccio.

Her mouth was drier than scorched hay, and she sipped the old glass of lukewarm water by the bed until her phone could no longer be ignored.

There's never going to be a good time to face Marco's response, she thought, reaching out and bracing herself.

Timidly, she peeped at the screen: sixteen missed calls from Marco and five messages.

Her whole body froze. Had he really taken it that badly?

> Laure, what kind of a response it that ...?

> This isn't the time for joking ...
> I'm being serious here

> Laure, did you see what I wrote to you?

> This is very important, I need to speak
> to you

> Laure, where are you? Pick up, *per favore!*

Laure was in shock.

This Marco really doesn't handle rejection well, she thought. *I couldn't have let him down more gently.*

Hastily, she scrolled up to reread the original message. Maybe, in her drunken state, it hadn't come across how she'd wanted.

> Doughnuts, thanks

Her eyes widened.

'Doughnuts, thanks?' What? No, she didn't know what that was, but that wasn't it.

Embracing denial, Laure began a frantic search for the heartfelt message that she had scripted, her blood pressure rising with every second. But, alas, there wasn't one. There was only 'Doughnuts, thanks'.

Her heart sank.

'Laure, you fucking idiot,' she whispered. *'Doughnuts?* ... You absolute moron.'

The response was all the more upsetting because Laure knew that she had desperately wanted a doughnut last night. On the way home, she had stood outside her favourite bakery and stared as the early morning pâtissiers laid out fresh sugary treats in the window. At the time, Laure had praised her restraint, pushing the craving from her mind in favour of the sleep she so desperately needed. But apparently, the sweet, soft dough had lingered in her subconscious.

Bon bah, this is clearly unacceptable. You need to sort this out, her brain said.

'You think I don't know that *"Doughnuts, thanks"* is an unacceptable response?' she snapped back.

After staggering out of bed, Laure gulped down another cold glass of water from the fridge, retched a few times and put her head in her hands.

It was midday.

In her mind, she could imagine Marco pacing like a bull somewhere in Rome, smoke flaring from his nostrils.

Muttering expletives, Laure retrieved her phone and began to type.

> *Ciao* Marco, I'm so sorry,
> I didn't mean to send 'Doughnuts' …
> I'm not sure what happened.

Her hands stopped, wanting to finish there, but she knew she couldn't.

> I think we should meet today and talk
> about all this. Your message took me by
> surprise. How about Da Antonio in an
> hour?

The second she pressed send, Marco's response came.

> Jesus, Laure. You had me worried!
> Thank God for your reply. I have been
> going crazy. Yes. Da Antonio, 1 p.m. It
> can't come soon enough

Laure popped two Ibuprofen. 'I've messed Marco around,' she said. 'I need to set things straight, then I'll find Viv.'

You're doing the right thing, her brain confirmed.

'Fuck off,' Laure replied.

Running a hand over her solid hair, Laure shuddered. Hygiene was the next priority.

The shower was a celebration of life. Laure shampooed, cleansed and scrubbed until the water around her feet turned from murky brown to clear again. As she stepped out, her mind felt clearer and she began consider how to let Marco down. He had decided the outcome of this story, but it wasn't what she wanted.

'I have to be brave and direct, *voilà,*' Laure announced.

Sounds ambitious, her brain replied. *I'd put my money on you collapsing into a simpering stress ball and telling Marco you'll give it a go.*

Laure shrugged. Her brain was astute. Was it about to become rich too?

Briefly, she envisaged her life with Marco as he rode out his life crisis. Puffing away, hitting the clubs, Jean-Maxime La Croix Montagne. She saw Viv sitting behind them, rolling his eyes whenever Marco spoke. No, no, no, it was too much.

'I'm sorry, it's just not meant to be, you and me,' Laure mewed into the bathroom mirror, trying her best 'sympathetic' but managing only 'constipated'.

Je ne suis pas convaincue, I am not convinced, her brain said.

In a bid for positivity, Laure pulled on a light-yellow sundress and tied her hair into a non-sexual ponytail.

The food-scarcity level in her house had been raised from 'moderate' to 'alarming' by the UN earlier that morning, and like a predatory dog, Laure skulked the kitchen, eventually sniffing out some old biscuits. Deep down, she hated that what she really wanted was a fucking doughnut.

'Tick, tick, tick,' whispered the clock, and Laure's eyes wandered over the shelves to a lonely bottle of Aperol.

Euh, non, her brain said, *you definitely can't go drunk!*

Laure left the house.

Out on the streets, there was a Saturday buzz. The smell of freshly baked dough and roasted meats drifted from the crowded delis, and all around, people were café hopping or perusing the vitrines of the small boutiques, chirping like contented birds.

The sunshine caressed Laure's skin, but she took no pleasure in it, knowing the golden light drenching her path was deceptive. At the end of it, Marco would be sitting under the veranda of Da Antonio.

The moment she spotted him, the guilt in her stomach sloshed through the thin barrier of confidence she had created, making her queasy. He looked tense and scruffy and was aggressively shaking a sugar packet. But upon seeing Laure, his puffy eyes flooded with hope.

This isn't going to be easy, Laure thought.

CHAPTER THIRTY-EIGHT

'That's what you got from what I said?' Part 1

Marco clambered around the table, seeing in Laure's face an end to his misery.

'*Sei qui,* you're here,' he said, reaching for her hand and leaning in to kiss her.

As his lips drew near, Laure's head twisted slightly and his mouth brushed her cheek.

Sensing the hesitance, Marco pulled back and searched her eyes.

Laure gestured that they should sit, her legs now shaking so violently that she was grateful to alleviate them.

'So, Laurrre,' Marco began, a light tremor in his voice.

Laure cut him off. 'Marco. It isn't going to work between us. I'm so sorry,' she said.

At first, the hope rippling in Marco's eyes was unchanged, then little by little, Laure saw the words sink in.

'*Cos'hai detto,* what did you say?' he asked, sure he must have misheard.

'This isn't going to work out,' Laure repeated, in barely a whisper.

'Laurrre,' Marco said, half-serious, half-jovial. 'I have to tell you, your jokes have my stomach in knots.' He tried to laugh, but nothing came out and his mouth flapped like a mechanical puppet.

Laure shook her head and stared at the ground.

Seeing this reaction, all the colour drained from Marco's face.

'I'm so sorry,' Laure said, her nails leaving deep grooves in her thighs as she tried to stay composed. 'I saw your text, but I can't do it. It's just …'

This time Marco cut her off. 'But Laurrre, what do you mean?' he asked, eyes wide and heart open. 'Believe me, I have thought about this over and over again. We fit perfectly! We like the same things, we make each other laugh, there is this chemistry. What more could we want?' His doe eyes stared out, imploring her to agree.

'Marco, I know we've enjoyed each other's company in the little time that we've spent together,' Laure said, taking a deep steadying breath. 'But the truth is, we don't really know each other at all.'

'But we do,' Marco said, holding her hand. 'You understand me and I get you. Laure, please … I think I've fallen in love with you.'

CHAPTER THIRTY-NINE

'That's what you got from what I said?' Part 2

Viviano hadn't slept at all. Laure was camped out in his head.

Why had she run off? Was she at home, safe, or had something happened?

He tossed and turned, and at ten o'clock, Mikey had awoken to find his friend balanced on the slackline in a grief-stricken pose.

'Viv, you're too much,' he mumbled, before turning to sleep again. But it was impossible. Viviano's nervous energy was permeating the room and minutes later, Mickey threw off the covers with a groan, and said: 'OK, fine. I'll get up, but you are so annoying.'

After showering, the pair traipsed towards the kitchen in search of coffee. No sooner had they entered, than Viviano's mum materialised in the doorway, announcing she had made breakfast.

Isabella looked them up and down, eyebrows raised. 'You boys just can't get enough of life, can you?' she said, before bustling off to fetch orange juice.

While they tested out their delicate stomachs with marmalade tart and sponge cake, Isabella subtly tried to establish whether her son had dressed up smartly for the first time in his life for a romantic date with Mickey.

Following a few clunky questions and a titbit about Estonia being the latest country to legalise gay marriage, Viviano turned to his mother.

'Ma, Mickey and I are not a couple.'

'Oh,' said his mum. 'Who was asking?'

'It's true, *Signora* C,' said Mickey. 'But I can reveal your son is in love.'

'What?' whispered Isabella, her eyes sparkling with excitement. 'Is it true, Viv?'

Viviano shot his best look of disdain at the two offenders.

'*Mamma*,' he said in a slow, firm voice. 'Thanks for breakfast, but we have to go.'

The two men cleared the table and made for the door, ready for a fresh session of the least fun game in the world – 'Let's find Laure.'

On the way out, Mickey slipped by Isabella and whispered, 'It's all true. I'll tell you later.'

Barely holding back a squeal, Isabella danced into the kitchen and began to sing.

...

By the afternoon, a suffocating humidity had set in and Viviano was making his way back towards Da Antonio for the fourth time, still desperate for any trace of Laure. Mickey had pleaded insanity at midday, preferring even his cramped squat to the incessant overthinking of an exhausted and lovesick Viviano.

As he walked, the woman without a story engulfed his thoughts, or Laure, as he now called her.

Last night, he had started to get to know her. Not in the way that he was used to, where his intuition filled in all the blanks, but little by little. The way she smiled when he had managed to make her laugh, her willingness to try new food and the dreamy amazement with which she had watched the bandit and he couldn't tell what she was thinking. Laure, he had discovered, was clever and kind, but most of all, he felt comfortable with her, and he believed she had felt the same.

All morning, their conversation on the bridge had whirred in his head. The idea that the heaviness lurking within was linked to guilt had unlocked something. Viviano had always believed that his dark thoughts and chaotic mind were unique to him, his own shameful secret, but was it possible they were actually symptoms ... something he could treat? Could he hope, one day, to feel different? Maybe he could look into therapy. The idea terrified him, though.

With every step, his desire to see Laure again grew. He had so much more to discover about her.

As Da Antonio's cream canopy came into view, Viviano stopped in his tracks. Laure was there. She looked radiant in a yellow dress and showed absolutely no sign that she had spent the night darting around the Roman streets with him. Sitting opposite, was the chiselled face of Marco.

CHAPTER FORTY

Run away

Viviano froze and a sharp pain seared his chest. Laure's hand was in Marco's and they were gazing at each other.

Like two infatuated lovers, Viviano thought, tears flooding his eyes.

Before anyone could see, he turned and started to run.

The destination didn't matter, Viviano just needed to get as far away as possible.

'I don't do this, I don't do this,' he repeated, sprinting past a blur of people and buildings.

When he could no longer breathe, he collapsed against a wall and began to cough and retch to the point of exhaustion.

'THAT IS ENOUGH!' he said, gasping for air. 'Look, at least she's OK. That's what you were worried about, wasn't it?' His eyes scanned the shabby alleyway and he shook his head. 'Stop this nonsense now. Sometimes things don't work out how you'd like them to. It's fine.'

Above him, a strip of pristine aquamarine ran between the two buildings, like a sky canal on which Viviano wished he could sail away. As he stared upwards, trying to bury his feelings, a wisp of dirty smoke seemed to descend from the beautiful blue. Then another, and another. One by one, the intrusive thoughts swooped down, like vultures coming to pick at his sanity.

What was I thinking about? What was I thinking about? What was I thinking about? His brain got caught in a loop, as slime crept over happy memories and sunk his self-worth.

Viviano hung his head. Suddenly, it felt so heavy. He hadn't missed his dungeon, but unlike the ache in his heart, it was, at least, familiar.

A cloud shaped like a burst balloon drifted lazily across the blue sky.

Perhaps I could make a costume like that, Viviano thought as he left the alley and wandered back into the urban jungle.

CHAPTER FORTY-ONE

'That's what you got from what I said?' Part 3

'You think you love me?' Laure repeated, staring at Marco from across the table.
Marco nodded.

It was all too much for Laure. 'Marco, I don't know what to say,' she said. 'Honestly, this is a shock to me!'

There was silence.

'I don't think I'm really what you want,' she whispered. 'And ... I don't think you know me.'

'Of course, I do,' said Marco, squeezing her hand and interpreting the doubts as fear. 'Laure, you're wonderful. You want to make the most of life, like I do, so why don't we do it together?' His earnest face begged her to see the light. 'I know it's scary, but ... let's try.'

'But it isn't true,' said Laure, feeling the whole façade fall away. 'None of it is.'

'What do you mean?'

For a moment, Laure was quiet.

'I don't really like to go out that much,' she said, closing her eyes. 'I'm more of a homebody. And I don't like cigarettes. I hate them, actually. I've been lying to you.'

As Marco listened, his eyes turned from liquid to stone and he pulled back, letting Laure's hand flop onto the table.

'Then, why did you say all those things?'

'I guess ... I wanted you to like me,' Laure mumbled.

'And now?' said Marco, his voice rising. 'Now that I do? Now what, Laure?'

Laure was silent.

'Is this all a joke to you?' he asked, suddenly interrogating her like a traitor.

'No, it isn't, of course it isn't,' said Laure. 'I'm so sorry.'

'I've broken up with my girlfriend ... *for you!*' Marco said, seemingly telling himself as much as Laure.

'I know. I didn't think you would do that,' Laure whispered, staring at the floor.

'I thought you felt the same!'

'I'm so sorry,' Laure said, fighting back tears. 'It was a mistake. I didn't think you would leave your girlfriend.'

'Oh my God,' said Marco, hyperventilating. *'O mio Dio, o mio Dio.'*

There was a loud clatter as he stumbled up, knocking his chair to the ground. Da Antonio was silent – everyone was watching the drama.

As Marco towered over Laure, serpents seemed to slither from his eyes. 'You are a bitch,' he managed to spit, before lurching off into the distance.

After he had disappeared, Laure slumped down onto the table.

CHAPTER FORTY-TWO
I've been an idiot

'Hey, watch where you're going, idiot,' said one man as Marco stumbled into him.

'Um, excuse me!' said another as he cut across their path.

'You need to pay more attention, young man,' tutted an elderly lady.

Marco barely heard the words as he staggered home, tripping over his own feet and bumping into passers-by. They shook their heads, believing he was a drunken nuisance. He couldn't see anything. Laure was roaring through his head like a fire-breathing dragon, hissing red hot flames over his thoughts, engulfing his clarity in toxic, black smoke and turning seven years of effort and partnership into crumbling ash.

How could I have misread the situation so badly? he thought, going back over their encounters. *How had she known just what to say?*

He hocked a thick globule of spit onto the ground. Laure had led him into a fantasy land, and he had blindly followed. Through the blackened debris, an image of Valeria appeared in his mind. He saw her anguished face, the confusion and her sadness.

I've been horrible, he thought bitterly.

Lost in another world, Marco wandered up the stairs, erupting into outbursts of incomprehensible mumbles until he reached the door.

The empty flat was a stranger and dank air pressed into his skin. Through the shuttered blinds, only minute streaks of sunshine permeated the dimness, scattering razor-thin threads of light across the room.

Casting his eyes around, Marco realised that this was the earliest he had arrived home in months. He thought about what it must have been like for an exhausted Valeria to return to this lifeless place every evening and not find him there. Maybe, given his behaviour, she had come to prefer it that way. Maybe she had groaned at the sound of his arrival and the prospect of another argument. All he could see were the places he had behaved poorly and tears began to roll down his cheeks. He pulled out his phone and dialled her number.

No answer. Just the machine.

'Valeria, I'm so sorry,' he said, his voice barely a whisper. 'Please come home. We need to talk. I'm so sorry. I was out of my mind.'

CHAPTER FORTY-THREE

Ma, Viv, dove sei? Where are you, Viv?

At Da Antonio, Laure uncrumpled herself. As she opened her eyes, she saw a coffee had been placed in front of her with a little biscotti on the side. Slowly, she took a sip and sent a grateful nod to Antonio. He didn't react.

Ça va? her brain asked. *Are you OK?*

'I don't know, really,' Laure said. 'It was pretty intense. But I'm glad it's over. I hope he doesn't hate me forever.'

That's probably asking too much, her brain said. *Maybe we can hope he moves house, instead.*

Laure nodded. 'That too,' she said, lifting the coffee cup to her lips and trying to gather her shaky emotions. 'I need to find Viv. I should have started hours ago.'

Laure knew it wasn't an easy task. The likelihood of bumping into anyone in the city was almost non-existent, let alone someone who purposefully hid.

'I'll start local,' she said, standing up and wandering towards Viviano's spot.

On tired legs, Laure scoured the area, rustling leaves with her fingertips and analysing dust patterns for footprints like a forensic scientist. But today, the vines had no stories to tell. There were no tell-tale trainers sticking out of the walls, or supersized tabby cats dangling between rooftops.

Not here. Maybe the piazza, she thought, retracing the route to where her night with Viviano had started.

On the way, last night's magic in the square danced in her mind and Laure peered around the corner, wondering if by chance, it might still look the same. But Piazza di Santa Maria had morphed back into the bustling market place of Sunday afternoons. Sweaty tourists were jostling each other among the various stalls, determined to return home with the perfect 'piece of Italy' for their loved ones, while market traders sang of samples and discounts. Any trace of the night's incandescent theatrics had been brushed away with the early morning road sweepers.

As Laure skirted around the edge of stands selling previously unseen pasta shapes and chillies from Calabria that would burn a hole through your tongue, her eyes darted around for anything unusual. *For anything Viv,* she thought. But it was like trying to find pineapple on a pizza in Italy. Around and around she spun, craning her neck to see over the crowds when, *SMACK,* out of nowhere, she hit the cobblestone ground, her limbs twisted like origami.

'*Mamma mia,*' a gruff voice said. '*Tutt'OK?*'

Looking down at her was the frontman from yesterday's swing band. Amid the chaos, she had barrelled straight over his double bass.

'I'm OK,' Laure said, brushing dirt from her arms and legs, her face burning with embarrassment. 'I'm so sorry about your bass. I hope I didn't damage it.'

'Nonsense,' he replied, extending a large hand and pulling Laure up. 'My girl is a tough old cookie.'

As they came face to face, Viktor studied the dishevelled lady before him and Laure heard his brain click. His sun-beaten cheeks stretched outwards making room for a broad grin.

'We meet again so soon,' he said, tapping his bass to keep the band's beat. 'Will you stay for a song?'

'I'd love to,' Laure stammered, 'but I'm really in a hurry.'

Viktor nodded. '*A fra poco allora,* see you soon then,' he said, and as quick as a flash, Laure evaporated among the crowds.

Had it not been for the unexpected encounter between her face and the floor, Laure reflected that she might have asked Viktor where to find Viv, but as it was, her cheek was bruised and she was still none the wiser.

An iron padlock and heavy chain barred the door to the secret rooftop, and anyway, Laure knew that he had no connection to the derelict site.

'He must be at The Sunshine Café,' she said, trying to stay positive.

Laure imagined Viv chatting away to the owners, and how his face would light up when she appeared. But after thirty minutes of twists and turns, the sound of a jazzy trumpet floated over, and Laure rounded the corner to see Viktor and the bustling Sunday market again.

'How the ...?' she said with a sinking heart.

Now, only a single location remained, and it was the one she was least keen on. A few times during their date, Viv had talked about the Gianicolo viewpoint, and his childhood memories and evenings spent there with friends.

It's an important place for him, n'est-ce pas? her brain said.

Laure agreed that it was nice. However, it was also at the top of a steep hill.

'For fuck's sake,' she muttered, wiping her sodden forehead with a sweaty palm. Why couldn't Viv's favourite place have been the pizzeria near her house? It was peaceful there, too, and delicious, and if anything, it had the decency to be positioned on a slight slope *down* the road. Also, you could book online.

You're getting off topic, said her brain.

'Fine, I'll go up the fucking hill.'

The first ten minutes of winding road were manageable. To avoid the direct sunlight, Laure revived a game she had played as a child where you could only step on the shady patches of ground – one foot in the sunshine and it would be death by burning lava. Under a canopy of trees, she tiptoed and hopped, pretending not to feel the ache in her feet. The distraction was short lived, though, and soon Laure stuck out her thumb for a passing taxi or car, but there were none.

164

Fortunately, her current location was a well-known 'hit-the-wall' zone for the unfit voyager, and the Gianicolo Gods had stationed a drinking fountain at the next corner. Laure happened upon it and leant in for a long, refreshing sip. It was so pleasant that she splashed a few drops up towards her face.

This is wonderful, she thought.

She leant in a little further, letting the cool stream graze her nose, then a little further. The cascading droplets were addictive and suddenly, her whole head was under the tap.

'Hu-hum.' A voice came from behind.

Feeling like someone was pissing on her party, Laure withdrew and turned to see a small queue had formed. More politely than she felt, she nodded and plodded on.

It was worth it, she thought, as her sodden hair sent trails of cool water down her back.

The path wound gradually up, and at last, Laure glimpsed the very top: a wide strip of promenade, sprinkled with towering parasol pines whose emerald tops looked like funky haircuts. Just beyond, the skyline of Rome shone in the sun.

In an unusual celebration at reaching the summit, Laure put her hands on her knees and began to wheeze.

'He must be here,' she said. 'He has to be. If I were the heroine in a film, all this effort would not go to waste.'

Her brain raised its eyebrows. *We certainly have a high opinion of ourselves today.*

Rome's Tetris buildings glowed golden in the light. Laure hopped up onto the viewpoint's wide ledge and began tiptoeing around the Sunday sun worshippers lounging in her pathway, half-expecting Viviano's face to appear in some strange form, just as it had yesterday.

Viv, Viv, Viv, Viv, she hummed like a mantra in her mind.

At the end of the ledge, she jumped down. Here, the promenade morphed into a gravely path which sloped through the trees towards the Vatican. The entire route was dotted with busts of soldiers from Italy's unification.

As if speed dating, Laure went along the line of marble gentlemen, staring each in the eye just in case one of them dared to wink back with electric-green eyes.

After drawing in close enough for a kiss with Luigi Masi, Brigadier General and commander of the Umbria brigade, deceased 1897, Laure straightened back up and stared down the sloped path, her eyes squinting in the sunlight.

Instantly, she too turned to stone. Jogging up the hill was not Viviano, but none other than the long-lost Davide.

CHAPTER FORTY-FOUR

I found you in the mountains

Davide was in lilac running Lycras which highlighted his lean yet muscular frame. By his side, a glamourous woman with swishy brown hair, full lips and a visor was breathing steadily. She looked like she had an excellent jogging technique.

Laure wanted to dive behind her new marble boyfriend or at least link arms with him and pretend they were together, but she couldn't move.

Davide had seen her too. It was so obvious that even he couldn't pretend. Instead, he waved guiltily, whispered something to his pro-jogger girlfriend, and began to slow down. She carried on, keeping her perfect pace.

'Hi, Laure …' Davide said, coming to a standstill by her side. 'I'm sorry … I don't know what to say. I'm sure you hate me. I just had so much going on. Some personal things that I couldn't share with you. I couldn't face it, so I disappeared.'

Laure had already heard enough.

'It's OK, Da,' she said, taking a deep breath. 'I know you stole those diamonds. I'm over it, anyway. I'm just glad they gave you bail.'

'Diamonds?' said Davide, looking completely baffled, like this wasn't the conversation he had scripted in his fifteen-second jog up. 'Laure, what are you talking about?'

His girlfriend was now watching the exchange from afar.

'I read it in the newspaper. Everyone's talking about it, actually. I know they caught you trying to escape through the mountains. It's sad that you didn't feel like you could tell me, but I guess everyone has their demons.'

'Laure, I didn't steal any diamonds,' Davide repeated.

Laure nodded. This time it was her turn to give the look, dripping with faux-sympathy. 'I know,' she said with a small wink, purposefully zipping up her bag and holding it tightly to her chest.

Davide raised a stunned eyebrow.

'I'm sorry, but I've got to go,' said Laure. 'I'm a foreigner here and I can't afford to be associated with criminals.'

As Laure departed, leaving a bewildered Davide frozen on the gravel, she turned and blew him a kiss. 'I hope jail isn't too hard on you,' she yelled in her loudest Italian, making sure his girlfriend and anyone around could hear.

Her heart was pounding. She pulled out her phone and typed to Eva:

Are you around?

Her friend replied immediately, accompanied by a smoky wisp of weed which puffed through the speaker.

Certo, passa a casa, come to mine

CHAPTER FORTY-FIVE

Deep breaths and weed

Eva lived with her parents, but you wouldn't know it. The house was so big, it was possible to never cross paths. Through their Venetian windows, Laure could see the crystal chandeliers dangling over fine art and dark-wood furnishings. She slunk across the front garden, past orchids and roses, and was calmed by the sound of a water feature trickling pleasantly into a stone basin.

The only thing not ornate or traditional about the residence was actually Eva who had decided to be as rebellious as possible while simultaneously never contemplating moving out.

The door opened and her friend appeared wearing a vibrant silk kimono. Her long hair was twisted into a high bun and her contacts were fire-coloured.

'*Amore,*' she said, taking in Laure's appearance. 'You look like you drowned in the Tevere and haven't come back to life yet. Come in.'

Laure nodded. '*Grazie.*'

She had missed her friend's candid way of sympathising.

Through an echoey corridor where Laure's sandals clacked on the floor, they entered Eva's bedroom. In reality, it was more like an apartment within the house. A large living area with an ensuite attached to it. No kitchen, though, of course. Her parents wouldn't hear of that, and frankly, Eva didn't have the patience to cook.

'I'll get you a cold mint tea,' Eva said, gliding over to a table with a selection of small glass pots, each containing a mysterious ingredient.

Sunlight poured into the room, casting an Eva-shaped silhouette on the floor, and Laure sunk down into a velvety blue sofa. Her friend lit a spliff and shook the match until it extinguished, leaving a wispy swirl undulating in the air.

'So, tell me, *bella,* what's going on?' she asked, blowing a cloud of smoke and handing Laure a jewelled glass.

'I'm not sure,' said Laure, her insides still in turmoil. 'I think I just did something hilarious, but I need a second opinion.'

Eva's amber eyes sparkled with endless intrigue.

'I saw Davide,' Laure said.

'Davide! *Ma scherzi,* you're joking?! The mysterious diamond thief!'

'Well, funny you should say that,' said Laure.

Eva snorted. 'You're not serious, Laure?' she said, eyes wide. 'Was it actually him?

What happened?'

'No, no, no,' Laure said. 'I was up at the Gianicolo, and I was soggy – I'd just stuck my head under a drinking fountain.'

Eva raised her eyebrows.

'I'll explain later,' Laure said. 'Anyway, suddenly, I saw him, jogging towards me, wearing Lycras like some kind of professional asshole. And he was with a woman – obviously a girlfriend – so, I guess that solves that mystery.'

Eva tutted. 'Cowardly bastard.'

'Anyway, he stopped and immediately launched into some weaselly explanation, but I shut it down. I ... I accused him of being a diamond thief and then I left.'

Eva was giggling. 'Laure, what?'

'Yeah,' said Laure. 'I can't really remember, but I'm pretty sure I yelled something about jail time as I left.'

Bravissima, piccola mia,' said Eva, coming over and hugging her friend. 'You were crazy and inspired. I bet he had no idea what hit him.' Eva reached out for Laure's hand. 'How did you feel when you saw him? Especially with another woman.'

'Actually, it didn't sting,' said Laure. 'I was expecting to have a heart attack, I've imagined bumping into him so many times. But even seeing his girlfriend, I felt overwhelmed, but not sad. The Lycras probably helped.'

'*Eh bene*, that sounds really positive, my love,' Eva beamed, rising to re-ignite her spliff. 'So, why do I sense you are so stressed?'

Laure shook her head. 'I have so much to tell you.'

'*Dimmi*, tell me,' said Eva.

Herbaceous fumes swirled around the room as Laure sipped her tea. Then the whole story began to tumble out, from the 'neighbour' Marco to 'the street statue' Viviano and everything in between. Eva listened, shifting only for the occasional drag on her spliff. The smoke trails mingled among the memories Laure was resuscitating, transporting them both back through time. By the end, Laure was horizontal on the sofa, feet propped up, and hands behind her head.

'So, what do you think?' she asked, looking over at her friend.

'What a rollercoaster you've had, my dear,' Eva said. She tilted her head from side to side, analysing. 'But, well, from what you've told me, this Marco lost his mind.'

'What do you mean?' asked Laure.

'I mean, *come on,'* Eva said, throwing out some dramatic hand gestures and re-joining her friend on the sofa.

'You only met him a couple of times! Why didn't he check in with you? No, no, no,' Eva tutted. 'This man did not think rationally. A simple text, for example: "*Ciao*, Laure, I think we have a real connection. I might end my long-term relationship for you, any thoughts?" To which you would've replied: "*Caro*, Marco, I've decided it's not for me, I'm afraid. Goodbye."'

Laure laughed and felt the oppressive weight on her shoulders ease. *It's amazing how a friend can make a shit situation seem OK,* she thought.

'This isn't your fault, Laure,' Eva continued. 'The problem is between Marco and his girlfriend.'

'I know,' said Laure. 'But I led him on. I took it too far.'

Eva shrugged. 'Meh, what is life without a little drama? No one wants to die bored.'

'I feel like I could come here and tell you I'd murdered someone,' Laure said, unable to hold back a smile, 'and you'd tell me the same thing.'

'Perhaps,' said Eva. 'It would certainly spice things up. We could bury the body here under the floorboards and frame my parents.'

'Your parents who have supported you your whole life?'

'I know,' said Eva. 'Deplorable behaviour, but … living under one roof isn't easy.'

'That's true,' said Laure. 'If they went to prison, you would only have to share the house with the dead guy.'

'He'd probably listen to my poetry,' Eva mused.

'He'd be dead, Eva. Anyway, in your scenario, do I just show up with this corpse slung over my back?'

'Hmm, could do. But if I'm honest, I'm not expecting such horrific things from you, *amore,*' she said, ruffling her friend's hair with an affectionate hand.

'Do you think I'm boring?' asked Laure earnestly.

'Of course not!' said Eva. 'Do you want to be a murderer?'

'I don't think so,' said Laure, snuggling down into the sofa again. 'Not right now anyway.'

Eva nodded in mock sympathy and Laure giggled, shuffling around to rest her head on her friend's arm.

'Thank you for listening to me today,' she said. 'I feel a lot calmer than before.'

'Anytime, *bella,*' Eva said, planting a kiss on Laure's head. 'Now go and find this Viv. I can see he makes your face light up.'

'I do like him,' Laure said. 'He seems like a nice guy. He's interesting and fun.'

'Well, then you have to tell him how you feel!' said Eva, arms raised as if she had just had an epiphany.

'I mean, Jesus, Eva, I have been trying,' said Laure. 'I'm all out of options!'

'Are you?' said Eva, suddenly stern. ''Cause it sounds like you've been to three places, and two of them were right next to each other.'

'It's a huge city!'

Eva tutted. 'On the other hand, you could always stay here,' she said, her pro-Viviano agenda suddenly sidelined by another train of thought. 'I do have some new poetry material to run by you – the sex series, of course .'

Laure nodded politely. *'Grazie.* But I really do need to find Viv.'

At the door, Eva wrapped Laure in a tight embrace and Laure closed her eyes.

'I love you, *bella,*' Eva said.

'Me too.'

'Now *vai,* go, go!'

'How do I look?' asked Laure, using her reflection in Eva's pupils to tidy her hair.

'Amore, like you've never ever seen a mirror,' Eva replied, 'but in a good way!'

CHAPTER FORTY-SIX

The fallen pieces

Marco's face was smushed into a cushion when the door creaked open.

Timid footsteps grazed the ground as Valeria entered and contemplated his pitiful figure. Just hours ago, this man had efficiently dismissed her from his life. Now, it was like he'd been deflated with a pin.

'Marco,' she said, her voice soft but firm as she leant back, arms folded, against the kitchen counter. 'I'm here. I got your message. What's going on?'

In the flat, resignation engulfed the air and the furniture had chosen sides, ready to be divided up in the event of a bitter uncoupling.

From a child-like position, Marco looked up and Valeria's face came across his blurry view. His heart fluttered. She was here. She had come to talk.

Sitting up, he gazed at his partner of seven years. She looked worn out, like a shell of herself. Every fibre in his body wanted to move towards her, to pull her into his arms and ask for forgiveness, but he held back. It wasn't that easy. Their relationship was bleeding, and a hug wouldn't mend it.

After a deep breath, Marco shut his eyes and began to speak. 'I just wanted to tell you I'm sorry,' he said, clearing his throat to lower the pitch. 'I'm sorry for every-thing – for my behaviour and how I've treated you. There's no excuse for it. I'm just sorry.'

In silence, Valeria listened, her expression unchanged.

'Lately, I really haven't recognised you,' she said. 'You've been a different person, a nasty one. That really scares me.' From there, her voice evaporated into a rumour, based on the logic that if the question was inaudible, the unwanted answer might never come. 'Why were you being like that?' she whispered.

For a while, Marco said nothing, and then finally, he addressed the festering pit of disquiet inside him.

'Honestly, I'm not happy,' he said. 'I don't think we've been happy in our relation-ship for a while. I guess I didn't know how to deal with those feelings, because we've been together forever, so I acted out.'

The truth cut through Valeria's skin like a razor blade. Her face contorted and she burst into tears.

'But the thing is,' Marco said, scrambling to continue, 'I really don't want to lose you. I'm so ashamed of my behaviour.' He stuttered, wondering if he was about to speak out of turn. 'But, for us to work again, if … if that's what you want too, things have to change.'

Valeria let out a low yelp, and tried to bring the tears under control.

The loyal dining-room table displayed its tissue box and, gratefully, she obliged.

'But you walked out. It didn't feel as though you cared about me at all.'

'I feel awful,' Marco said, shaking his head. 'I was so frustrated, Valeria. It's fighting, fighting, constant fighting. That's what our life has become. I just wanted it to stop and I started to feel like maybe we weren't right together anymore.'

'But it's the way you changed,' Valeria said, her whole body trembling. 'I thought maybe …' she hesitated, staring at Marco's face, the face she had kissed, playfully bitten, despised but undeniably loved. Fear possessed her eyes.

'What it is?' Marco asked.

'Did you meet someone else?' Valeria whispered.

The ticking clock on the far wall whose noise had forever gone unnoticed, was suddenly deafening. Marco stared down at the ground.

The week played out in his head and Valeria's tears rained down on his mind. There, clinging just above the flood, was Laure, clasping onto a wall of his brain as if it were a jagged cliff above the sea of tears.

Did I meet someone? he asked himself.

'No, I didn't,' Marco replied. 'Not really.'

'Not really,' Valeria said quietly. 'What does that mean?'

Marco looked up and her hazel eyes attempted to search his conscience.

When he spoke again, the tone was resolute. 'I didn't meet anyone,' he said, as in his mind, Laure's grasping hand lost its grip and she was swallowed up by the salty water, drowning, forever, into nonexistence.

'I was being selfish and I wanted an out, but it was a mistake,' Marco said, closing his eyes. 'Please forgive me.'

At that moment, Valeria took some time, blocked Marco out and retreated into her thoughts. As if wandering through an exhibition, she saw all the memories they had shared together, through the years. She acknowledged the lurking grey areas that still persisted and considered her own self-worth.

'I'm not sure if I can forgive you,' she said eventually, streams of tears running down her cheeks.

Hearing these words, Marco wilted inside, but he forced himself to continue. 'Well, I guess that's the first thing we need to figure out,' he said, sliding off the sofa and onto his knees. 'Valeria, I wish I could take it all back. Please believe me when I say I won't ever treat you like that again.' His almond eyes were raw. 'But, I think we have to be honest. We stopped behaving respectfully towards each other a long time ago.' He shuffled closer. 'I know I can't justify what I did, but it was the culmination of some awful months. We've been terrible to each other.'

'You know how stressed I've been!' Valeria said, her voice rising.

'You see!' Marco said, cutting her off. 'It's this! I can't do *this* anymore! I can't bear it.' Again, he shuffled closer. 'I know you're tired and you're a big boss now, I get it. The pressure is immense. But at the moment, we don't exist as a couple, Valeria. Maybe the old routines and expectations that used to work for us are outdated, and we need to find a new way of being together.' He traced a timid finger along her wrist. 'I'm happy that you're thriving at work, but I also don't want to sacrifice our relationship.'

From the corner, the fridge hummed its approval – it was a good point.

'I guess, I get frustrated,' Valeria whispered, 'because you had your busy time, when you were over-worked and unpleasant to be around and I had to put up with it. All the outbursts and the months of your snapping, so I felt like I deserved my turn. Like, I could treat you badly because you did the same to me.'

'I know,' Marco said, nodding. 'I was impossible, and you put up with a lot, but ... amore ...' he said, tentatively, 'you also cheated on me.'

For the briefest flicker, their gaze held in a deadlock and then a dumbfounded smile broke across Valeria's face and she placed her head in her hands.

'Cazzo, fuck,' she said.

Through tears of delirium, Marco laughed. 'I'm laughing,' he said, 'and believe me, I forgave you. I know it was a mistake. I understood and I still understand. But you have to know it still hurts me sometimes. You act like it's nothing, and maybe it was to you, but it still happened.'

'What a mess,' said Valeria, sinking to join him on the floor. 'So, what do we do?'

'I want to fix it,' said Marco, his voice shaking. 'If you do?'

Valeria shut her eyes and nodded. 'I do too,' she said. 'But I agree that things have to change.'

Relief flooded Marco's face and he breathed the sigh of an ocean.

For a while, Valeria's gaze drifted away and she was silent, contemplating a stray starling tiptoeing across the window ledge.

'I'll speak to my boss about reducing my responsibilities,' she said, finally turning back. 'I need more of a work-life balance.'

'You can do that if you want, Vale,' Marco said, 'but I know you like your job, and you're really good at it. You deserve to progress.'

'I do like it,' Valeria said, nodding. 'If I'm honest, I don't want to pull back, but maybe I can set some boundaries instead. I'll try and delegate, which I am supposed to do. That way, I could switch off more when I'm not at the office.'

'I think that would be healthy,' said Marco. 'And I'll be around more, for you, when you get home. I can take care of the day-to-day stuff, so life is not so stressful outside of work.'

'That would be so nice,' said Valeria, as for the first time since she could remember, a feeling of happiness blossomed inside. 'I promise, we'll get back to having more fun together again.'

'I know,' he said, reaching for her hand.

Leaning over, Valeria rested her head in Marco's lap and he bent towards her. They both knew they were at the limits of exhaustion.

I want to believe that this can work, Valeria thought as she lay there. *It's a new chapter in our story.*

At some point, the couple began to move around each other, slowly and carefully, until they were woven like fabric on the floor. There, they stayed, drifting in and out of sleep.

In the apartment, the furniture made peace. After all, they all agreed they were nicely arranged together. The fan purred like a contented kitten.

As the hottest hours of the day began to subside, Valeria pushed herself up and gently ran a hand over Marco's hair.

'Shall we go and get a coffee?' she asked.

'*Sì,*' he replied, half-awake, half-dreaming.

Little by little they untangled. Marco leant over and kissed Valeria, feeling a sense of stability and peace return to his body. It was as if he had been standing at an awkward angle for weeks and someone had finally tipped him upright.

CHAPTER FORTY-SEVEN

Little by little

Through the muggy air and fog of tourists, Laure could just about spot her street in the distance. After leaving Eva's, she had continued the search, engaging in alley explorations and interrogations of astronauts, musicians and one chubby man dressed as cupid. Viviano was MIA. Lost in a myriad of dead ends, Laure had become an ambling mess, but despite the misery, she refused to give up.

Higher powers decided to intervene.

At a leisurely pace, a motorino tootled towards her. Laure nodded to the driver in acknowledgement and commanded her weary legs to get out of the way, but they were no longer cooperating. Consequently, the bike ran straight over her foot. The driver shook his head, disdainful of her poor reaction time, and drove off. As Laure went to give him the finger, she saw, as if in slow motion, how little droplets of sweat flicked from her arm, catching the afternoon sun, before spraying the pavement. She tried to hurl insults at the *bastardo* driver, but her mouth was parched. In that moment, Laure understood it was time to go home. By some small miracle, the moto-collision appeared to have left her foot bruised but otherwise unscathed. The higher powers patted themselves on the back.

At last, her building danced ahead, its walls wavy in the sweltering haze which played tricks on the eye. Laure crept up the stairs and into her flat. Not a soul was stirring next door and guilt pricked her insides as she recalled the encounter with Marco.

Did I break up a relationship that could've been salvaged? she wondered.

The apartment welcomed Laure from the odyssey with open arms, concerned for her wellbeing. The shower seemed to gargle a hymn about rebirth and Laure dived straight in. But though the water cleansed her body, it was unable to clear her mind. Every droplet was loaded with a fragment of Valeria and Marco's demise: an insult, a puff of cigarette smoke, a 'casual' text, a weak sob. Relentlessly, they pelted down on her until Laure was soaked in shame.

As she closed her eyes, an image of her and Viviano on the bridge the night before appeared in her mind, and she thought about their conversation. He had said she was too hard on herself. Over the course of her life, that was almost certainly true.

'What's happened with Marco and Valeria is done,' she said aloud, her voice barely audible over the cascading water. 'I don't feel proud of how I behaved, but I cannot take all the blame either ... Maybe I need to start focusing on my own life, not other people's.'

When she finally opened her eyes, the water was just water again.

Laure wrapped herself in a towel and shuffled out of the bathroom. In her wardrobe, a satin slip dress caught her attention – burnt orange with a square neckline. Laure had bought it on a whim from a Paris charity shop many years ago, but to this day, she'd never had the courage to wear it.

It's bright, just like Viv, she thought, noticing how the fabric shimmered in the evening light and how she could not stop herself from evoking that colourful human at every occasion.

Pulling the dress over her head, Laure tried to channel him with her thoughts.

Where are you? she asked, scanning her imagination but finding only the remnants of weed and mint tea on the tip of her tongue.

What if he doesn't want to see you after you ran off? What if he's changed his mind about you? her brain asked.

'It doesn't matter,' Laure replied. 'I have to try. I don't want to be afraid of life anymore.'

For the first time ever, her brain was silent.

Laure picked up her phone and messaged her friend Julie back in Paris.

> *Mon chou*, do have the name of the job coach you were seeing a few years ago?
> You found her helpful, right?
> I think I'd like to get some advice.
> *Merci, ma belle*

After pressing send, she sat at her desk and typed 'Volunteering, hospitals, Rome' into the search engine.

I should start trying things out, before committing to anything, she thought. *To see if I actually like it or whether I'm just trying to please someone else.*

Several options to explore came up and Laure pinned the page, feeling for the first time in a long time, like she was taking control of her own fate.

'I've got to go out again,' she said. 'I know Viv is looking for me. We have to cross paths.'

In the kitchen, Laure stuffed a bit of old sandwich into her mouth, spat it straight into the bin and then made for the door. But as soon as it swung open, an arctic chill swept over her body. She was face-to-face with Marco.

CHAPTER FORTY-EIGHT

Fuck

He was leaving the flat. Just behind, was a woman who must have been Valeria. Her attention was consumed by the zip on her handbag which appeared to be stuck. Marco had frozen, his dark eyes filled with a mixture of fear, confusion and disbelief, as if Laure had come to him as an unwanted apparition and he couldn't understand why.

Noticing he had stopped, the woman glanced up. *'Amore?'* she said, lightly touching his shoulder.

This reminder of her presence sent Marco into a tailspin. Laure saw his breath falter and eyes search frantically around for an escape route.

From behind, the woman was not privy to any of this. She sighed, showing bemusement at Marco's lack of neighbourly etiquette, stepped around him and beamed at Laure.

'Ciao! Sono Valeria. Piacere, nice to meet you,' she said, extending her hand.

'Oh, *ciao,'* Laure managed to stutter, her anxiety so intense she could not even appreciate that the pair were apparently still an item.

'You live next door to us!' Valeria said, seeming to dial up the enthusiasm as she waited for Marco to engage. After an enquiring glance behind, she continued, 'Sometimes I see you coming into the building from our window, and I knew you lived next door. *O Dio,* God, that makes me sound like a stalker! What I mean is, I know you're our neighbour and I've wanted to introduce myself for ages.' Valeria inhaled, visibly pleased to have made it through the sentence, but wondering why this was so difficult.

Silence followed and she smiled once again at Laure, who smiled back, all the while hoping for imminent death.

Behind Valeria, Marco's face had turned to stone and Laure knew that the penny had dropped. His eyes were fixed upon her.

Valeria, on the other hand, was ready to leave. 'OK!' she said, exasperation tinging her voice. 'Well, we were just heading out. Are you as well?'

'Oh, yes,' replied Laure weakly, her palms clammy and her heart palpitating.

'Perfetto,' Valeria said. 'It's a beautiful evening.'

She began to walk down the stairs, leaving Marco and Laure together. Halfway

down, she turned to see her boyfriend still hadn't moved.

'Marco?' she said. *'Vieni?* Are you coming? Have you even introduced yourself to our neighbour?' She gave Laure an apologetic look, before continuing towards the floor below.

Finally, after what felt like an eternity, Laure's ashamed gaze met Marco's. They were alone. His nostrils flared and his eyes bore into hers, cold, like an assassin. Every inch of his body was shaking and it looked as though he might lunge for her, sending Laure four storeys down to the stone floor. Laure felt his disgust seep into her and eat away at her insides.

'Amore?' Valeria's perplexed voice rang out again and her head appeared around the stairwell.

As his eyes fell upon Valeria's innocent face, Marco appeared to soften.

He turned back, but made no eye contact. 'Nice to meet you, Laure,' he said robotically, but loudly enough to appease Valeria, before walking down the stairs.

She was waiting for them on the next landing, but something about her had changed.

'How do you know her name?' Valeria asked, staring up at Marco.

Marco stopped on the spot, clearly confused by the question, and then suddenly he looked flustered. 'She … she told us,' he said, trying and failing to sound convincing.

There was silence.

'You're lying,' said Valeria, as cold as ice. 'I know she didn't. I was just thinking as I walked down the stairs that I needed to ask. When I introduced myself, she didn't answer.'

Standing a few stairs up, Laure said nothing.

'Is that your name? Laure?' Valeria asked, finding Laure's shadow-cast face. Her earnest tone demanded a response.

Laure nodded, unable to look away.

'Right,' Valeria whispered.

In between the two women, Marco had begun to squirm.

'I knew something weird was going on,' said Valeria, looking back at Marco, her hands trembling but her voice calm. 'I could feel it as soon as we met her. You began acting so strangely.'

'I haven't,' Marco insisted. 'I wasn't …'

'Stop it,' said Valeria, shaking her head. 'Stop being so weak.' A tear slid from her eye, but she swiped it away. 'You know, when we were talking just now in the flat, I was going back and forth, back and forth in my head. I told myself, "This man really messed up, he treated me badly, but someone you love deserves the benefit of the doubt."'

'Amo—' Marco intervened again, but Valeria wasn't taking questions.

'But here you are,' she continued, seemingly lost in her thoughts. 'Here you are being deceitful. Here you are humiliating me again, almost immediately. It's everything I was worried about, everything I had to convince myself wouldn't happen anymore.'

'I can explain,' said Marco, the sentence coming out as a desperate wail.

'Your time to explain was this afternoon,' retorted Valeria, 'when we were sitting together, crying. That was the time to be honest even though it would have hurt. That was the time to turn a new page.'

The strength of her energy seemed to create a force field around her. She took one step towards Marco, and Laure saw her stand tall.

'I can see the type of person you are now,' she said, staring him dead in the eye. 'It's crystal clear. I don't trust you. You don't deserve my love. It's over.'

Valeria glanced up at Laure who was still standing, stationary, on the periphery of the disarray.

'What good fortune that we bumped into you, *Laure,*' she said with a frail laugh, before turning and bolting down the remaining flight of stairs like a sprinter out of the blocks.

CHAPTER FORTY-NINE

Still I, I can't feel the heat

Marco stood paralysed in front of Laure, staring at the door through which Valeria had left him' – it would be forever imprinted on his mind.

Laure realised that at any moment, Marco would destupefy and she didn't know how he would react. As quick as a flash, she also began to run, bounding through the door and tumbling out into the sunlight. She took a corner and another, gaining more distance, before collapsing behind a row of bins which lined the pavement like colourful Lego blocks.

Her heart racing, she lay there until the adrenaline coursing within gradually flowed into the gutter. Even the stench of rubbish smelt like the sweetest roses compared to the fetid air she had just left behind.

Not far away, she could hear Marco. 'Valeriaaaaaaaaaaaaaaaaaaaaa, Valeri-aaaaaaaaaaaaaaaaaaaaaa, please come back, *ti prego, per favore,*' he yelled at the top of his lungs.

Valeria has long gone, Laure thought, still shocked by the turn of events. *Actually, I think it might be for the best. In the end, they didn't seem happy ... Anyway, that's their decision,* she reminded herself.

As her panting calmed, the reality of Laure's resting place set in. Acrid odours of decaying food invaded her nostrils and splodges of unidentified gunge lay dotted around like mines. With a shudder, she scrambled up and peered around the corner of a bin for an unhinged, heartbroken thirty-something-year-old. The coast was clear, so Laure cautiously began walking towards Da Antonio, shaking out her limbs and brushing dirt from her dress on the way.

Under the café veranda, Antonio was folding napkins when Laure sidled over and touched his arm.

'Laure,' he said, leaning over to kiss her on both cheeks, and wondering why she smelt like bin. 'What can I do for you?'

As they stood together, Laure realised she had never really had a proper conversation with Antonio. Feeling shy, she looked up at him.

'Antonio, I'm looking for someone. I'm wondering if you can help me.'

'Go on,' said Antonio, his light eyes sparkling with curiosity against his golden, leathery skin.

'He's often around here,' Laure said, trying to be casual. 'He's called Viv. Most of the time he stands over there, dressed like …' she hesitated.

Antonio listened.

'Well, dressed like a tree,' she finally said. 'I mean, he might dress as other things too, but definitely a tree …' she trailed off.

'*Tranquilla,* don't worry,' Antonio said, putting Laure out of her misery with a warm smile. 'I know Viv. He was here earlier, actually, around the same time as you.'

Laure's heart stopped. 'What? When I was sitting with Marco?'

'*Sì, sì,*' Antonio said, with a nod. 'I have to say he left very quickly. Looked a little disappointed, *povero ragazzo,* poor lad.'

'Oh *mon Dieu!*' said Laure, her face crumpling like a piece of waste paper. 'Did you see where he went?'

'Well, he was back a little later, in his usual spot,' Antonio said, shifting his head from side to side as he recalled the memory. 'He waited there a while, but he seemed deflated somehow.'

As he spoke, Laure couldn't help but detect inconsistencies in Antonio's demeanour. Although he was making all the right overtures, she noted a light bounce in his heels and his furrowed brows belied a touch of smugness, as if he was impressed with how he was accompanying Laure on her tumultuous journey.

'I just can't believe this,' Laure said, staring down at the floor. 'Nothing is going right.'

Seeing the crestfallen figure before him, Antonio could no longer keep up the act. 'Hey,' he said, lifting Laure's chin, his thick Italian accent flowing like a melody. 'Laure, whatever are you so sad about? Personally, I have been enjoying watching you stomp all over these men's hearts. So dramatic, like a Shakespeare,' he said with a theatrical hand flourish. 'The whole point is to have them falling head over heels for you, isn't it?' Antonio laughed and his capped teeth shone brightly. 'Now, Viv, Marco,' he said, turning one hand over and then the other. 'I don't know how many men you need, Laure! But go on, enjoy it! We men don't need an easy time, we've had it easy for centuries.' He gave her a wink.

Through tearful eyes, Laure managed the beginnings of a smile. 'I don't think I was stomping,' she snuffled.

Antonio brushed her arm. 'That's better, my dear,' he said, before turning and strolling back inside. '*Mamma mia,* these women! One man just isn't enough these days,' Laure could hear him saying, shaking his head melodramatically as he walked away.

Wiping her eyes, she wandered to Viviano's spot. Over the intense search period, Laure had come to develop a complicity with the tangled vines. Now the leaves quivered, seeming to whisper that Viv wasn't around. She stared up at the sky, searching for a fresh idea, but the heavens didn't care about the fate of Laure and Viviano. As her eyes drifted back down the wall, they landed upon graffiti she was sure hadn't been there before. The lettering was several feet tall, in shining scarlet paint. After taking a few steps back, Laure could read the whole thing.

SONO SCAPPATO SUL PONTE
I'VE FLED TO THE BRIDGE

Instantly, she knew it was him.

Laure turned and began to sprint towards the river, weaving through the crowds and almost losing a shoe on the way. Hardly able to breathe, she scanned the area, trying to discern a familiar figure in the sea of bobbing heads.

In the sky, the starlings were dancing, and there, right in the middle of the bridge, was Viviano, gazing out over the water.

Laure ran closer, unable to believe he had materialised. As her view improved, she saw that he was fishing. Seemingly with all the time in the world, he flicked out the spindly rod and watched as it plopped into the Tevere's flowing waters.

Oh, this fucking guy, she thought. *Why wouldn't he be fishing?*

'Viv,' she said, stopping just a few feet away from him.

As the woman without a story appeared before him, Viviano's face lit up.

'I've been looking all over for you,' Laure blurted out, finding no capacity to organise her words. 'What you saw at the café – with Marco – it's not what it looked like.'

Above them, the starlings were creating a kaleidoscope of shapes across the pale evening sky.

'It's OK,' Viviano said, taking a step towards her.

'No,' said Laure, 'I was telling him it wasn't going to work between us. I don't want to be with him. I never did.'

Relief shone in Viviano's eyes. 'Really?' he asked.

'Really,' said Laure. 'God, I looked and looked for you, and then I spotted that bonkers message about being at the bridge!'

'I'm sorry,' said Viviano, shaking his head. 'That's my flair for the dramatic. I wasn't even sure you'd see it.'

'You're a lunatic,' Laure laughed, taking a few steps closer.

'When you ran off this morning, I didn't know what had happened to you,' said Viviano. 'We searched everywhere, Mickey and I. Then I saw you with Marco and …' He trailed off. 'I mean, I was just relieved that you were OK.'

Laure's eyes found his timid gaze. 'Just relieved?' she asked.

Viviano turned pink. 'No,' he managed to stutter. 'I did feel disappointed. Just a little, you know?'

'I'm so sorry,' said Laure. 'It's just—'

But before Laure could offer more explanations, Viviano cut her off.

'I like you, Laure,' he said.

Now Laure was pink.

'And I-I also want to say thank you,' he stammered. 'Some of the things you said, they opened my eyes.' For a moment, he hesitated. 'I'm going to go to *Signora* Solari's funeral next week. If I had missed it, I would've regretted it forever, and that's thanks to you.'

Laure couldn't help but laugh.

'Why are you laughing?' Viviano asked.

'I'm sorry,' said Laure. 'Everything you're saying is so wonderful. I'm so glad for you and … I wanted to tell you, you've helped me too. It's just I don't think the sentence "I like you" has ever been followed by a funeral anecdote.'

Viviano snorted.

'But … I'm sorry,' said Laure. 'Gosh, I'm just flustered. I really am so glad that—'

As she was speaking, Viviano leant in and Laure froze. For the briefest moment, she thought he was going to kiss her. Instead, his lips brushed past and he swooped down and planted a kiss just above her hip bone, causing her to shriek. Slowly, he moved around. Laure felt him kiss the middle of her spine and then the tip of her right shoulder.

'Viv, what on earth are you doing?'

Spiralling around, Viviano's lips grazed her lower neck and he moved his body in close, wrapping his arms around her. Here he stopped and their eyes met.

'You're unique,' he said.

Softly, Laure kissed him, noticing every sensation – the shape of his mouth, the roughness of his chin. Her mind floated like a cloud.

'So are you,' she said, pulling away just for a moment and beaming, before searching once again for his lips. His tongue tasted like kiwis and sunshine.

While caught in the moment, oblivious to the throngs of people milling by, something brushed Laure's arm and hit the floor with a thud. She nestled into Viviano, feeling the beat of his heart, the warmth of his chest. There was another thud, and another and then, in quick succession, a clattering of noises all around.

Turmoil erupted on the bridge. Gasps, shrieks and cries rang out as people sprawled out in all directions, nearly knocking Viviano and Laure to the floor as they fled. Still, the pair noticed nothing. Eyes closed, they were interested only in each other and this small square of happiness they had carved out. Then something whacked Laure squarely on the head.

'What on earth?' she said, the words muffled through Viviano's lips.

Reluctantly, they opened their eyes and looked around.

'Oh *mon Dieu!*' Laure gasped.

'The birds!' said Viviano, his mouth falling open. 'The birds, Laure! They're colliding! They're falling!'

Across the sky, thousands of starlings were hurtling into one another. They clashed and crashed, falling out of the air like doomed dominoes and plummeting to Earth.

The bridge was empty – everyone had run for cover. From underneath building arches and bus stops, stunned faces stared out, and hundreds of phones captured the chaos.

In the middle of it all, Laure and Viviano stood, shielding their heads as bird after bird bounced off them and gathered around their ankles.

'What shall we do?' Laure asked, gazing around in shock. 'I guess one of them finally put a foot wrong.'

'They're not dying,' Viviano said, staring at a bird pile. 'Look, they're just struggling. Let's try and help.'

Carefully, he gathered a starling from the floor, cradling it in his hands. Then with a swinging movement, he tried to release the bird back towards the sky, launching it outwards and letting go. The starling looked fragile, a shadow of the proud dancer it usually was, but after a timid start, a few dips and zigzags, it began flying upwards once again.

'It's working!' Viviano said. 'Laure, come and help.'

Laure watched in amazement as Viviano launched another, then tried herself. The starling felt so light in her hands and it quivered nervously. Then with a swoop, she swung her arms and let go. As the tiny bird soared into the sky, Laure let out a whoop.

'This is totally insane,' she yelled.

Laure and Viviano's curious actions were gaining traction among the crowds who were gradually emerging from their hiding places. Little by little, a mass rescue mission began. Hundreds of people spread out over the bridge and began saving the starlings, crouching down to retrieve them, before giving them the extra boost they needed to fly again. Everywhere you looked there was a kind of euphoric chaos.

Soon, there were more birds back in the sky than on the ground, and they were soaring, creating formations more beautiful than Laure had ever seen.

Every time another was launched upwards, it joined its family, slotting seamlessly into the dance.

'Wow,' Viviano said breathlessly.

'They just needed some help to get back on track,' Laure said as the starlings performed loops across the sunset. 'Maybe they needed to fall to reset.'

Viviano put his arm around her.

Printed in Dunstable, United Kingdom

76431804R00105